Hidden Motives

A Corruption Universe Romance

By J. F. Posthumus

Black Anvil – Blue Rose Press
An Imprint of
Three Ravens Publishing
Chickamauga, GA USA

To my eldest son, Chris.

Who answered all my questions and gave advice and suggestions when I needed it. This universe wouldn't be what it is without you.

Ar scáth a chéile a mhaireann na daoine.

'til Valhalla, son.

Table of Contents

Chapter One

Alyssa strode through the primary corridor of the vessel's fifth level. She was an assassin for the IMD, hidden in plain sight, for over five years. Today, she played a very familiar part, although not the one most suited to her training.

Displaying the confidence needed to pull off the deception, she kept her back straight, strolling the corridor with pride in her step. As she traveled past several other human crewmembers, she took note of who watched her and made mental notes of who avoided looking at her all altogether. She hadn't earned her rank or position, real or deceived, by being unobservant or ill-prepared.

Everyone on duty wore their official uniform of Earth's Interstellar Military Division, complete with the insignia of the IMD. Crewmen wore drab gray jumpsuits with high collars and seven-inch touchscreen computers woven into either forearm. Officers of every spacecraft wore red two-piece uniforms, while. medical personnel wore white. The latter being a holdout from ancient Earth days when doctors wore long white jackets.

The individuals rank and purpose were displayed by cloth stripes and patches on the opposite forearm. The division's four-pointed star within a circle adorned the right breast of the jumpsuit. A small disc was on the left, which currently displayed green on each person's chest, including Alyssa's. This was the IHD, or individual health display of every person who wore any type of uniform.

Green meant healthy, yellow warned of declining health, and red was near death or in mortal peril. In case of death, the disc displayed a brilliant white, which also served as a beacon for other personnel to locate the corpse.

The downward-slanting trio of black stripes indicated Alyssa's rank of sergeant. The white square patch above the stripes indicated she was part of Military Affairs and Inventory. The division referred to as M.A.I. on reports and formal situations, and the reason why many crew members gave her a wide berth.

Members were often called the "Mai-bees" during less formal conversations because they were "always buzzing around in everyone's business."

Dealing with beings who wanted to do less than a job required, or prejudice against someone who could hold a person accountable for doing less than what a job required, were a constant. That fault in sentient beings was one of the unfortunate traits that never seemed to evolve away or go completely out.

Regardless of whether it was humans, Xoutians, Alphanians, Jupes, or any of the other known races, there were always people among them who just wanted to hate. Fear and the controlling grip it had on some beings? It seemed to be a universal curse of existence.

Those facts did not make much difference to Alyssa. With her practical good looks, golden hair, and blue-gray eyes, she'd experienced plenty of suspicion, expectation, the whole volley of human emotions thrown her way even before she'd put on the uniform. She usually made those emotions work in her favor or was able to avoid the need to engage them in her work.

Because she wasn't actually one of the "Mai-bees," her work did not consist of making sure paperwork was all in order, triplicated, and stored away for later review. Nor did she spend her days checking that all gear and equipment provided by the IMD was present and accounted for. In fact, she spent most days out of the gray jumpsuit.

All one hundred thirty-five centimeters of Alyssa Zelaya was in exceptional physical shape, conditioned in multiple ways of war, combat, and weaponry. The only persons on this particular ship who were privy to her actual duties consisted of the captain and the sergeant at arms. The latter still went by the antique Earth title of weapons master on the *ESS Rambler*. The captain, Richard Spivey, had made no qualms about transporting Alyssa and her handler, Boran, to her latest assignment and then back home to Earth.

The *Rambler* was now coming into orbit around the blue-and-white planet they all called home. Captain Spivey had requested that Alyssa come to the bridge.

Alyssa came to the starboard entrance of the bridge. She held the palm of her left hand against the dark panel next to the ceramic door. The ID chip beneath her skin sent a burst of information to the panel, identifying her to the ship's primary database. Her clearance to the bridge was verified in milliseconds by the system. The board illuminated a medium blue color. A low buzz accompanied the large door sliding aside.

The bridge was circular in shape, with workstations jutting out of the walls. Chairs were molded into the floor, rising up at the stations. Restrictive belts and panels adorned the chairs. The most complex and sturdy pair of chairs sat to either side of the large central platform in the middle of the floor. The captain and first officer usually occupied those seats.

The platform presented 3D displays of the ship, inside and out, and the surrounding space for as far out as the sensors and information could provide. Inventory lists, crew reports, and literally every bit of data that could be obtained about any aspect of the ship, crew, and current situation were on call.

Instead of both senior officers, only the second-in-command was at the platform. He gave Alyssa a curt nod. She responded with a crisp salute. The first officer pointed to a door to her right.

"The Captain's waiting for you in his office."

Alyssa nodded. The door opened as she approached, allowing her to enter without breaking stride. Inside the practical and formal office, Alyssa discovered her handler was keeping Captain Spivey company.

The captain stood behind his large antique white desk. His dark skin and features were complimented by the red command jumpsuit he wore. Spivey looked pleased, perhaps relieved, at her arrival.

Boran sat at one of three chairs facing the desk. His olive-colored complexion and jet-black hair were at odds with his gray jumpsuit. He looked out of place, like someone pretending to be a soldier or crew person, but who had no idea how to act like one. He slouched in the chair, his dark eyes narrowed at her.

"Finally," Boran grumbled. "We can debrief, and I can get back to wearing real clothes again."

It was no exaggeration to declare Boran unfit to be a soldier in the traditional sense. He was lazy with his appearance, physical training, and any attempt to blend in wherever the jobs took them.

His skills lay in the direction of clearing customs, falsifying documents, and knowing the tells of his charge, also known as her. He could make sure no trace of her as an assassin could be detected. He knew when she needed meds, meals, tools, and silence. For those specialized talents, Boran was part of the IMD that did not have to measure up to the more rigorous aspects. And he reveled in that fact.

Alyssa allowed herself a smirk when she recalled that Boran's idea of real clothes consisted of outfits better suited to the last quarter of the Twentieth Century. All the worst ones in her opinion.

Parachute pants, flannel shirts, and platform sandals, oh my.

"You don't have to be here," Alyssa countered. "You chose to attend."

"I make sure you don't forget important details, darling," said Boran.

"Like how much credit you want to have on those successful missions."

Settling back into his seat, Boran flashed a smile. "We've had nothing but successful missions. You're welcome."

She looked over to the captain with an exhausted expression. Captain Spivey was quick enough to interpret the cue and began the debriefing.

Five minutes into Boran explaining why she had been successful on the mission with his help and support, Alyssa let part of her mind wander. At some point, she would need to supplement the schmoozing and self-congratulatory sermon with facts and what occurred, minus any frivolity or exposition. The way her handler was going on, though, it might be a while before that happened.

Nostalgia crept into her thoughts. She had spent the past five years working as an assassin, without a single failure. That was thanks to the failures she had suffered and learned from since she first entered the IMD programs at the age of fifteen. The programs had saved her from a very unsavory and desperate existence.

While destitution had been decreasing from Earth's existence for a few decades, it was still possible to be homeless, hungry, and at odds with societal laws just to survive. The choices she had made between being orphaned and being taken into the program had put her on a rocket sled to the latter lifestyle.

"I believe this is where Sergeant Zelaya can tell me the details," she heard the captain say.

Her mind and focus snapped to him. Boran looked a bit put out but didn't vocalize any objections. He schooled his features to look pleased before he nodded to her.

"At this point, enough data was gathered to postulate the target's weak points, blindsides, and breaks in the schedule. I made entry into the target's home the following evening. They had minimal sentries, per the observed pattern, due to the off-world lover being at the residence. Once I made my way to the sleeping quarters, I was ready to fire the poison round from the electric short rifle into the target's soft palate," Alyssa reported in a crisp, professional voice. "They snore quite heavily, and often doze with slack mouths that put humans to shame."

"I've heard that about Xoutians," Captain Spivey interjected, "but never witnessed it."

Boran replied, "It's probably because they have more in common with canines than primates for evolutionary cousins. Never knew a big dog that didn't snore loud enough to wake a corpse."

Captain Spivey gave Boran a cross look, likely objecting to the comparisons between Earth dogs and the inhabitants of Xoutsiis.

The most hospitable planet near to the star Sirius, long known as the Dog Star, had given birth to a single bipedal species with several hundred sub-species. These beings had exceptionally large snouts and jowls, in addition to thick hair. The jokes, nicknames, and other mockery came swiftly after the Xoutians were known to humanity.

"To continue," she rejoined. "A clear shot presented itself within the first one hundred seconds. The shot was taken, I exited the residence, and used the weapon's self-destruct charge to destroy the evidence."

"Thank you, Sergeant."

Alyssa nodded to the captain. "If that will be all?"

She felt certain that was it since she noticed her handler getting up from his seat. Boran was already walking towards the exit when Spivey gave her a curt nod and salute.

Once the salute was returned, she pivoted on her left heel and strode out after her handler.

Conversation wasn't rare between the sergeant and her handler after missions. This time, however, no words were spoken by the latter. Alyssa took that as a cue to not initiate chatter or questions.

The silence didn't bother her. She had little in her repertoire for small talk. There were no questions about the finished mission. If something came up, they had neighboring cabins on this vessel, and he could ask her easily. Thus, she expected to be behind Boran until they arrived at their respective doors.

"You need to come in my quarters first," Boran stated as he paused in front of his door. Even as he spoke, the eye-level sensor at the cabin door was scanning his retinas and skull to identify him. "It's business," he assured her. "We have a visitor."

Alyssa had halted just before she reached the sensor for her quarters.

This was new. Visitors during a mission meant a change in some aspect. But this one was over.

"If this is some foolish attempt to surprise me," she threatened. She had never enjoyed surprises and he knew it.

Boran shook his head and stepped aside when his door opened.

"See for yourself," he invited.

Peering into the room with the caution of a soldier expecting gunfire, she saw a single individual sitting at the small table in her handler's guest quarters.

The person's face was obscured by shadow. Whoever it was had deliberately sat in front of the single lamp that stood by the table. All she could make out was the person had short light-colored hair and the upright posture of a career in the military.

"Hello, Aly," came a strong female voice. "Or would you prefer I address you as Sergeant Zelaya?"

"Um, no, that's fine," Alyssa said, which was no more than an attempt to keep herself from sounding nervous or not speaking at all. "It's a pleasure to see you again, Admiral."

The person in the room stood and walked to her. Within four strides the light from the hallway illuminated the wiry physique, solid white hair, and distinguished features of First Admiral Jaquilen Lynchen, head of IMD since its inception.

She was well past the traditional age of retirement while still being the most qualified person to be in charge. She had also personally recruited one Alyssa Marie Zelaya at the age of fifteen into the assassin's program, in addition to being her sponsor, counselor, and parental figure in lieu of biological ones.

Admiral Lynchen had given her the nickname "Aly." They had seen each other maybe twice in the past year. When Alyssa had begun to take "active" assignments, the admiral had spent the first year personally briefing her for each one. After her handler came into the program, the two women saw less and less of each other.

Some small, still insecure part of Alyssa Zelaya often wondered if it was some perverse punishment for doing her job so successfully.

The military of Earth had never, in any time or place, been a place where personal relationships were encouraged or nurtured. The vast, unknown dangers of space had only hardened that tradition. It mattered not at all if those very circumstances made such relationships all the more needed for a healthy being.

"Well done on your last mission, Aly. You never fail to deliver on your assignment parameters."

The adulation began to make Alyssa smile, but something kept it from reaching her eyes or spirit.

Admiral Lynchen had, on the occasions she appeared after a mission, given her similar praise. However, the use of the word "last" had never been included before now.

Dread and suspicion tried to creep into her mind, even as she attempted to stop her emotions from showing physically.

"Thank you, Admiral," she managed to reply with a pleasant tone. "I do what is asked of me by the Corps."

That response had routinely been the one that pleased the admiral most. Alyssa took little comfort that the familiar smile and nod were given in response this time. The admiral's smile, like hers, hadn't reached the eyes. Another variation from past experience.

"Come and sit, Aly," Lynchen invited, motioning toward the table. "I will be just a moment."

Alyssa saluted and went to the small table where she took the only other chair. The one the admiral hadn't previously occupied. Once seated, she realized Boran was still at the doorway.

He was having a conversation with the admiral, and he wasn't happy about something. The two of them were speaking low enough to keep even her augmented hearing from making out what they were saying.

"What in the old Hells am I supposed to do, then?" Boran asked through gritted teeth.

She had witnessed him do it enough to know it by sound alone.

What the admiral said in reply was garbled. Obviously, the bio-implant in her eardrums was malfunctioning, it interpreted the words as "throw yourself out an airlock." Her next statement was a little clearer, and louder, as Alyssa clearly made out the words "You are dismissed."

Even if she had doubted her own ears or the mechanical enhancements, Boran's response, which was an abrupt stiffening into a more alert stance followed by a speedy exit, verified what that final sentence had been.

Curiouser and curiouser. Her concern deepened.

The door was closed, then secured. The admiral returned to the table and sat across from her. Alyssa struggled to keep her body posture and facial expression neutral.

"You have an assignment, Aly. Without question, the most important of your impressive career," Admiral Lynchen stated, her posture and expression never changing.

"Very well," Alyssa replied, still doing her best to remain calm and appear emotionless.

A small holo-projector was placed on the table. The flat ten-centimeter disk lit up. The display was three space vessels immediately recognizable to her as a pair of destroyer-class ships escorting a single transport craft. The destroyers were half the size of the transport hulk, each holding a crew of no less than one hundred.

The transport might have as many personnel as either of the fighter ships, depending on the number of automated systems on board and what kind of cargo it carried. The destroyers always reminded her of old Navy fighter ships, such as F-14s, just expanded to allow for much higher crew numbers and super-sized weapons. The transport was the usual uneven rectangle of metal, ceramics, and whatnot that earned them the nickname "garbage scows" by, well, just about every being that didn't work on one.

The destroyers seemed to crumple inward at multiple points on their surfaces. The blue glow of the transport's engines flickered and winked while the craft began to tilt downward. It slowed until it fell behind the destroyers.

Next, the pair of destroyers began to come apart.

Intermediate pinpricks of light flashed before being snuffed out by the vacuum of space. Within ten seconds, there was no structure left of either fighting vessel. Only debris moving in every direction. The transport was stuck at a thirty-degree slant down from the Y-axis.

It might have been moving, still, but the hologram displayed nothing that she could gauge movement against.

Alyssa didn't have words to speak. She was staring at the recorded carnage and destruction.

A vessel, which resembled a highly crafted dagger with engines working organically into the hilt's end came into view and stopped above the transport vehicle. Alyssa was instantly fascinated. The ship was unlike anything she'd ever seen, even as a theoretical model. The design was alien and beautiful all at once.

It took a few moments for her to realize that Admiral Lynchen had paused the display. The debris, transport, and unknown vessel hung without motion above the holo-disk. It took a conscious effort to pull her eyes away from the ship and back to the admiral.

"Where was this?"

"Sector Three Pluto Delta, Omega eight," replied the admiral.

"At the end of our solar system," Alyssa murmured.

"Exactly. A completely unknown assailant with no prior contact or provocation intercepted the latest attempt to transport goods and personnel from our system to the Alpha Centauri bases."

"This isn't an enemy of the Alphanians or Jupes?"

The first response was an appraising glance, followed by the admiral saying, "No. The Xoutians, we think, know something, but have declared these are not adversaries to their system or fleets."

"The Xoutians aren't easy to decipher. They might be telling us the truth, but too many humans get caught up in trying to find something deeper in the 'puppy dog eyes' they all have. I've heard many complain that it's unsettling that they don't bark or growl."

"You feel the semi-gaseous, crystalline beings of Jupiter and its moons are more understandable?" Lynchen suggested. Her eyes twinkled, and a smirk appeared on her lips.

"To quote many people I've heard say it, at least they're local. Not that proximity to our planet is any reflection of how we should measure anyone. But it does seem to make a difference."

"Somehow, it does to a great many," Admiral Lynchen agreed. "Those people tend to forget that was only the case once we encountered beings from outside our solar system. I recall all the hate, paranoia, and fear from our first contact with the Jupes."

"In any case, we have little to no information on this ship, or any possible crew it may contain?" Alyssa guessed.

Admiral Lynchen nodded.

Alyssa frowned. What did this have to do with her? She was a part of eliminations, not recon or first contact. Her idea of diplomacy and negotiation consisted of knowing how many targets she had versus how many rounds were in the weapon she carried.

"Which comes to why you're going out, immediately. We need as much intel as possible on this new threat," the admiral explained. "You have a knack for getting out of… unexpected circumstances, which is paramount for this mission."

"But I'm really not a pilot."

The admiral held one hand up and continued. "The plan is for you to be in a single pilot cargo vessel, which will appear to have a failed engine, with minimal life support. The unknowns only disabled the primary drive of the cargo transport, leaving the crew more or less unharmed and able to signal for help. We feel they will be less aggressive to a solitary, helpless ship. If they take you aboard, you will gather all the intel you can, make your way off-ship, and fire up the beacon when you're clear and ready to return."

Alyssa recognized her death sentence the moment the admiral stopped talking. Her expression remained neutral, but it felt as if her body temperature had dropped ten degrees. This wasn't something she was expected to come back from.

It was the folly of assassins to believe they would retire. Sooner or later, they would be perceived as a threat to their employers and dealt with in the same manner that they had been hired to do so many times.

The words were a memory of Alyssa's first instructor, Santo Remus.

He had taken her and the rest of the training squad out for celebration after each of them survived the first exercise, a record never accomplished before. Somewhere around the tenth shot of tequila, Remus had slumped in his chair between Zelaya and another student.

Looking to the ceiling, he lamented that he was training each of them for slaughter. The other student laughed and went for another drink. Alyssa had asked what he meant.

Remus spoke those two sentences before passing out. He never made any mention of it or acted like that was his deepest lament after that. Six months later they all left to their next instructors.

Alyssa hadn't thought of that statement in years. But it had never been lost in her mind.

She focused hard on the admiral and went through the motions of mission briefing.

"I understand," Alyssa said. "How long do I have before extraction? Will I need to be fitted with a different tracking implant?"

The second question was a lure.

Alyssa normally was tracked all through a mission by her handler. If she was meant to be extracted at all, something with a much longer range would need to be on her. Or more precisely, in her, to be tracked if she wasn't on a planet. She wanted to see what excuse the admiral would give.

"There is no set time frame for extraction. You will be fitted with an experimental implant that only becomes active when you dislocate your left shoulder."

The bit about the implant was unexpected, and likely utter rubbish. The implant would be, at best in her reasoning, a burst transmitter that sent as much information obtained from her experiences as possible onto IMD satellites.

She would be left to die wherever she was once the implant was activated, if it did anything at all. The ship she would be piloting would have the highest level of sensors and transmitters, giving the precious data the IMD did care about a chance to reach them. She was expendable and being put out in the cold. There was no doubt in her mind.

"Let's hope this new adversary doesn't get extra creative with torture. The implant might go off before I've gotten as much info as I can," Alyssa heard herself say.

"Whatever information you can recon will be the highest level of useful," countered Lynchen, her tone dismissive and deflective.

"Do I collect anything from my current quarters before the mission starts?"

"Your quarters have been cleaned and swept. We proceed to the launch bay on the port side to get you underway."

Alyssa nodded her understanding, stood, and waited to follow the admiral out.

Words from her instructor played over and over through her mind on the walk to the launch bay.

If you stay good at this job, sooner or later they have to get rid of you. You become too much of a threat. They can't outwit you, they can't flank you, and you have more intel on them than they do on you.

She had never really wanted to think it would come to that.

Granted, Alyssa knew she was a valuable asset and could do her work over and over with success. The truth was that she figured to be retired long before any kind of "asset is now a threat" scenario came across the big command's virtual desks. A couple of years, perhaps fifty contracts, and they would retire her to some obscure locale or on a base to train newbies in any of the skills the work required.

Five years, over four times that many successful missions, and she'd foolishly allowed herself to forget that warning along with all the others.

Perhaps she should have been looking around instead of straight ahead just over the admiral's right shoulder. Take in the sights of everything one last time.

No, she chided herself. *That would be a change in behavior. One that the personnel that were no doubt watching her on video feed would catch.*

There was a moment spent wondering how many armed and highly-trained soldiers there were standing ready to drag and stuff her into the oversized coffin waiting for her. The thought passed, and she kept her focus all the way to the bay.

Chapter Two

The journey went quicker than Alyssa would have expected. Probably because the corridors had been void of people. Another unavoidable indication was that she was taking her last walk. She had no clue how she was going to survive what was to come. If she were honest, she expected her death to come in the empty vacuum of space. Alone and forgotten.

Her dark thoughts came to an end when the admiral stepped to the left. Alyssa stepped up beside the admiral.

Before her was a prototype ship, sitting forty-odd meters away. She knew it was a prototype ship due to the audacious and unfamiliar design of its sleek exterior. Unlike the standard attack vessels or single/dual crew fighters, this ship's exterior had a dull matte finish across the hull and no lighting.

A stealth craft for space.

The wings swept forward. Some bizarre cameras were installed at the tips where there should have been launchers, plasma cannons, or any kind of defensive or offensive weaponry. The nose end of the ship was blunt, save for the navigation dish at the tip. It was the only pointed piece on the ship.

That piece of equipment was the same flat charcoal color as the rest of the exterior.

Standing at the ramp stood the Chief Medical Officer, often abbreviated to CMO, and a nurse. She hadn't met either while onboard, so she only knew the CMO's name. Dr. Loyd Higgins. He had short cropped curly hair. Both he and the nurse wore the standard white uniform. Neither appeared pleased. The nurse was carrying a small bag.

"Not even a porthole to read the stars by," Alyssa said.

"We need to test a few new ideas. The navigation and imaging upgrades will take you where we need you to go."

Alyssa grunted at the admiral's words.

"We finally cut the esthetics and put a submarine in space. Although I suppose the ship needs to look impressive for our new neighbors," she rejoined.

The admiral stiffened but said nothing. Alyssa walked to the ship, not caring that the higher-ranking officer had to catch up.

As she entered the ship, the admiral followed behind her. Doctor Higgins and his nurse brought up the rear. The brunette nurse carried a small bag.

Once inside, the doctor turned to Alyssa. "Let's step into the back of the ship for this."

Without another word, he herded Alyssa towards the back of the ship. The nurse set the bag on a small shelf in the head. Without a word, Alyssa unzipped the front of her jumpsuit.

The nurse rolled Alyssa's sleeve back to reveal her shoulder. Holding the sleeve back with one hand, the nurse used the other to remove an object from the bag. The long cylindrical object was smooth with only a few grooves. One end was rounded on top, while the other end was flat. She handed it to Higgins.

Higgins examined it for a moment, then gave a brief nod.

"This will sting," he stated as he pressed it against her skin. "Ready?"

"I doubt it can be worse than being shot," Alyssa stated, giving a nod. "Go on."

Higgins gave a slight smile. "One. Two. Three."

As he said the last word, there was a soft click. Alyssa winced at the sting caused by the hypo inserting the chip beneath her skin. She could feel the small chip moving through her body before stopping. Rolling her shoulder, she glanced at the spot. There was nothing to show anything had been injected.

"Good girl," Higgins stated, handing the hypo back to the nurse who remained silent. "Safe journey."

"Thank you," was all she could manage. It took far more effort to not scoff. The journey away might be safe, but she doubted the end would be. The return would probably be nonexistent. She doubted the military would even bother collecting her body. If there was anything left to collect.

How long have they been planning this? she wondered to herself as her sleeve was unrolled and moved back into place. Her thoughts continued as she zipped the uniform back up. *This was definitely an experimental ship. Was it what they used to remove their unwanted assassins? And this was the first I've ever heard of it?*

The nurse and doctor turned and headed back to the hatch. Alyssa followed behind them to where Admiral Lynchen awaited her.

"Let's start the pre-flight check. I'll instruct you on the controls," the admiral stated, moving to the front of the ship.

Alyssa followed behind. Her question about if they used this for many of their assassins was starting to sound more like the truth. Otherwise, how did Lynchen know the ship and its controls so well?

The pre-flight check was less tedious than Alyssa expected it to be. She only had to memorize a minimal number of controls before the admiral was satisfied and ordered the launch.

Maneuvering the single-person ship out of the bay wasn't difficult. She'd never trained to be a pilot, so she was impressed by the fact the tractor beams weren't required. Considering everything was done by autopilot made it that much more impressive.

Had whoever programmed the ship known it was going to kill someone? Or did they see it as just another job placed before them? She would never know the answer to those questions or others.

Unable to see out of the ship, she checked the coordinates of the computer as the ship flew through the empty vacuum of space. There were still hours left on the journey. Leaving Alyssa to occupy herself with learning everything she could about the ship that hadn't been taught to her. Though the craft was small, there was still a lot to discover. It took those hours for her to find the explosive charges that had been placed for the faux sabotage.

There was nothing false about the sabotage.

The two kilograms of compact nitro compound had been placed directly under the closet-sized fusion reactor that propelled the ship. The explosion would spray radioactive material that would show up like a beacon on

Earth equipment. There was no doubt it would grab the notice of a race with more advanced technology.

Going out in a blaze of glory, indeed.

During the hours traveling, Alyssa had come to loathe those who had put her in this situation. In spite, she ripped the compound right out of its housing in the bomb. Her plan was to see how many flushes it would take to jettison the payload out of the ship's single toilet.

She was halfway down the length of the ship, heading towards said toilet, when the cockpit exploded. The interior hallway bucked around her, and she went shoulder-first into a wall. It wasn't the shoulder with the implant, which Alyssa found ironic even as pain threatened to take her into unconsciousness.

The damn cowards set a second bomb to incinerate me while I sat in the pilot chair. Why did they go to this much trouble? Why not kill me and put my corpse in this rigged vessel?

It was her final thought before the ship lurched again in response to the atmosphere and the forward quarter of the ship abruptly not existing. Bulkheads sealed the section she was in, fans pushed precious air around her. But the whiplash she suffered at that moment tore muscles around her neck and spine.

Alyssa watched the nitro block drop from her numb fingers as all of her senses succumbed to the invading blackness.

Chapter Three

Some things were a constant in Alyssa's life. Such as the smell associated with any sort of medical facility or sickbay. It didn't matter if they were alien or human. Regardless of the race, Alyssa had never noticed a lot of variance in sickbays. It seemed the tang and cloying scent of disinfectants were similar no matter where she happened to land.

She'd been a patient, in one way or another, many times during her twenty-five years of life. In fact, in her particular line of work, sickbays and hospitals were inevitable. Sooner or later, she'd be injured or sick and require medical attention. As part of the IMD, her physicals had also been at a hospital or medbay of some sort.

This time, the scent that assailed her even before her eyes opened was akin to a light mint and citrus scent. It didn't fit with her knowledge of any sickbay she'd ever landed in or visited. Either she was in the most unusual sickbay ever, or she had been deposited in a room on an ally's ship after being treated.

Considering she hadn't had a window to look out, it was impossible to know who or what had been around when her ship exploded.

At least I'm not dead, she thought as her eyes adjusted to the dim lighting. Her brows furrowed slightly. *Why am I not dead?*

As her eyes adjusted to the light, her first sight was the ceiling above where she lay. A strange bubbly texture gave the off-white ceiling a calming effect as Alyssa stared up at it. The bed beneath her was firm but not uncomfortably hard. The pillow beneath her head contained the citrus and mint fragrance.

Definitely not human, she decided. Even as the question of how she survived kept churning around in her head. *Or any race I know.*

Anxiety rose at the realization there was nothing human or familiar about the room. None of Earth's allies had ships with sickbays even remotely similar to this one.

Panic set in the moment she realized she wasn't wearing her uniform. Instead, she was wearing a snug-fitting jumpsuit that wasn't anywhere close to what she'd been wearing prior to the explosion. From her neck down, she was covered by an unknown material.

She wouldn't have known it if her eyes weren't seeing it, and her skin wasn't sending signals to her brain. The material was light and breathable. The color was what humans would refer to as "gunmetal-blue" lending towards black with a high shine. However, it was the texture of the material that she was unfamiliar with. The texture felt and looked like nothing she'd ever experienced in her whole life. It almost seemed to be alive, thrumming with a heartbeat.

What. The. Hell? Where *was* she?

Alyssa tried to remember what happened after cracking her head on the doorframe and her shoulder hitting the wall. There had been blood. The sound of fire and smell of smoke. Then, nothing but blackness.

Her shoulder no longer ached and when she moved it, there was no pain or stiffness. Lifting a hand to her head, she couldn't find any blood or a scab. Just hair and scalp. Running her fingers through her hair, she pulled it forward to better examine the strands. The golden strands were the same as they always were, as far as she could tell, anyway.

Did the aliens rescue her? If so, why? She hadn't been wrong: she'd been sent to die, and she hadn't expected the explosion. Why would an alien race who had so far attacked her people decide to rescue her? Did they know she'd been sent out to die? How had they rescued her from an exploding ship?

"Ah, so you are awake," a dulcet male voice said, breaking into her thoughts. The owner of the voice moved towards her.

Alyssa struggled to sit up. Being prone went against everything she'd been taught. Not that she was in any shape for hand-to-hand combat, but she still didn't like being on her back as an unknown being approached her.

"No, no, don't get up. Though it appears you are well once again, I'd rather not chance you relapsing." There was a pause as he stopped just within Alyssa's eyesight. "Our information of your race is not complete, so I hope you will forgive any… difficulties that may arise with attempting to heal you."

He didn't sound as though he was truly sorry. Nor did he appear apologetic, Aly thought as she stared up into his face.

She opened her mouth but couldn't speak. She blamed it on having a dry mouth and throat. It was better than thinking it was due to the power the man exuded. He gestured, and there was a responding sound of booted feet moving in the room.

Alyssa wanted to ask him who he was but couldn't manage to get herself to form the words. Whoever this man was, the uniform he wore was different from those worn on Earth.

Like her suit, his was a snug jumpsuit of the same material. Except his was a metallic teal bordering on an unearthly reptilian green. He wore a military insignia, an image of an encircled plant and what looked like a motto above it, on the vest at his left breast. The plant reminded her of a closed rosebud surrounded by blade-like leaves. She couldn't see any distinguishing marks on his uniform. None that she could recognize, at least. he wore what resembled a chamberless gun on his right hip. The unusual silver-gray metal didn't reflect any light. On his left was something akin to a sword in a leather sheath. The hilt appeared worn, yet well cared for. There was little chance either was worn for decoration.

Why would an alien race have a need for a sword? Alyssa wondered before tucking it away for later. For now, she needed to focus on the current situation.

This being moved with purpose, his shining eyes taking in everything with an intensity that made them seem luminous. His movements were more fluid and measured than any athlete or performer she had witnessed. The poise and body language was somewhat familiar to her. As someone who had dealt with commanders of ships, fleets, whole populations, that familiarity left her with only a little doubt he could be the one who commanded whatever ship she was on. His confidence alone would have captured her attention, but she couldn't tear her eyes from his chiseled features. The man wasn't young, yet there were no lines or blemishes on his skin. Not even the laugh or smile lines found on any human or the other races she'd met.

His silver hair and brows matched his piercing silver eyes. She had an instant's desire to run her fingers through his hair to find out if it was as soft and silken as it appeared. Training overrode the insane thought, and she tore her eyes away from his face. For a moment she wondered if amusement flashed through his eyes.

Did he know what her thoughts had been? Could these aliens read minds? Then again, perhaps he had the same effect among his own people?

He was certainly handsome enough to draw the attention of any female. Muscular, powerful, probably domineering, with smooth pale white skin to go with his silver hair and matching eyes.

What woman wouldn't be attracted to someone in a powerful position with looks to match?

It had always been her weakness, and she knew it wasn't unusual or even uncommon. She had encountered enough females of various races to know power, in every form of the word, attracted others.

Another alien appeared beside her bed. This one was possibly female, since her physiology was similar to Alyssa's, although this being had hair so dark it reflected purple and blue highlights.

Alyssa turned her attention to the newcomer who was a polar opposite to the man. Her unblemished dark-olive skin reminded Alyssa of natives of the Mediterranean. Gold eyes glanced above Alyssa's head. If the situation had been different, she would have been fascinated by these beings who appeared human in so many ways, yet completely alien in others.

"Thank you, Master Healer Zh'oros," the unknown man said as the woman offered a glass to Alyssa.

Accepting the glass cautiously, Alyssa tried to not stare at the woman and failed miserably. Not only was this woman's appearance a complete contrast in color, but so were her clothes. Unlike the man standing at the foot of her bed, this woman wore a silver, almost white, jumpsuit.

On the left shoulder of the woman was an emblem of a gray tentacled mollusk. A pair of wings were spread wide to each side of the shellfish. A single black stripe wrapped around the woman's wrists. Alyssa suspected the emblem stood for medical personnel while the stripe denoted her rank. Whoever she was and her position, her eyes kept shifting to something above the bed. She would also turn to view something behind the bed, as well.

Monitors, probably, Alyssa thought. Due to the angle, she couldn't see anything above the bed she was currently resting on.

Deciding these beings wouldn't rescue and heal her just to poison her, Alyssa took a small sip from the glass. Cool water flowed over her lips and down her throat. Trying to not gulp greedily, for fear of having the refreshing beverage taken from her, Alyssa stared at the foot of her bed. Better to stare at it than at the woman's full lips, long lashes, and blemish-free features.

These people would give any human on Earth a complex.

Alyssa wasn't ugly, but she wasn't movie-star beautiful either. She had scars, lines, and blemishes. The desire to hide was growing with each passing moment she was with these aliens, and she didn't like it.

"Who are you?" she finally asked, cradling the glass in her hands.

"I am Commander Mc'narrd." He bowed his head slightly. The smile on his lips didn't meet his eyes. "My people are from K'lais. We are not, I'm certain you noticed, a docile race. You are a lowly sergeant. Your name is Alyssa Marie Zelaya."

"That's correct," Alyssa replied, trying to keep her voice calm and unemotional.

Though he was obviously the more dangerous being in the room, Alyssa wasn't going to dismiss the other simply because she didn't wear any obvious weapons.

When Mc'narrd didn't speak, she asked the obvious question. "You rescued me. Why?"

His smile widened the slightest bit. "It is far easier to capture and contain a single person than a large number. You entered our territory in a single-being ship, dropping off relay beacons prior to being disabled from an explosion." He paused and the smile turned sly. "The first one, I should say. There were multiple. Your ship exploded due to them. It seems your owners didn't want you to return home."

"Why me? You've attacked other ships before I arrived," Alyssa pressed, a shiver racing down her spine. She deliberately ignored his comments about the bombs. It was better than allowing herself to dwell on how badly the admiralty had wanted her dead. "And I have no owners. I'm not a slave."

"Indeed. Slaves aren't paid," he retorted thoughtfully. "Either way, your ship is destroyed, the beacons you released have been destroyed, and you are now my captive."

There weren't enough profanities to convey everything Alyssa felt. This was, indeed, the worst scenario she had ever been in. But that didn't mean she would be stuck here permanently.

She was adaptable, and at the very least, she would survive.

"Does it not bother you that your people wanted you dead?" he asked.

Alyssa stared at Mc'narrd, trying to control her emotions. She knew she'd been becoming too good for the government to keep alive. It had been only a matter of time before someone killed her, one way or another. Not that Mc'narrd needed to know that. At least, not yet.

Finally, she asked, "Why have you destroyed all other human ships that came this way?"

"It was not all of them," he replied, his voice a shade colder.

"Very well. Almost all of them," she conceded. After all, they only disabled the cargo ship.

He gave a slight nod, his tone shifting to what it was previously. "Have you not seen what your people do to each other? Why would any sane species want you around, or trust anything your governments offered? Your history is filled with hatred, murder, genocide, and wars. Wars over resources, currency, and which star you wish upon."

Mc'narrd snorted and shook his head. If he was bothered by her not answering his question, he didn't show it.

"You Earthers are problematic. Even now, you kill your own people simply over the ability to eat," he concluded.

"How... how do you know all of that?" Alyssa managed to sputter out.

Mc'narrd knew far too much about her people's history, and to be honest, she could not blame his people for not wanting humans anywhere near their worlds.

Mc'narrd sighed. "You Earthers are also very slow in intelligence. It should be rather obvious: Your race has been broadcasting their every deed from the moment your people launched a satellite into the stars. Anyone could pick up your broadcasts and listen, or view them, with ease." His eyes trailed towards the right and seemed to see through the walls at something beyond them. "Although, considering the crude vehicles and technology which you use to travel, I shouldn't be surprised at how slow your comprehension is."

Alyssa tried to come up with a witty retort, or any retort for that matter. Unfortunately, none came to her lips. She was still too foggy from the explosion and head injury to think of one. At least, that was her story, and she was sticking to it. It had nothing to do with how frighteningly accurate Mc'narrd's words were or how hard they hit home.

When she remained silent, staring at him with her blue-gray eyes, he smirked and continued speaking.

"The vainest race in creation, the Zuell, thought Earthlings were worshiping them. They came to visit, lost one of their ships, and the rest vacated as quickly as possible. They show up, see what humans are like, and then leave. Can you comprehend how poorly, how horrible you have to be, for beings who live for being praised and worshipped to decide, as you would say, 'fuck this, I'm out'?"

He remained silent, so apparently, he was waiting for her to say something.

Alyssa sighed.

"Okay, yeah. My race is pretty horrible when you put it that way." She paused, her sluggish brain finally catching up to a small detail that should have actually been pretty damned big. "Wait… how can you understand me? Do your people also speak our language?"

Mc'narrd snorted, and his perfect features twisted into a look of disgust. On him, it still looked attractive.

Zh'oros took the moment to retrieve the glass of ignored water from her hands. Then the woman moved out of her sight once again.

"No, absolutely not." He reached up to his ear and removed a small clear earbud. He had to turn his hand slightly so the light reflected off the edges of it. He replaced the bud. "We have universal translators. Our people share knowledge and help each other. Your people broadcast every language you speak throughout the galaxies. Because of those reasons, we can understand each other perfectly. Though we do have a common language used by all members of our federation, the translators are given to every being, regardless of race, free of cost."

"We felt it best to allow you to have one. So there would be no misunderstanding of words between our races," Zh'oros stated, ignoring the sharp look from the commander. She deftly plucked something from Alyssa's ear and held it in front of her. Then it was replaced. "The one you're using is only a translator. The ones we use within the military also double as communicators. Or 'comms' as we call them."

Reaching up, Alyssa carefully removed the device and stared at it for several long heartbeats. Then, she replaced it, shifting it until the device was comfortable in her ear.

Damn, she thought. It was considerably more comfortable than the ones Earth offered.

The universal translators offered on her planet were also expensive as hell and only the military were given the translators without a fee. Those were implanted into anyone who served to keep them from being damaged easily. And their translators certainly did not double as communicators.

The K'laisians were far ahead of Earth on so many things. Alyssa feared that if the aliens truly desired, they could invade and eradicate humans with ease.

"Oh. Nice," she finally said quietly, shifting uncomfortably on the bed. Folding her hands on her stomach, she looked at her fingers. "So, why did you rescue me? If you hate humans so much? I prefer that term over 'Earther,' by the way."

"I have always wanted a pet, and I like a challenge," Mc'narrd replied easily. Alyssa's head snapped up, and she glowered at him. He smirked. "Why were you sent alone into our territory?"

"My people wanted information on you. We hoped you'd be more like cats." His eyes narrowed, but his expression remained otherwise emotionless. She smiled pleasantly as she added, "You certainly have the ears, but do you purr?"

"This must be the sense of humor that humanity so prides themselves on," the commander replied with a bored tone. "How pathetic."

Alyssa's face flushed even as she gaped at him.

Damn. She wanted to blame the lack of a quick retort on her injuries, but knew that wasn't why she was faltering. He was too good at everything.

"Remind me again why you even want to trade with humans? What could we possibly offer that would interest you?"

"We like your skulls. It's fascinating how much space is taken up by the brain. Especially in light of how little of it gets used," he countered.

"Well, I certainly can't argue the fact that most humans act like sheep," she replied, trying not to laugh. "But if you're hoping for an interesting hunt, you're going to be sadly disappointed."

Her eyes trailed slowly from his head down his chest to his waist. It took more than a little effort to keep her mind out of the gutter. He was fit, muscular, and made the uniform look good. In fact, she suspected he could make anything look good on him.

"No, you don't seem like the lazy hunter type. Much too muscular for that."

The alien laughed. It was very similar to how her own species laughed, but more musical.

It was a sound Alyssa could have listened to for hours. Or even days. It reminded her of the ancient Earth fairy tales about elves and their musical voices. The elves in those stories had laughter that sounded like tinkling bells. His laugh didn't sound like bells, but it was the sweetest sound she'd heard so far in her twenty-five years of life.

She was thankful he couldn't see the goosebumps on her covered arms. The shiver of pleasure she somehow managed to suppress.

"Very good," he allowed. "To truly answer your question, your planet has materials that we do not find easily, and some of your architecture is envied. A valuable business could be made for humans who would teach or build similar constructs for my people. For example, the ancient skill of building with, I believe it's called, bamboo? We have many similar plants in our home system, but none have used them as efficiently."

"That makes sense," Alyssa replied, nodding. "So what is it you want from me? I'm not exactly an ambassador for my people."

Talk about an understatement, she thought.

Her people wanted her dead. A fact the aliens knew. She knew the admiralty of Earth weren't going to be too pleased to learn she was still alive. She rubbed her left shoulder, wondering if the chip was still active or if whatever the K'laisians did to heal her deactivated it. Or even if it had been removed.

Which brought up the question of if she still had her augmented hearing. Or if that had been damaged by her healing or removed while she'd been unconscious. Her guess was on the latter. If the aliens were so sophisticated with everything she'd seen so far, they could not have missed her implants. And if they'd found them, they'd probably removed them. Her own military would have and she doubted such procedures changed much between races.

"If I wanted to learn about a species, beyond the most basic behavior, I wouldn't choose a politician, lawyer, or career military personnel. Civilians present their own list of difficulties depending on their intelligence and constitution." He nodded towards her. "You offer an atypical option. Your own people offered you up as bait. Dead bait, at that. How loyal will you be to those who sent you out for slaughter? How untainted will your opinions and knowledge of your race, planet, military and political systems be?"

"Even if I did agree to help you, what makes you think my people would listen to me? Especially since, as you say, they sent me out to die?"

Yes, she had been sent to die, and it was very relieving to know she was still breathing. Most sane, or even semi-sane, beings wanted to live. But did that mean she wanted to betray her people? Admittedly, her loyalty to Admiral Lynchen had died with her ship. And she owed little to nothing to the IMD. It was the innocents of Earth she was mostly concerned about.

For all she knew he was weaving a fanciful and elegant trap so he could go in, slaughter the humans, and take over as the supreme ruler.

Not that she'd mind kneeling at his altar, so to speak. Not if he looked as good naked as he did with clothing on.

The laugh rang out again. He kept smiling as he explained, "I'm not expecting you to be an ambassador to your people. You can help me better understand how humans actually live. What they count on, what they need to thrive. At least I'm not preparing to torture you for such."

"So, what do I get out of all this? Aside from surviving?" Alyssa asked. She wasn't certain death wouldn't have been better. But she was thankful she wasn't dead. Talk about a dichotomy. On the plus side, at least she didn't have to worry about testing out the training for torture. "Regardless of if I help you or not, my military will believe I betrayed my country. I'll be killed one way or another if I return."

It took all her training to keep the pain and heartache from showing. She was an exile at the least. Her people would brand her a traitor and want her dead. Spending the rest of her life forever looking over her shoulder was not appealing at all.

"That will depend on what you decide you want." A simple sentence with so many possibilities.

It left her wondering what she actually did want.

Chapter Four

Mc'narrd watched Alyssa's expressive blue-gray eyes. They revealed more than anything else about her. Hope mingled with fear and apprehension. He knew she couldn't return to her people, yet she had no home with his race. The possibility was there. He'd given her a sliver of hope. Now, she needed to stew on it.

"I'll leave you to decide," he said, allowing a tiny smile to form.

"Am I a prisoner?" she asked.

"For now," he relented. "Prove you're worthy of something better, and I might be willing to grant it."

Without another word, he gestured to Zh'oros and strode out, leaving Alyssa Zelaya alone.

The human was intriguing. She didn't bend or buckle, despite being a captive on an alien ship in what she must have seen as enemy territory. Petite by human standards, if their intel was accurate, she was far from ugly.

"You're certain she's healed without any serious side effects?" Mc'narrd asked Master Healer Keris Zh'oros once they were outside the room.

Zh'oros sighed. "We don't know enough about human biology to know the answer to that question. I did warn you before using the nanites. The good news is she isn't dead. Nor did she have a severe reaction to being injected with them." An amused smirk stole across the healer's face. "A fact you seem very pleased about."

"Obviously. The dead don't speak," Mc'narrd deadpanned.

"Nor do you find them so amusing," Zh'oros retorted. "She appears to be stable. But without knowing a baseline for her, or humans in general, we're guessing. My suggestion remains the same: We keep her here in isolation until we're certain she isn't going to relapse. If she has any adverse effects, we can treat them as they arise." She paused a moment before adding thoughtfully, "Perhaps next time we should take the human prisoner before their ship explodes."

"It isn't as though that was planned," Mc'narrd snapped. "Had we known, we could have taken steps to prevent the explosion before it harmed her." He turned to the one-way window into the human woman's room, watching as she curled up on the bed like a wounded animal. "We need her alive and well for this to work in our favor."

"The devices she had implanted in her are secure. Technology and Security are going over them. So far, she's not showing any ill effects from having them removed." Zh'oros paused, eyeing the commander. "Only you and my medical staff have access to her room for now. If her condition changes, I'll inform you."

"Good," Mc'narrd said, tearing his eyes away.

He felt torn between going back in the room and reassuring Alyssa that all would be well and promising to find the humans who had tried to kill her. Someone so strong shouldn't be curled up in a ball. Even if the situation was far from ideal.

Alone on an alien ship, suffering from a near-death ordeal would probably leave one confused, disoriented, emotionally injured, and uncertain.

"Time will tell if her spirit is broken," Mc'narrd murmured.

"If it is, we can treat that, too," Zh'oros reassured him.

Mc'narrd nodded. Healers were trained to deal with both physical and psychological illnesses. Those who went into space learned how to treat any race, as well as being given leeway towards treating any new race they encountered.

Her eyes twinkled as she asked, "Are you planning on being a daily visitor, Commander?"

"No," he replied.

He stifled a sigh. He wouldn't mind teasing the human more. She had a backbone and wit to her that few of his own people dared to throw at him.

Clearing his throat to keep a smile from showing, he turned his back to the isolation chamber. "I will give her time to consider her situation but Ac'kyll will be taking point. I'll be back whenever she makes her decision on what she wants to do."

"Very well," Zh'oros replied. Mc'narrd gave a nod and began walking away, but before he was five feet away, she called after him. "Were you serious about that pet remark?"

Mc'narrd looked over his shoulder at the head healer of his ship and tipped his slowly towards his left shoulder, then back up in a wink. She burst out humming loudly and shook her head before turning away. His own humming was soft and skittered as he headed for the lift. He churned over everything the human did and didn't say.

Once inside the lift, he tapped the screen for the second level, then pressed another icon. A chime sounded.

"Yes, Commander?" the First Officer, Ashyna Ac'kyll, asked.

"The human is awake, and I've left her isolation chamber. The meeting will take place in ten minutes from now. Get the party together, and meet me in Room Three."

"Yes, sir," Ac'kyll said.

Within minutes, Mc'narrd strode into the briefing room. A simple room, it held an oblong table with eight chairs around it, each with a small terminal in front of it. A view screen took up most of the far wall. There were no decorations on the walls or the table. Even the view screen was void of any decoration.

Four K'laisians occupied the same number of chairs, leaving three other seats vacant, including the one at the head of the table open. Ashyna Ac'kyll sat at the other end. They all fell silent as he moved to the head of the table. Between them sat the Masters of Communication, Security, and Policy. Unlike most other meetings, the Master of Weapons and Master of Navigations were not included in this group of senior command.

With the current antagonistic behavior with the humans, Master of Weapons Issyl Li'kox was best served at the helm. The Master of Navigation was also at the helm for the same reason as the weapons master. Zh'oros was still watching over the human in their medbay, so she was missing.

Policy Master Ardor ,K'rell suggested, "Shall we begin with a review of our orders?"

The suggestion was more in line with an order, and every person in the room knew it.

Mc'narrd stifled any emotional reply and instead gave a curt nod.

"Good," Policy Master ,K'rell began. "Our most prevalent order is that of announcing our presence and intent, officially, upon the space-faring species of the third planet of this system."

"Our official position is even now being subverted by the species in target," stated the communications master, Dairra Ar'ath. Her narrowed silver eyes settled firmly on ,K'rell as she continued. "The battleships escorting the transport vessel altered the convoy's course to intercept us. They attacked. We defended ourselves. Even if our vaunted policy master wanted to further disagree with my interpretation of the humans' communiques within their military? Our discovery of the obvious lure they set out, and the sacrificed member of their race, vilifies that agenda. They are trying to make us out as enemies."

"A sacrificed being that currently lounges in our medical ward," rejoined the policy master. His gold eyes were wide, perhaps a bit panicked, as he spoke the observation.

"Before the useless debate on that point begins, we should finish the list of orders," insisted First Officer Ac'kyll.

Mc'narrd felt a smirk form on his lips. His choice of first officer knew how to leash this group. Ashyana Ac'kyll would perhaps be a better commander than he was once she was given a ship to command.

"Yes, to the orders." ,K'rell refocused. "Under our primary order, we have the following stipulations: Learn enough of their habits and weaknesses to have an effective approach when officially making our presence known to the humans' notice. Make no overt actions to heighten their sense of alert. Do not compromise our own security or emplacement."

A few grunts around the table acknowledged this initial rhetoric of information.

"The second primary is to establish favorable trade agreements with the humans if possible. The understanding that we will not allow them to interfere with our already established routes in this system need not be brought to their attention at this time."

Mc'narrd waited for it and was not disappointed. His first officer, along with the communications and security masters, all rolled their eyes up the instant the policy master looked back at his interface.

The commander wondered if the humans acted similarly to personnel who had an exaggerated sense of importance in their calling.

"Finally, we are to report all information, without exception, to the High Command," ,K'rell concluded.

"Where they will engage their infinite wisdom to assess what best to do with said information," Mc'narrd added with as little irritation as he could manage.

The policy master's satisfied smile and nod to him did nothing to quell the urge to make an offending sound or gesture.

The members of the High Command had long left the stars, trading a commander's chair for an office desk. Often lightyears away from what the commanders encountered. Though they were all military and had spent time traveling the universe, it seemed many forgot what they'd encountered. The difficulties they faced. The fact they, too, had been second-guessed by those who weren't there. When the difference in seconds could cost a ship its life. Along with every being aboard. Fortunately, there were some who remembered. Those were the admirals he preferred working alongside.

"Considering the humans are requiring a different course of action and our distance from Command, we will have to adapt to the current situation," Ac'kyll stated. "The Earthers chose to send Alyssa Zelaya on a ship they sabotaged." She turned to Master of Security Eldonn Ra'dett. "Have you received the report on the human's now-destroyed ship?"

Ra'dett nodded, a somber expression on his pale-skinned face. "The ship's explosion began near the front. From our scans prior to its destruction, it occurred near or at the pilot's seat. Had our human been sitting at her console, she would be dust and particles alongside her ship."

"Were there other charges set?" Mc'narrd asked, already knowing the answer. He ignored Ra'dett's cold declaration of the truth, refusing to admit the thought of the human woman being dead bothered him.

"Yes. After we rescued the human, we discovered explosives beside her. We extracted her and the explosives safely." Ra'dett's face twisted in disgust. "It's a primitive but effective explosive that they used. She apparently located and disarmed one bomb but missed the others."

"How many total?" Ac'kyll asked.

"Four."

"Fark. They must have really wanted her dead," Ar'ath said. "From the records we've acquired, Alyssa Zelaya is a noted and successful assassin for her race. Why would they send her on that ship, let alone want to eliminate such a valuable asset?"

"That is a good question. A few possibilities come to mind," Mc'narrd replied.

"From what the analyst masters have concluded of this species, they remain quite obsessed with self-preservation for individual sake," interjected Policy Master ,K'rell.

The first officer replied, "You suggest that she became a theoretical adversary to someone of a higher position?"

"Given what I've read from the analysis reports of this species, yes. That often seems to motivate action more so than even personal gain." ,K'rell answered.

Security Master Ra'dett said, "If not for the excessive number of explosives and their placement aboard the alien ship, I would have thought they sent a professional killer to have the best chance of surviving an abduction or rescue."

The words settled around the group as Ra'dett turned his eyes on Mc'narrd. The commander gave a nod, encouraging him silently to continue.

Ra'dett shook his long silver hair before continuing. "The decision makers of her employment do not know enough about us to make a tactical judgment about what would be most effective. The best choice in those circumstances is to send someone who is best at infiltration and cares only for survival at high cost." He paused, turning his gaze to Mc'narrd. "Humans are what they call themselves, yes?"

Mc'narrd gave the security master an affirmative gesture.

"This human would qualify as a good gamble in that scenario," Ra'dett concluded.

"Except from what you said, and the timing of the explosions, even I could tell they wanted this human dead," Communications Master Ar'ath stated. "From what we've intercepted, humans would kill off their own soldiers in their past, or place them in impossible situations.

Perhaps that is what happened to the human?" Ar'ath tipped her head to the side in thought. "Or we could simply ask the human at a later point."

"Even if she were to be interrogated, there is no guarantee she would tell the truth," ,K'rell argued. "This race is unpredictable at best, and probably even more unstable. How do we know she won't say anything for fear we will kill her otherwise?"

"It is certainly a possibility, considering her own people sent her to die. She's among an unknown race, believes we attacked first and doesn't know why we rescued her," Mc'narrd stated. "It is also possible she will tell the truth knowing her fate rests, quite literally, in our hands. To tell a lie, in her mind, could equal death from us. She is aware she cannot return to her home and her people. She has also acknowledged her people desired her death."

He suspected the human had known she'd been sent to die even before setting foot upon the ship, but hadn't been given any sort of escape prior to being loaded onto the ship. He wasn't going to voice that thought. Not at the moment.

Silence filled the room. After several moments, he spoke again.

"Let us ask. Call Master Healer Zh'oros," Mc'narrd ordered.

The comm chimed before showing the healer on the wall opposite the door.

"Yes, Commander?" Zh'oros said by way of greeting.

"Is there a way to determine if the human is lying or telling the truth?" Mc'narrd asked without preamble.

Zh'oros leaned back in her chair, a thoughtful expression on her face. "If we built a baseline for her, it's possible. We would have to have enough accurate answers to questions to create that baseline, though." Her gold eyes drifted to ,K'rell, who was opening his mouth to speak. "It would not be one hundred percent accurate, since we do not have enough knowledge of the human race, or even this particular human to be accurate beyond question. Nor do we know a lot about their physiology or psychology."

"What about the knowledge we've intercepted?" Ar'ath asked.

"Let me be clear, I speak only for the medical side of things." Zh'oros waited a few moments before continuing. "Everything we have intercepted is questionable. As with every other race's communications we've intercepted, it isn't considered truth beyond question until we have opened communication and trade with that particular race. Sometimes what we intercepted wasn't interpreted accurately. Other times it was completely inaccurate."

Ra'dett shifted in his chair. Mc'narrd gestured to him. The chairs were comfortable, so the only reason for the security master to shift was to subtly call attention to himself.

"There are many variables with the human. Her military attacked us first. Yet in the transmissions we've intercepted, they claim we fired first. The fact she isn't cowering in a corner or trying to attack can mean many things. The main ones being: she's waiting for a better opportunity to attack, she's still trying to grasp the gravity of her situation, or she is willing to turn against those who were willing to not just sacrifice her to an unknown enemy but kill her."

There was a spattering of agreement from most in the room. ,K'rell, Mc'narrd noted, remained silent.

Security Master Ra'dett held a hand up to silence ,K'rell when the man began to open his mouth. "I would advise against allowing the human out of isolation until we can trust she won't try to attack us. Even then, she should not go unescorted around the ship."

"Considering the unpredictability of humans, it would be foolish to allow her access to the entire ship, even escorted," Mc'narrd stated. "She is an alien. As such she has no knowledge of how our people act, think, or react."

,K'rell and Ra'dett appeared slightly mollified.

"Would it be possible to give her limited access to our knowledge base?" Mc'narrd asked Ra'dett. "Perhaps by way of an interface that isn't linked to the subnet or databases? If she requests a way to learn about our people, I want a method available."

"And not have to worry about her possibly hacking into our computers?" Ra'dett asked. He chuckled. "I doubt she would be able to manage such a feat, but it would be best to not chance what the human can do. I will have one of my subordinates work on it and will look it over personally."

"Good. We will discuss who will have access to the human after she is released from isolation whenever it happens."

"So what are we planning on doing with your pet?" ,K'rell demanded. "There is no way to be completely certain she won't turn on any of us."

"There is no way to be certain our own people won't turn on another," Ac'kyll mused. "We are in a contained vessel for months at a time, sometimes years. Many of our own people have broken mentally and emotionally under the stress and isolation. This human is more isolated than any of us." She paused and turned to the healer. "What is the human's mental state currently?"

"From what I can determine, she is showing the typical range of a prisoner," Zh'oros deflected. "You are correct, though, First Officer Ac'kyll. The human is alone. She knows she cannot return to her people. If she is not allowed to speak to beings it is possible— probable even— that she will end up depressed, anguished, possibly even willing to self-harm or self-destruct. If we are going to use her in any fashion, she needs to socialize."

Mc'narrd remained silent, keeping his own thoughts about the human to himself. He suspected she would not lack for crew willing to talk to her. His couldn't help but wonder how she would react to an alien race. Was her wit and cleverness unique to him? Or something she would throw at anyone?

Zh'oros paused, before shaking her head. "We have yet to encounter any race or being that lives in complete solitude and isolation. I don't believe humans would be that different, though I suppose it is possible."

"I am still uneasy with the idea of the alien socializing on board our ship. At least until we have more knowledge of her species," Ra'dett objected.

"No one is suggesting that we go and open the cage immediately," Mc'narrd replied in a stern voice. "And this is *my* ship. Not the property of this collective."

That seemed to finalize the debate.

Mc'narrd nodded. "We proceed according to the Master Healer's recommendation. All other ship functions continue as usual. Our course remains as is. Dismissed."

The protocol master stood, turned on his heel, and strode out. The door slid closed behind him. The atmosphere of the room shifted considerably.

"Now that the watchdog for Command has departed, what is the real plan with the human?" Ra'dett asked, leaning back in his chair.

"Comm Override. Record to my file and copy Admiral Ad'dari only," Mc'narrd commanded.

Admiral Torlla Ad'dari, a three-star admiral renowned among their people, had personally debriefed Mc'narrd prior to leaving K'lais on their current mission. His orders came from her and they encompassed far more than what ‚K'rell had spoken earlier.

A private briefing with an admiral, especially Ad'dari, was not uncommon. The unusual fact was she'd required their briefing be classified to a security clearance of the highest level. Admiral Ad'dari had permitted him far more latitude than he'd been given so far in all his years of command. Complete with permission to omit whomever he deemed from meetings, recordings, and anything in between.

Ad'dari brooked little argument from even her peers amongst High Command. Her skill at Duelling was as infamous as her sharp tongue and quickness to issue a Challenge. She'd quickly risen through the ranks, spent several decades as the commander of a ship, and settled into being a High Command admiral quickly. Those who didn't respect her insight, certainly respected her knowledge and ability to choose the right commanders for each mission she was in charge of.

Which meant he could alter the recordings to only those with the security clearance of a battlecruiser commander and higher without concern of reprisal. The required security clearance did not include the current policy master of his battlecruiser. Mc'narrd was confidant none of those within the meeting room would inform ‚K'rell of what was spoken.

"Override acknowledged. Recording access acknowledged and complete," the feminine voice of the comm reported.

"Now that ‚K'rell can't try to access this, we can continue without concern from him," Mc'narrd stated. "We have more fluidity with the humans than what ‚K'rell wants to admit or acknowledge. My orders came directly from Admiral Ad'dari prior to our departure from K'laisian space. Having the human on board may be a security risk, but I have zero doubts you can handle it, Ra'dett. Especially since she's not going unescorted anywhere."

"Who will be given access to her?" Ac'kyll asked.

"To begin with, you and myself, as well as Master Ra'dett," Mc'narrd replied. "Those within this room at this time will be on the allowed list once she is permitted outside the isolation chamber, as well as Master Healer Zh'oros. I will reevaluate as time progresses."

"Do you think she will actually be of use?" Ra'dett asked.

"I believe so, yes," Mc'narrd replied honestly. "The woman was an assassin. As such, she would know more about the darker side of the human race than a soldier." He smiled slightly at the uneasy expressions his crew were trying to hide. "Our own people are far from peaceful. The humans simply haven't found a peaceful way to control their murderous behavior."

"Considering their history is rife with war, that's putting it mildly," Ar'ath stated. "Our own history isn't lacking bloodshed, but we found a method to remove the cold-blooded murdering that humans are still doing." She paused, before continuing in a wary tone. "Are we certain we even want to open trade with such a bloodthirsty race? One that appears to have little respect for any laws?"

"We trade with other races who are even more bloodthirsty. Such as the Va'nu'ians. They spend their entire lifetimes using murder to rise to better stations and plot against each clan in an effort to rise above each other," Ra'dett stated dismissively. "Knowing what a race is like, and what motivates them, makes it easier to negotiate. You learn their strengths, their weaknesses, and how to work around their fears."

"Any other questions or concerns?" Mc'narrd asked. The crew looked at each other but remained silent. "Very well. The human will remain in isolation until you have a plan, Ra'dett." He stood. "Private record off."

The comm chimed and the rest of the crew stood as one group.

Mc'narrd turned and strode from the room, his mind churning over everything said. Yet a pair of blue-gray eyes kept slipping into his thoughts. Perhaps for the first time in decades, he was distracted by a woman. One with golden hair, startling eyes, and a steel spine.

Shaking his head, he entered the lift and headed for the ship's gym. With luck, exercising until he was too tired to think would cure himself of the human's image haunting his thoughts. He doubted it, but it was worth a try.

Exercise to the point of exhaustion did nothing to help Mc'narrd banish Alyssa from his thoughts. Despite collapsing into a deep sleep, Mc'narrd still dreamed of the woman's expressive eyes, sharp wit, and capricious nature.

There was no denying the human woman had wheedled her way beneath his skin. He wasn't entirely certain he disliked it, though. She intrigued him in a way none had managed since he'd entered the military.

His door chimed, indicating a visitor as he thought about his not-so-unwilling captive.

"Enter," he called.

"Good morning, Commander," First Officer Ac'kyll said, stepping inside Mc'narrd's room. She smiled slightly. "How long do you think it will be before ,K'rell demands to be allowed access to the human?"

"I give him a day after she's allowed out of isolation," Mc'narrd replied. The thought of Alyssa spending time with ,K'rell bothered him, though he wasn't entirely certain why. "He can wait until we're certain she can hold her own against such pompousness."

Ac'kyll laughed. "I've seen the recordings of your interaction with her. I suspect there will need to be someone to ensure no Challenge is invoked from either."

Mc'narrd snorted. The idea of the tiny human woman Challenging the policy master to a Duel amused him. Until he considered the fact it could end in her death. As far as he was aware, she wasn't familiar with using a bladed weapon, which concerned him.

Official Duels were issued among their people to settle arguments and disputes. Often, the Duels ended in death. If someone died during a legal Duel, there were no punishments. One of the reasons anyone who killed in cold blood was given a death sentence. There was no need to resort to killing anyone in any other method. Not when you could employ a Champion of your choice, to better ensure your win.

Shaking the thoughts away, Mc'narrd turned to the task at hand. "Are you ready to meet the human?"

Ac'kyll gave a nod. "If this goes well, we will need to decide on someone who can take time away from their current post, yet is in the chain of command."

Mc'narrd frowned. "We'll worry about that later."

His first officer gave him a curious look, but didn't say anything else. Mc'narrd brushed it off. Who would be given access to the human would come later. Much later.

"Where will you put the human once she is out of isolation?" Ac'kyll asked as she followed Mc'narrd from his quarters.

Mc'narrd didn't pause as they traversed the corridor to the lift. "Beside mine."

"You mean the quarters that adjoin yours? Your non-existent mate's quarters?" Mc'narrd gave a stiff nod. Ac'kyll cleared her throat. "Ah."

"What?" Mc'narrd demanded as they entered the lift. "Can you think of a better, safer place to put her? None but myself would dare enter those quarters without approval from her or me. "

"No. No argument at all," Ac'kyll said, her eyes fixed on the lift's wall. "All ships are equipped with quarters for the commander's mate. It's a part of command due to rarely being on our home planet."

"Those who have mates and are career military are allowed to have their partners with them onboard, also," Mc'narrd countered. "Commanders are simply given extra room for their mates."

"And you're allowing a human to take the room designated for your mate."

Mc'narrd shrugged. "If there were a mate to concern myself about, I wouldn't consider having the human there. For now, it will work to keep her safe from the crew, and the crew safe from her."

"Of course," Ac'kyll stated.

The lift's doors opened, preventing Mc'narrd from arguing. Even if he did like the idea of having the human close to him and easily accessible. It was merely so he could speak with her and ensure her health. Nothing more.

Though, as he neared the isolation chamber she was being held in, he couldn't deny the fact his pulse was quickening. Or the fact he was eager to see her again and learn more about the woman who invaded his dreams.

Chapter Five

The empty room gave Alyssa time to think about the conversation with Commander Mc'narrd. Despite being a highly successful assassin, Alyssa knew plenty about solitude. Every year, she had gone through training to prevent herself from snapping if she were captured and placed in solitary confinement. Little had she known, those lessons would come in handy in an isolation chamber on an alien ship.

When the door opened, she sat up, ready to meet whoever was entering. She couldn't stop her pulse from speeding up, but she could keep her features emotionless. Even the fact the commander was accompanied by a female crewman couldn't keep her from being glad to see him again.

"I believe the term on your planet is 'good morning'? Is that correct?" asked the commander.

"Uh, yes. It is," Alyssa replied, her eyes shifting from the woman to the commander.

The new woman was beautiful, though more austere than the commander. Her dark hair was braided back tight against her scalp in a bun. Her demeanor was stiff and cool. If Alyssa hadn't known who commanded the ship, she might have considered this new woman. Though she lacked the complete confidence held by Mc'narrd.

"My first officer owes me an extra shift. She was certain the greeting was 'what the fuck do you want?' Or similar," Mc'narrd said through what she presumed was a smirk.

Startled, Alyssa couldn't help the bark of laughter that escaped. "No, that's when you're angry or upset and don't like the person who shows up."

"What is a 'fuck'?" the first officer asked

Alyssa opened her mouth, then closed it suddenly, looking down and away from the pair. She could feel warmth creeping along her cheeks.

It had to be Stockholm syndrome she was experiencing— an ancient phrase still used to describe when someone grew affectionate towards their captor— because of the beauty of the K'laisians. She was certain the fact she hadn't been with a guy for far too long didn't help either.

The first officer touched her collar and said something in some unknown language. Alyssa's brain tried to claim it was singing, despite knowing it had to be their native language. So transfixed by the woman's melodic voice, Alyssa did not hear the translation from the earbud still in her ear.

"Poor manners, turning off your translator and speaking in our language." Mc'narrd narrowed his eyes at the first officer before stating, "You're fully aware she has a translator."

Refusing to meet the commander's silver eyes, Alyssa admitted, "I'm afraid I didn't catch the translation."

Mc'narrd raised a brow, his lips twitching as though he wanted to smile. There was only a slight hint of amusement in his voice as he explained. "She wants to know why your eyes sparkle when you make that sound. It is laughter, isn't it?"

"Yes, it is," Alyssa replied, thankful for the explanation, and subsequent distraction.

Why, after decades of training, did this man throw every lesson she'd learned out the proverbial window? She'd learned how to seduce and not be swayed by a pretty face. Yet here she was, all but swooning and begging this man to take her.

Clearing her throat and shoving those thoughts to the side, Alyssa asked, "So, why are you here?"

"Answer our question, and we will answer yours," Mc'narrd replied, amusement in his eyes.

"Oh, well. A 'fuck' is a figurative word we use when angry. Or upset. Or when someone feels like they're doomed," Alyssa replied, not meeting their eyes. "Used that way, it's meant as an emphasis on demand to know what the person wants."

Her responses were thoughtful sounds and exchanged looks between the pair.

"We have similar words," the first officer stated. "Often used the same way."

"As to why we are here? This is my first officer, Ashyna Ac'kyll. She will be observing you as well, often in my absence. I thought it best to make the introductions," Mc'narrd said.

"My caution was amplified because the oddity within your eyes is a signal of vicious intent among we K'laisians," Ac'kyll replied.

Alyssa said, "Oh, there's a different, um, ocular oddity for that in my case. And many humans."

"Could you explain?" the first officer asked.

"The one that comes with laughter is often referred to as a twinkle, the other is usually called a gleam or 'hard' gleam in the eyes," Alyssa offered.

"Could you produce a 'hard gleam' for us to see for comparison?" the first officer countered.

Alyssa felt her temper flare at this woman's presence and what felt like smarmy attitude. Her face felt stony, and she felt the edge of her lip curl upward.

"Ah, I see the difference," Ac'kyll said in a more pleasant tone. "Thank you."

This took Alyssa by surprise. She felt a little flabbergasted and looked to Mc'narrd for some idea of what to expect next. The commander, damn him, appeared to be looking off into space. This only lasted for a moment, but Alyssa noticed the first officer doing the same thing just before Mc'narrd focused back at her.

"My first officer meant no hostility nor offense."

"Uh huh." Alyssa retorted. "And who are you both listening to? Communicating with?"

The other woman gave a solemn look at her while Mc'narrd made an odd humming noise, his eyes amused and unflinching.

"Our master healer of the ship. Who informed us that your statistical health readings shifted, possibly indicating anger," Mc'narrd explained.

"It wasn't funny," the first officer said in a lowered volume.

"Oh my gods, is that humming how you laugh?" Alyssa blurted.

Ac'kyll hummed in response. The commander gave that almost-smirk of an expression again.

"Very good. You are as observant as I suspected, Alyssa," the commander stated.

"So the first time we talked, you laughed like a human to what? Put me at ease?"

Mc'narrd gave her a single nod. "As I stated, you are observant."

Alyssa couldn't process if she were dumbstruck by how cleverly she had been played, or if it was because her skin had goosed up when he had said her name for the first time. Or both.

Probably both and more, she silently reasoned.

Though it was technically the second time, this time it was spoken differently. It was just her first name spoken with some warmth. The first time had been a statement of fact, as though he'd read it from a dossier. Not as an actual person he was talking to.

"We shall leave you for now. One or both of us will return later in today's course." Mc'narrd offered.

"That's it? That's all you came here for?" Alyssa asked, trying to grasp at something, anything, to make sense of what just happened.

"Would you prefer we stay?" rejoined Ac'kyll.

Alyssa blinked. She opened her mouth, shut it, and then sighed.

"Well, actually, if I were to be honest? Yes." She met Mc'narrd's gaze and allowed herself to be drawn into their silvery depths. Perhaps not the wisest decision. But at the moment, she was willing to take whatever pleasure she could find. "I have the answer to your question. About what I want." Mc'narrd's head bowed, but he didn't break eye contact. "I want to survive. I... I don't want to die."

There was an exchange of looks between the K'laisians.

"We have no plans of executing you," explained Mc'narrd. "Should you give us a reason to, you would be given the chance to defend yourself."

"What do you plan on doing once you're finished with me, though?" Alyssa asked, only slightly relieved by his words. "You all are aware that I was sent to die on that ship. There's no reason for me to deny that fact. So, once my usefulness with you is done... then what? I can't go back to my people."

Her jaw clenched unconsciously even as her stomach twisted with the words. Never in all her twenty-odd years had she ever thought she'd never be able to return to Earth. Despite the fact she had no family or true friends, the planet was still her birthplace. She had enjoyed having a place that was hers. Now, she had nothing but memories. Memories and a desire to find a way to survive in an alien world.

"There is an abundance of time to discover what course your life can take from this moment on," observed Ac'kyll. "You have no need to worry about how your existence will end."

Alyssa forced herself to look away from Mc'narrd's eyes. The first officer was studying her intently.

Before she could say anything, the commander spoke. "Why did your employers want to murder you?"

"I was too good at what I did. Too successful," Alyssa answered, trying to sound neutral. Though she knew the bitterness seeped into her words. "I was an assassin with no failures. Unfortunately, with my employers, once you become too good at something, you become a liability. I thought I would have time to find a way out before I reached that point." She paused and shook her head slightly. "I was wrong."

"That confirms what we've learned," Mc'narrd admitted. "It doesn't explain why they would want to exterminate what should be a valuable asset."

"Because people– humans in this case– are usually scared of something. Wealthy and powerful people are mostly afraid of their own mortality. So if someone gets as good at my job as I was? They fear that the person could kill them or reduce their status in some way. And then it becomes time to exterminate the exterminator!" Alyssa felt out of breath when she finished her explanation.

"Your employers were afraid you would turn against them." Ac'kyll stared over Alyssa's head as she spoke.

"Are you certain it was not because of your last assignment?" Mc'narrd asked.

Alyssa felt as though someone had punched her in the solar plexus. She stared at the commander for several long moments. For most of her life she'd been sworn to silence. Trained to not speak of anything she did. The assignments she was given and carried out.

And now, she had zero reason not to tell someone.

"My last assignment was the assassination of Rumusvi Gnech," Alyssa replied. "A Xoutian ambassador. He wasn't even the first Xoutian I'd been assigned to eliminate. Before you ask: no, I do not know why he was targeted for elimination. That falls under 'do not need to know' for assassins."

"The lack of knowledge concerning why the Xoutian was targeted is troublesome," Mc'narrd admitted. "Since that could lead directly to measures we've seen in other races. A process of eliminating all witnesses, minus the beings in political positions to order such missions."

"Welcome to the wonderful world of a professional killer," Alyssa said with a sigh.

"It's not so different from being a soldier during active warfare," Mc'narrd replied. "But K'laisians allow for soldiers to be aware of why they are targeting any being. The motivations are stronger when it's more than a matter of patriotism and blind duty to a philosophy."

She considered his words and couldn't find an argument against them. As she was processing the whole theology he had put forth, Ac'kyll posed another question.

"What about your family? What do you believe they have been told?"

"What family?" Alyssa replied. She gave a disgusted snort. "I have none. I grew up in an orphanage. I was approached and offered a unique opportunity: I could remain in the orphanage and be kicked out upon my eighteenth birthday or enter a government program. I was told I'd receive the best education possible. In return, I would be theirs until my 'retirement'." Alyssa shrugged dismissively. "I accepted the offer and became an employee of my government. My aptitude tests placed me in the program specifically to train as an assassin."

"There must be someone who cares about you..." Ac'kyll trailed off as Alyssa shook her head. "You have no one? Not even friends?"

Alyssa snorted, trying to ignore the heartache causing her chest to tighten. "Friends are a liability in my line of work. The only person who may have cared was my handler. Though I wasn't close to him, either. Not in the way you mean."

"So no one would demand to know about you after the mission. Not to any concerning amount," Mc'narrd mused aloud.

"No," Alyssa replied, ignoring the coldness creeping into her veins. She hated talking about her past, but was willing to do so for these beings.

"A rather lonely life. Did you never want for more?" Ac'kyll rejoined.

"I had the occasional lover," Alyssa admitted. "And friends would have been nice, but I was dedicated to my job. It was all I ever knew. All I have ever known." She paused and shifted her attention to the first officer. "What would you do if you left the military? What does any of your crew do when all they've known is life in the military?"

"All our people are required to spend a year in the military or the police service," Ac'kyll explained. "After that year, they either continue with the Service or they find a position in civilian life that best suits them and their skills and talents." The woman's lips turned up into a slight smile. "Those who eventually retire from the military, or can no longer continue due to illness or injury, find positions best suited to them planetside. Our world's belief is 'in service, we prosper'."

"So, everyone is promised a job? No matter what?" Alyssa asked.

"Those who can work, do work," Mc'narrd answered. "Eventually you retire, but even then, many continue to offer their knowledge in one way or another. It is our way, which is undoubtedly different from your people."

"Your people are very different from mine. Most humans prefer to work to succeed in life, even while envying those who are born into a life of luxury," Alyssa replied. Sighing, she shrugged. "Humans aren't always lazy. Though there are plenty who would rather not have to work to improve their place in life. It all depends on the person."

"What about you?" Mc'narrd asked.

Alyssa started. For the first time, she didn't know exactly how to answer that question. She'd only ever known her life with the IMD. First in the programs, then as an assassin.

"Growing up, I was jealous of those who had a family. I always wanted one, but no one ever adopted me. When I was accepted into the government program, I promised myself I would work hard and become the best. That way I could provide the life I wanted without having to rely on anyone else."

"Did you stop wishing for a family? Or is that no longer a desire for you?" Ac'kyll asked. Her eyes never wavered from Alyssa.

"Who would want an assassin as a wife?" Alyssa asked in return. It was a cold truth she'd come to accept years ago. "As wonderful as it would be to have a husband, even children, I always had to be realistic. Who would want someone who has learned how to tell if a person is lying? To spot their weaknesses and exploit them?" She shook her head. "Not that it matters now."

"Why do you say that? As we have said before, we have no intention of killing you," Ac'kyll said. The first officer sounded exasperated to Alyssa, but she had no way of knowing if that was accurate with the K'laisian.

"Why would a K'laisian want me as a wife? Partner? Mate? I'm not exactly the prettiest being on this ship. Far from it. Not if what I've seen so far is the norm. Besides, I'm a complete alien and so far no one has said anything close to complimentary about my race." Alyssa paused and gave a slight chuckle. "Not that my people have done anything to deserve to be liked or trusted."

Ac'kyll's eyes darted to Alyssa before returning to whatever they were watching behind her. A monitor of some sort, Alyssa guessed. They were monitoring her for something.

"If we were to allow you out of this room, what would you do?" Mc'narrd asked, abruptly changing the topic.

"Whatever you want, I suppose," Alyssa replied. Mc'narrd smirked, and she felt her cheeks grow warm. "Within reason, of course."

"Of course," Mc'narrd parroted.

Alyssa felt her blush deepen. "I would like to learn more about your people and your culture. If possible, I'd like to help you with your objective of opening trade with my people."

Ac'kyll's eyes didn't leave whatever she was watching as she spoke. "What if we lied, and you learn we want to take over your planet?"

"Then I guess Earth is fucked," Alyssa replied with a grin. "Can I make requests on who you take out first? Since I do happen to know the chain of command on Earth?"

Both of the K'laisians' eyes narrowed. The humming sound came again, from both. Mc'narrd finally smiled and gave a more human-sounding laugh.

"That can be discussed," he said.

"Did I say something wrong?" Alyssa asked, still smiling. She looked from the commander to the first officer then back to Mc'narrd again.

The commander's smile ate away at any concern she might have felt. She suspected he knew it, too. Or perhaps she was jaded because it was a skill she'd used against her own targets. She should have felt off-balance and uneasy. But her mind kept sliding into the gutter, especially when he smiled. Something about him suggested she could trust him. To do what, she didn't know. But she found herself wanting to trust him despite the fact he was an alien race.

"No, that was... amusing. Was your suggestion not meant to be humorous?" asked the first officer.

"No, it was meant to be humorous, for the most part," Alyssa replied. She relaxed on the bed. "I do know the military's chain of command, though. And I *am* sincere in wanting to help you."

She wanted to add more but didn't want to play all her cards just yet. These people did not need to know she was bitter about her intended death by the admiralty. Or the fact she knew her position was tenuous at best. After all, her position had never been one with any sort of power. She doubted they were aware of all the information she possessed. Or her knack for deciphering codes.

Assassins didn't exactly climb the ranks or grab a powerful position anywhere. They were the seedy, dirty, unknown underbelly of her world's government.

"I will have to ponder your offer and present it to my command staff," Mc'narrd stated. His voice had not changed in pitch, nor had his expression changed since he and Ac'kyll had laughed.

Alyssa started to feel more at ease.

A new crew member entered the chamber carrying what looked to be a tray. As the crew member came closer, she couldn't discern the gender but had no care of that. Gender fluidity had come a long time ago on Earth and while it was less common, it was still accepted. The contents of the tray were looking more familiar.

"We haven't synthesized any of the food from your ship yet." Mc'narrd explained. "However, we brought a serving of what was most plentiful from the storage. We presumed it to be your preferred choices."

"Oh. Wonderful. That looks like gefilte fish, brussel sprouts, and... I don't know what that mushy gray stuff is," Alyssa said, refusing to look at any of the K'laisians in her room. "That was very kind of you to do, though I'm afraid my ship was stocked with the leftovers from other missions."

She didn't add that her food stock probably included expired foods.

"This is an embarrassing situation," observed Ac'kyll.

Mc'narrd interjected, "I thought the food masters had determined the gray matter was something called 'potted meat'? Is there some manner of animal that grows like a plant on Earth?"

When he noticed that his first officer and Alyssa wore similar expressions of disbelief, he made the connection.

"None of this is food that you enjoy. Yes, Ac'kyll, this is embarrassing. Perhaps we can have a different variety brought in."

He gestured to the crew person, who made a hasty retreat.

"I wonder if any peanut butter or crackers survived," Alyssa mused aloud.

As it turned out, both had. So, her first true meal aboard the K'laisian spaceship was peanut butter and crackers. And the most bizarre wine she had ever tasted.

Chapter Six

Boredom was a familiar companion to Alyssa. Normally she could content herself with something to read or research. Or even reviewing the files for whatever her next target was to be. This time, confined to an otherwise empty room, she was at a loss on how to keep herself entertained. Her only options were sleep or stewing on her new, unknown place among a world of aliens.

She had no hope of returning to Earth. No matter how much her body desired the commander of the ship, she didn't have much hope there, either. Allowing her thoughts to churn on Commander Mc'narrd definitely wasn't going to help her.

"I suppose it's too much to want something to read while I'm in here," she said aloud.

Instead, she took in her surroundings. Nothing startling about four walls and a floor. The bed was a small erected force field, which had enough give to be comfortable. The tiny emitters appeared to be built in the floor. Then she noticed how organic and flowing everything was.

The emitters weren't actually built into the floor. The curves and lines of the construction of her whole surroundings flowed easily into one another. The appearance was as if all of it were hand-carved from a giant block of the same material. Whether it was made that way or achieved by some other means, Alyssa could not tell. She did find it pleasing to her eyes and mind.

Her eyes followed the walls to the ceiling above her, which glowed with a soft, steady light that illuminated the chamber. The glow was constant and ebbed when she lay down. She hadn't seen it go completely out. Lowering her lids until she was barely peeking through them, the lights lowered, but didn't go completely out. Opening them, she watched as the light intensified. It didn't reach an unpleasant level. But it also didn't shift to where her eyes could discern any details above.

Sighing, she sat up on the bed trying to figure out what she could do.

After a few moments, the room's door slid open. Her eyes leapt to the emblem she now associated with the medical staff before shifting to the rest of the medic.

A few inches taller than her, the K'laisian was definitely male. His silver hair was cut short, and he also had the same pale skin tone as Mc'narrd. He even had the same shade of silver eyes.

"You requested something to read?" he asked in a friendly voice. It was maybe two octaves higher than the commander's tone. He held out a tablet to her. Seemingly not concerned about her being a possible threat. "Healer Zh'oros suggested you may find this of interest."

Alyssa accepted the offered tablet.

Slim, it was smooth and cool to the touch. Lighter than anything she'd ever used, it had delicate etching along the edges. Looking closer, she realized it was scrollwork. As with the light in the room, the tablet adjusted to a pleasant setting that wasn't harsh to her eyes. Turning the tablet over, she found the back of the tablet was also textured. It reminded her of tree bark or maybe leaves.

Flipping it back over, she looked up at the medic.

"It is a history of our people," the medic replied.

"Could I ask you a question?"

The medic nodded. "I will answer if I can."

"Why does your commander wear a sword?" Alyssa asked. She gestured towards the medic, who she had to admit, was as handsome as the commander. Even if he didn't appeal to her the same way the commander did. "He is the only one I've seen wearing one."

The medic tipped his head to the side. "The medical personnel are rarely Challenged. Medics also rarely have need of any weapon. If you were a perceived threat, you would be receiving meals through the door." He smiled brightly and she found herself smiling in return. "Since you are not, you are given better treatment.

"But you asked about the weapons. The carrying of weapons is a personal choice. Some do, others do not. There is a more rigid standard involved with service-issued weapons, but you are on a military ship." the medic gave her a smile and continued "Commander Mc'narrd chooses to wear his preferred weapons along with his service-issued sidearms when interacting with new races."

"Challenges? Would you explain that more to me? Such as what do you mean by 'preferred weapon'? What other weapons are used by your people?" She paused before adding, "What is your name?"

"I am Medic Ba'lyn." He bowed slightly. "Duels are our method of settling disputes. Not always to the death, though that isn't uncommon, either. Challenges are invoked when two parties are displeased with each other. A time and place are agreed upon and Champions are chosen, if they are desired. Depending on the Challengers, the choice of weapons may differ. For example, our commander is renowned for his skill with a sword. First Officer Ac'kyll prefers a collapsible spear." He nodded towards the interface in her hands. "There is a section on Duels and Challenges there."

"Thank you for answering my questions," Alyssa said. "I look forward to learning about your people and the culture."

"I am happy to be of service," Ba'lyn replied. "I am certain Commander Mc'narrd or First Officer Ac'kyll would be willing to answer any other questions."

"Have you ever been Challenged?" Alyssa asked before he could leave. Eventually she'd get the nerve to ask if there were any K'laisians who weren't perfect. Until then, she was going to try to not envy their perfection and beauty.

Ba'lyn's smile grew slightly. There was a twinkle to his eyes, and Alyssa found herself liking him even more. Searching herself, she had to admit, there was no physical reaction to the medic.

So what was it about Mc'narrd that appealed to her on a physical level?

"Everyone is Challenged at one point or another in their lives. Those who are chosen for space exploration are those who can defend themselves without our Gifts." The smile grew into a broad grin. "Everyone on this battlecruiser, I assure you, has been Challenged multiple times, and all of us are skilled with our preferred weapons. Before you ask, I prefer a sword."

"Why a sword? Even I know knife wounds can be some of the nastiest to treat. Swords can often be worse than a knife."

The medic lifted a single silver brow. "Do humans often use swords or knives to inflict injuries on each other? Is that how you know that?"

"Actually, I've been stabbed before and had to have the injuries treated," Alyssa replied, deflecting his question away from her personally. If these beings used bladed weapons, it was best to not inform them she was skilled in the art, also. "Compared to a typical bullet wound, knife wounds take longer to heal and become infected easier."

"What is a 'bullet'?" Ba'lyn asked. His brow furrowed. "Is that a type of weapon?"

"Yes. Well, it's ammunition used in a weapon. Bullets are specially made metal casings. Inside the casing is gunpowder, which is an explosive. They're small cylindrical objects with pointed tips." Alyssa shrugged. "I'm not the best at describing these things, so my apologies if it's confusing."

"Ah," Ba'lyn murmured. "Interesting. Do your people also Challenge each other to settle disputes?"

"If only," Alyssa muttered. "No. My people tend to either resort to filing charges with the local police or fighting it out physically. Sometimes guns are involved, but usually it's one-on-one if they choose to make it personal." She paused, before adding, "Though, centuries ago, dueling was a very common method of settling disputes. It became 'uncivilized' and eventually a thing of the past. The distant past."

"You must enjoy history if you are aware of that," he replied.

"I was an assassin. I chose to learn about the cultures of my targets. In my experience, it aided in my ability to blend in with those people. I learned early in my training that to understand a group of people, or a race of alien beings, you have to learn their history. Their culture. If you read enough of my people's history, you'll quickly learn that humans frequently fail to learn from past mistakes. There is a saying among my people, though it isn't often followed: if you forget your history, you're doomed to repeat it." She chuckled. "Admittedly, it often made my job easier."

"Humans are very confusing," Ba'lyn remarked.

His skin darkened along his cheeks. It reminded her of humans when they blushed. Oddly enough, it made him appear more human, and Alyssa found herself liking him even more.

"I apologize. That was rude."

"Maybe, but it was certainly accurate," Alyssa said, the grin still on her face. "No apology is required when I can't argue the truth of the statement. If it helps, I find my own people confusing often."

"Is that normal?"

Alyssa laughed and nodded. "Very much so, I'm afraid."

His head snapped up suddenly, and he stared over her head. She turned to look but didn't see anything. Sighing, she turned back to find the medic looking at her again.

"I am sorry, but I must go now," he said. He even sounded sincere to her. "I thank you for answering my questions."

"No, Medic Ba'lyn, I am the one who should be thanking you. I do appreciate your time and patience. I hope I didn't get you into trouble for asking you so much," Alyssa replied. "If so, I apologize, and I hope Master Healer Zh'oros realizes I'm the one to blame for pulling you into the conversation."

Ba'lyn grinned again. This time it was a boyish smile that made him appear even more elfin to Alyssa. She really hated not having her library of antique books. Hopefully they went to a good home and not into a disposal somewhere.

"No, I won't be in trouble," he reassured her. "If you wish for anything else to read, please let us know."

"I will. Thank you for the tablet," she said.

"Tablet?" he asked. She held up the gift he had given her. He hummed lightly. "Ah. We call them 'interfaces'."

"Then thank you for the interface," she said, bowing her head to him.

Ba'lyn gave a bow, then turned and strode from the room. Alyssa watched him go and stared at the door for a few moments before turning to the tablet. She'd have to remember to call it an interface. Even as the tablet… interface lit up, her mind turned towards treacherous questions. Questions she didn't dare ask aloud.

How much were these people playing her? How much did they already know? Were they questioning her to see if she'd lie? It was definitely something her people would do. Though her own people would probably also resort to threats of torture, if not torture itself. It had happened before, after all.

Shaking her head slightly, she reclined on the bed, propping the tablet up on her legs. No time like the present to start learning about the people who rescued her. Maybe, if she were lucky, she could find a home with them.

Plus, it would hopefully take her mind off the commander. Maybe. Probably not, but she could try.

Chapter Seven

Mc'narrd and Ac'kyll watched the recording of Ba'lyn interacting with Alyssa in Zh'oros' office. Mc'narrd forced his expression to remain emotionless while Alyssa laughed, seemingly at ease with the medic. He was secretly pleased, though, to see she wasn't showing any actual desire for the medic.

"It appears her reactions to you, It'zarry, are unique," Zh'oros commented. "Perhaps you can use it to your advantage."

"Perhaps," Mc'narrd replied.

He pressed a button and stopped the recording after Ba'lyn left the room. The interface shifted to the room where Alyssa was being detained. The human was intently looking at the interface, obviously reading it.

"How long has she been reading the interface?"

"Since Ba'lyn left," Zh'oros replied. "She's been reading it intently the entire time."

"What are you thinking, Commander?" Ac'kyll asked.

"I'm thinking she should be allowed out of isolation. She won't be allowed outside her quarters unescorted, though. If she's going to help us, we need to show we are better than her race."

"She will need exercise that the isolation chamber won't allow," Zh'oros added. "I will continue monitoring her vitals and alert you should they change drastically."

"What about those who object?" Ac'kyll pressed.

Mc'narrd smiled. It was anything but pleasant. "I do not believe anyone will Challenge me for this decision.

Especially since High Command gave me explicit orders to do as I need to open communications with her planet."

Ac'kyll sighed but didn't say anything.

"Please inform our Master of Security of the change."

"Yes, Commander," Ac'kyll replied, obviously not pleased but resigned to his decision. She turned and strode from the healer's office.

Zh'oros hummed. "Considering an intimate method of opening communication, 'Zarry?" Mc'narrd frowned, and the healer hummed louder. "I have to monitor everyone, Commander. That includes you."

Mc'narrd smirked. "It's a 'sacrifice' I'm willing to make."

"Tread carefully. There are some who wouldn't think twice about Challenging you if they think you're betraying our people."

Mc'narrd snorted. ",K'rell can get stuffed and placed in a museum. I don't plan on initiating anything intimate with the human. For all we know, she is attracted to anyone in command. Or it's part of her training as an assassin. Time will tell."

"What do you plan to do about her?"

"She will need to learn our ways and make a life with us," Mc'narrd replied. "Or she can choose another of our ally planets. Unless her people can be convinced to accept her without fear of killing her."

"What do you believe?" Zh'oros asked, leaning back in her chair.

"I believe what the woman has said. She has shown to be an intelligent being so far. I'm willing to give her a chance at living."

The healer narrowed her eyes at Mc'narrd. "My friend, you are playing a dangerous game. But then, you have always been one to take risks and play the long game. I just hope I'm around to heal you should it ever go badly."

"Her own people sent her here to die. They didn't even care how she died. Slow and painful or fast and painless. It made no difference to them." Mc'narrd clenched his fists before releasing them. "Alyssa knew it, too. She is aware of the cruelty of her people. I suspect she also knows the other end of that spectrum. We need someone who knows what the humans will do when they realize their plan failed. Not only at killing a person with knowledge, but at not garnering the information they sought."

"So Security and Science have figured out that homing signal the human's ship left behind?" Zh'oros asked.

Mc'narrd nodded. "I'm allowing them the chance to play with it. It's been a boring mission until now. They may have some entertainment with such primitive technology."

"If it doesn't make them weary trying to make it interesting," Zh'oros countered.

"They said Engineering and Navigation are conferring with them," Mc'narrd said with a grin. "Until we have more information on what to expect from the humans, we aren't remaining in the same area. They also can't locate us as long as we remain cloaked. So I'm fine with giving the crew some leeway on playing with the box."

Zh'oros hummed again. "I'm certain they will keep the humans scratching their heads if that's the case. Keep me informed on your plans." She paused, a mischievous grin curving her lips. "And if I should set up a chamber for a certain pompous fool."

Mc'narrd hummed in turn. "I'll let you know."

Giving the healer a slight bow, he departed the office and headed for Alyssa's isolation chamber. Pressing his palm against the interface beside the door, he waited until the device flashed green. The door slid open with barely a whisper. Alyssa jumped, almost dropping the tablet. She caught it before it fell to the floor.

"Good catch," he complimented her. Her cheeks slowly turned red and he smirked slightly. "Perhaps you will permit a question?" When she gave a nod, he continued. "What is it called when your cheeks turn red?"

"Oh, um, it's called 'blushing'," Alyssa replied. "It's something humans do when they're, um, flustered."

Mc'narrd kept his features the same. His own people did something similar, except their skin merely darkened. It did not shift colors, like hers did.

"Now that is a lie," Zh'oros' voice said via the comm in Mc'narrd's ear. "At least according to my readings, it isn't a truth."

All their earpieces were linked. Their technology allowed them to listen in on any conversation onboard that wasn't on a private frequency. Those in the command line, the senior crew especially, could change between the various departments aboard the starship with ease. Those of lower rank had a set of frequencies they could use, but it wasn't nearly as extensive as those in the line of command.

Anytime someone wanted to speak to another specifically, all they had to do was say that being's title and name first. The comms did the rest. It did not matter what rank or department the being happened to occupy.

It also meant the personnel could listen in on conversations. Such as what Zh'oros was now doing with him and Alyssa. The higher in the command structure, and security clearance level, the more a being had access to. He and Zh'oros were able to listen to anyone at any time.

His command crew were directly below him and Zh'oros, as was ,K'rell, despite the policy master not being in the direct line of command. At the moment, Mc'narrd was thankful the policy master disliked the comms with a passion. As such, ,K'rell barely used his unless it was to berate someone or a being spoke to him directly.

"Are you certain that flustered is the correct word?" Mc'narrd asked in what he hoped was a tone that the human would interpret as somber.

The color in her cheeks grew. Mc'narrd didn't dare say it, but he found the feature endearing. Yes, it made the fact she was alien more obvious, but it also added to the attraction he felt towards her. Sometimes being in command made his life difficult, especially when it came to females.

"The color in your face has deepened, meaning more of your blood is pushing to the surface of your skin. Is this a health concern?"

The question felt sloppy coming out of his mouth. How he hated his impulses in regards to beings he felt attracted to! His command impulses were, thankfully, far more successful.

The distinct humming from Zh'oros rang in his ear. He also wished he could tell Zh'oros she was not helping him at all.

"Oh, no. Not a health concern," Alyssa replied. She rubbed her cheeks while averting her eyes. "Humans also do it when they're embarrassed. Or shy. Or other strong emotions."

"I'm fairly certain you didn't embarrass the girl," Zh'oros said. "Perhaps it was a different 'strong emotion' you triggered?"

"So this would be... which emotion?" Mc'narrd tried to not sound as eager to know the answer as he actually was.

He knew the translator was giving accurate feedback of the words they were saying, but he didn't know if emotional tones were relayed correctly. For that, they'd already discovered fundamental differences in how emotions were expressed between the races.

"Fine, I'm embarrassed," Alyssa admitted.

"Her readings are showing that as a half-truth, if I'm reading this correctly," Zh'oros stated.

"It seems our people have something else in common. We are uncomfortable making mistakes or being clumsy in front of others as well," Mc'narrd replied, deciding to not push it. Better if he didn't force her to lie again.

He hoped his smile was "human" enough to put her at ease.

"I'm surprised you're here, when you said your first officer would be my main contact," Alyssa said, smiling.

"That eager to be rid of me?" Mc'narrd asked, a smirk pulling at his lips.

"No!" she exclaimed, her cheeks reddening once again. "That is, I enjoy our conversations. I just didn't expect a commander to have so much free time."

There was no doubt in Mc'narrd's mind that she was flustered. Perhaps she was truly attracted to him, after all? That it wasn't a ploy for some unknown ulterior motive of hers.

"For now, I am free," Mc'narrd allowed. "At least long enough to escort you to the quarters you will use while aboard my ship."

"I would love that," Alyssa said, her eyes meeting his own for a few brief moments before she lowered them.

In his own people, females did that as a way of admitting attraction for the other being. Acceptance of a sexual suggestion. Since she was not K'laisian, Mc'narrd couldn't help but wonder what the action meant from a human.

She sighed and held her arms out in front of her, wrists close together. "I'm ready to go, sir."

The laughter in her eyes betrayed her actions. Mc'narrd suspected the human knew she wasn't going to be led away in restraints. Yet she gave the outward appearance of such.

"Teasing again, Alyssa?" Mc'narrd asked, raising a brow.

"Maybe a little," she admitted, a grin flashing across her face as she dropped her arms.

Shaking his head, he gestured towards the door. "Unless you plan on trying to run around the ship, you can go without restraints."

"I don't know, sir. That could be fun. Is it like a maze? Would I get a piece of cheese if I found the right exit?" she asked, glancing up at him from the corner of her eyes.

Mc'narrd laughed as the human did, aware it kept Alyssa at ease around him. From the comm in his ear, he heard Zh'oros humming loudly.

"I think you might have finally met your match, 'Zarry," Zh'oros finally said in a breathless voice. Humming followed the comment. "Best hope High Command doesn't object."

He didn't think High Command would object should a relationship develop. After all, it wasn't as though K'laisians didn't take other races as partners, or even life mates. As long as he succeeded, they could have little to object about. He hoped.

"You're very quiet," Alyssa stated as Mc'narrd guided her through the halls. "This won't cause difficulties with your crew, will it?"

Mc'narrd started before studying the woman beside him. "My crew follows my orders. Those who do not suffer the consequences."

"That doesn't mean difficulties won't arise if they think you're allowing an alien to roam somewhat freely, certainly without restraints. Especially if they believe it is a bad idea," she countered.

"You know how beings think very well," he commented.

Alyssa shrugged, her eyes darting around the corridors. Mc'narrd noticed her body was stiff. As if she were alert and on edge. Prepared for an attack from any angle. She seemed to notice everything around her.

"I had to learn to read people. To know how they think, act, or what they might believe," Alyssa admitted quietly. "As an assassin it was part of the job."

"Did you enjoy being an assassin?" he asked gently.

Another shrug from the human. "It was all I knew."

"But did you enjoy it? Did you enjoy extinguishing the lives of other beings? Did you not wish you could have done something different with your life?"

Her steps faltered, and Mc'narrd watched as she closed her eyes.

"Zh'oros," he said quietly.

"Her readings are similar to when you left her, after she first awoke," Zh'oros replied, her tone somber.

Mc'narrd watched as Alyssa drew in a deep breath before letting it out slowly.

Her tone was lower and shaky as she spoke. "It was a skill I could do. My trainers and the psych docs said it was like I had a switch I could turn on and off." She shook her head as she stared in front of her at something Mc'narrd could not see. Perhaps reliving unpleasant parts of her past. "But did I enjoy it? No. It was a job. It kept me alive, and I was damned good at it."

"That was all truth," Zh'oros stated. "Not even a hint of a mistruth or lie."

"Then we will need to find a new skill for you to utilize with as much aptitude and accuracy as you did your former one," Mc'narrd stated. He took a chance and placed a hand on her left shoulder. She looked up at him startled. He added in what he hoped was a soothing tone, "Something you will enjoy."

Her face turned pink and she glanced away, a smile on her lips.

"That would be lovely," she said before biting her lip.

Humming came from Zh'oros. "Definitely *not* embarrassed that time."

Mc'narrd rubbed her back before dropping his hand. He noticed Alyssa took a step closer to him after he moved his hand, but didn't say anything. Thankfully it was only two short corridors and a corner before they arrived at the door to her quarters.

"Stand before the door, please," Mc'narrd said, nudging Alyssa forward.

She glanced at him before doing as requested. The door slid open without a word.

"How?" she asked, even as Mc'narrd led her into the room.

Mc'narrd moved into the center of the large room. He couldn't help but think how empty the room was and how it matched his personal life.

"Every room on board this ship is programmed to its occupant. Scanners and sensors, as well as cameras, are built into everything. It's to prevent unwelcomed, and unwanted, entrance into a being's room. Or into unauthorized areas," Mc'narrd explained, not giving her the full truth behind it.

She did not need to know the details about her current quarters. Or the fact that when his crew discovered the human was in the quarters meant for the commander's mate, many would most assuredly be very displeased. To say the least. Especially since many of them had hopes of acquiring the quarters for themselves.

Not that he could blame them. Aside from his quarters, these were the largest onboard. No one would dare enter the room without an explicit invitation. Whoever occupied the quarters could program the door to let in no one, including the commander himself. Only Ra'dett and Zh'oros would be able to override those commands.

That wasn't the only benefit, either.

There was a small sofa with a short table and two matching chairs on each side of the table on one side of the room. A large viewscreen sat opposite the sofa. A writing desk with both a comm station and paper was secured to the opposite wall with a single cushioned chair positioned before it. Further into the room was a bar, typically filled with the favorite libations of the commander and his mate. Currently the cabinet set into the wall was empty.

The bed in the sleeping chamber was large enough for two beings with room left over. A sonic shower and vestibule had its own small room. The sonic shower was large enough for two beings, also.

Of all the quarters onboard, these were designed for comfort and luxury. As the commander's mate, it was up to the mate to bring a sense of 'home' to the ship. Or at least to the commander.

Most commanders kept the quarters decorated and made to appear as though someone used them. Even if it was only the commander. Or the commander and his current lover, if said commander did not have a mate.

Mc'narrd did neither. He had his own quarters and did not wish to intrude on what was not his. Even if it was within his right. Sometimes he questioned that decision, but now he knew it had been the right one. Alyssa was staring around the room, searching the walls and furniture for any sign of someone else.

"These cannot be the typical crew quarters," she finally stated. She turned directly to him, hands on her hips. "These aren't your quarters, either. So where am I?"

Mc'narrd's eyes narrowed slightly, a smile curving his lips. "How do you know they aren't mine? I did say I wanted a pet, after all."

Alyssa glowered at him before folding her arms across her chest. "Very funny. These quarters are too empty to be used by anyone. Even you, Commander."

"The quarters are reserved for special guests," Mc'narrd replied. It wasn't exactly a lie.

"That's as close to a lie as I've ever heard you say," Zh'oros stated. "And I'll be hoxed if the suit isn't showing it as a truth."

Alyssa didn't look convinced, but she didn't say anything.

"You will be absolutely safe within these quarters. No one will enter without your permission. Unless you wish to return to the medbay, or the brig?"

"I'll pass on the latter suggestions," Alyssa said quickly. She took another look around the room before turning to him. "Thank you for this."

"Allow me to show you around, and then we will discuss your new schedule," Mc'narrd said. "But first, you may enjoy this."

Crossing to a small table, he picked up an interface and turned back towards her. She crossed to him, accepting it from him. She looked from the interface then back to him.

"What is this?" she asked.

"This interface has considerably more information than your previous interface. Since you've already read through the other multiple times, it was suggested you might enjoy something with considerably more information," Mc'narrd explained. He kept his voice pleasant and even, despite the delight he felt towards her surprise.

"Thank you," she repeated. There was no mistaking the joy in her eyes.

"You are welcome, Alyssa," he replied warmly. "Shall I show you your quarters, now?"

Alyssa nodded and followed him as he gave her the tour. The questions she asked were intelligent, and he realized quickly that she could be a benefit to any world that appreciated intelligent beings.

Leaving Alyssa in her quarters, Mc'narrd turned to the two guards stationed outside the room.

"Inform me if she tries to leave," he ordered the pair.

They nodded, then resumed their positions on each side of the door.

Mc'narrd turned and strode down the corridor. Stepping onto the lift, he touched the interface for the bridge. He forced his thoughts away from the blonde-haired alien female currently residing in the quarters meant for his mate. Dwelling on her would do him no good. He had a mission to complete. Either she would help. Or she would not. Until they had that answer, there was little he could do regarding her.

The lift's doors opened and he stepped onto the bridge. As with most battlecruisers, the bridge was two levels with the main viewscreen curving along the nose of the ship. The top level of the ship held the communications array and science station with security divided on each side of the lift door. Typically the Security Master and three personnel. When Ra'dett was not there, it was the next highest ranking K'laisian and three other guards.

The 'lower' level– lower by way of only a handful of steps– held the command chair and the consoles for navigation, engineering, and weapons control.

As he stepped onto the bridge, the crew turned, saluted, then returned to their stations. He crossed to Ar'ath at her console instead of heading to his command chair.

"Have there been any more communications from the human ships?" he asked, studying her interfaces.

Ar'ath turned in her chair to look up at him. "The communications are coded. Security and linguistics are working on it, but they may have to reach out to other departments for aid."

"Do you believe your human would be able, and willing, to assist?" Ac'kyll asked as she stepped up to Ar'ath's station.

Mc'narrd tipped his head to the side thoughtfully. "Perhaps. She did offer."

"Do we want to appear as though the only thing she is useful for is information?" Ar'ath asked, turning to face both superior officers. As Mc'narrd and Ac'kyll turned their attention to her, she tipped her head from side to side in a shrug. "If we wish to show we're better than the humans, approaching her immediately for information may not be the best option."

"There is also the question of how accurate her intel will be," Ra'dett said, crossing to the trio. He leaned against the railing that wrapped around the upper level. "But I do agree with Dairra."

Dairra Ar'ath smiled at the Master of Security. Mc'narrd raised a brow at the pair. They met his gaze evenly, and the commander wondered if they were involved in an intimate relationship. Not that such was frowned upon. They were both consenting adults of equal security clearance levels. Provided it didn't interfere with their positions, relationships were not his concern.

"We will approach the sergeant at a later time," Mc'narrd stated. He gestured towards the interface in front of Ar'ath. "What have you learned in regards to the humans' communications?"

Ar'ath met Ra'dett's silver eyes a final time before she turned back to her interface. Touching the screens she pulled up a view of the current sector. Small icons representing three ships appeared on the screen. A brilliant blue line traveled from one to another, with a third line shading into red as it ended in an empty space.

"The three ships we're aware of are transmitting encrypted, coded messages. There is another outside our range involved in the transmissions," she answered. "Whether the fourth ship involved is another human vessel or an ally of the humans, we do not know. Without moving closer to the third ship, there is no way to tell."

Mc'narrd frowned. "That would place us too far outside this area, as well as away from our current allies in this sector."

"Are you certain we don't want to question the sergeant for what knowledge she currently possesses?" Ac'kyll asked, her voice soft.

"Would she even have the codes we need?" Ra'dett countered. "She was an assassin. What's the likelihood she'd have the level of security clearance required to decode transmissions between their warships? Even the Va'nu'ians do not give their assassins those types of codes."

Ac'kyll frowned, but didn't respond. There was no argument to be had since the Master of Security was correct.

"We will continue our current course," Mc'narrd said, his gaze traveling around his command crew. "We'll remain cloaked and our transmissions silent. The less visibility we present, the better. As we are outside of direct communications with High Command, the silence will not be noticed. In fact, I suspect it would be expected if they were informed of our current situation."

",K'rell will not be pleased with that decision," Ra'dett commented.

"I'll handle our policy master," Mc'narrd replied calmly. "Until he holds my title, *I* still make the commands on this battlecruiser."

Humming filled the room, even as his crew exchanged smirks.

"In the meantime, I'll confer with Zh'oros about the health and mental state of Sergeant Zelaya," Mc'narrd said. His eyes met Ra'dett's and he smiled slightly. "She will need to be introduced to you. We'll need to arrange that tomorrow."

Ra'dett gave a nod and pushed away from the railing as Mc'narrd turned towards the few steps leading down to his command chair. The conversation shifted to when and where to meet for Ra'dett's introduction and how best to conduct it.

By the time Mc'narrd's duties were finished for the day, it was well past the time he typically concluded his day. As commander, his duty was to his ship and crew. Ensuring everything ran smoothly. Questions were answered, reports from other departments read and signed. He also had his own reports to file. And even once his general tasks were done, he had those concerning the humans and their erratic behavior.

So far, the humans' transmissions they'd been able to intercept were not helpful towards their mission. Nor were those from their allies. The only news that was of any interest had come to them just before they'd rescued Alyssa. That had been about the assassination of a Xoutian ambassador. One of their allies. Mc'narrd had his own suspicions about that, but it wasn't of grave importance at the moment.

As he relinquished command, Mc'narrd retired to his quarters. His eyes glanced towards the door linking his rooms with Alyssa's quarters. With a quick shake of his head, he was on his way towards his well-stocked cabinet when his comm gave a series of chirps.

"Mc'narrd," he said, recognizing the sequence changing the comm to a private frequency between him and Zh'oros. Since it was at an odd hour, he chose to address her informally. "What's wrong, Keris?"

"It appears your human is active and her levels are… strange," Zh'oros replied.

"Strange… how?" he asked.

"If she were K'laisian, I'd say she was growing increasingly restless. As though she were trapped and unable to find something to stimulate her mind or body."

A smirk flashed across Mc'narrd's face at the statement. He could think of many ways to do such, but he shoved those thoughts away.

"I'll check on her," he said instead.

"If she is growing restless, we will have to adjust her schedule accordingly," Mc'narrd could hear the warning in her voice. "If she is similar to K'laisians, such behavior can and will lead to harm. Mental, if not self-inflicted physical, harm."

"Arrangements will be made, once we determine what is troubling her."

Zh'oros hummed. "I'm certain you'll figure something out. Zh'oros out."

Sometimes Mc'narrd truly hated all the data the bio suits sent to the medics.

Crossing to the door, he touched the interfaces. Instead of opening the door, he chose to chime the room. To allow her the choice of allowing him entrance.

Chapter Eight

Alyssa stared at the tablet in her hands, her departing gift from the commander several hours prior. It contained considerably more information on her rescuers. From their history to their culture and even their biology. It was all fascinating, but even she could only read so much before growing bored.

She'd explored her quarters, going over everything a second time after Mc'narrd left, examining all the nooks and crannies. All the furniture and rooms. Including all the cabinets. There was no sign of anyone else ever living in the quarters, though there was also no dust to be found, either. Not that she'd seen any dust anywhere on this vessel. Everything had a polished shine with sleek curves and soft edges.

After sitting on the sofa reading for several hours, she stretched languidly. Her body was restless. This was, perhaps, the most downtime she'd ever encountered in her entire life. Or, at the very least, for as long as she could remember. Numbers flashed on the interface she held, as well as the larger one near the sofa. But she had no clue how those eight numbers matched up with Earth's times. Her internal clock, however, suggested it was the same as some ungodly hour in the morning. When she should have been sleeping.

Yet, here she was, wide awake. Walking around her quarters again, she ran her hands through her hair. Her eyes settled on what reminded her of a computer console and she sighed heavily. She was still a prisoner. Regardless of how comfortable the cage was, it was still a gilded cage.

Turning her back on the console, she ran her hands over the short shelf in front of the empty cabinet. There had to be something she could do. Or she was going to go stir crazy. Something she had not been trained to prevent. Her training to not snap in solitary confinement had not included being placed in a room of luxury. Or what to do when her mind kept wanting to shift to one of her captors.

Were they captors? Or her saviors? She was so conflicted and there was little she could do to figure it out.

The soft sound of a chime rang through the room. It reminded her of a doorbell.

"Come?" she said uncertainly, looking around the room.

From behind her, she heard a door opening. She pivoted around to face whoever had found a new door into her quarters. Her eyes widened as she found Commander Mc'narrd standing in a doorway. Behind him she could see what appeared to be personal quarters. The view vanished as the door slid shut.

"That appeared to be someone's personal quarters behind you," she said accusingly. "You cannot tell me all quarters are joined."

"No," he replied simply, his silver eyes twinkling. At her frown, he chuckled. "You appear restless."

Alyssa studied him for several long minutes. It made sense they would be watching her, but it still left her feeling uneasy. Shaking away the feeling, she gave a brisk nod.

"That's because I am," she replied, not moving. With him in the room, she had a great many ideas on how to cure her boredom. None of them were ones she'd dare speak aloud, though. "I am not accustomed to not having so little to do."

"And what would you like to do?" he asked, closing the distance between them.

An innocent question. Yet warmth flooded her face. She glanced down and away from him. That was a dangerous question. And she was not about to answer it the way her mind wanted to. She had to get control over whatever was causing him to affect her so strongly.

"Alyssa?" he asked and she could feel his closeness without having to look up. "Are you well?"

Raising her eyes, she found him watching her, that damnable smirk fixed on his face. On most beings she'd want to wipe it off them. But on him? She liked it. And she suspected he knew it, too.

"Yes," she replied, using the same tactic he'd used earlier.

His laugh and slight bow revealed he knew exactly what she was doing. Perhaps even approved of it. She also suspected someone was conversing with him on the comm they all wore. Not that it mattered. She enjoyed their verbal sparring and teasing. It was far preferable to anything else.

"Very good," he allowed. "May I ask what you did prior to requiring rescuing?"

That was not nearly as helpful as he thought it would be, she acknowledged. Since there were plenty of times she'd find someone to take as a one-night stand. Not that she believed Commander Mc'narrd would ever be someone to do such. He reminded her too much of the humans who wanted something long-term. And as an assassin, that had never been an option for her.

Instead, she tucked a non-existent wayward strand of hair behind her ear. Glancing away from him, she shyly said, "I had one hobby that I wasn't supposed to do. Or know how to do. In fact, if it was discovered, it might explain why the admiralty wanted to kill me."

Mc'narrd appeared relaxed, but Alyssa noted the subtle shift of his body. "What was that?"

Glancing up from beneath her lashes, she admitted, "I enjoyed breaking codes. While I was training to be an assassin, and for a year or two after I finished, I knew someone who taught me. He… Well, we liked each other and spent a lot of time together. I had a knack for cracking codes and he enjoyed teaching me."

"Someone you were intimate with, perhaps?" Mc'narrd suggested, his voice calm and even.

Alyssa nodded, squeezing her eyes shut even as her chest tightened. She'd been a fool to believe the government would have allowed them to have a relationship. Even just a physical one.

"Assassins aren't allowed to have relationships," she said, finally looking up at him. Her eyes were haunted, her voice filled with old pain and heartache. "There were fewer and fewer who showed more than a physical interest as I became better at my profession. After Alistair, I knew there was no possible way I could have a relationship while I was an assassin."

"Did you kill-"

He didn't even finish the sentence before she felt as though she'd been slapped. She stared at him, feeling her body grow cold. Shaking her head, she couldn't even open her mouth to say anything.

"Forgive me," he murmured, closing the last bit of distance between them. His hands settled on her shoulders. "I am sorry. That was cruel and needlessly harsh."

"No," she said, looking away from him. She swallowed hard, drawing in a deep breath before letting it out slowly. "It was a fair question. But I did not harm him. I don't even think it was love. Nothing more than a childhood crush."

A warm hand touched her chin, lifting her face up until she had no choice but to meet Mc'narrd's eyes. Compassion filled their silvery depths and she found herself drowning in them.

Oh, hells, was she ever in trouble.

His thumb brushed over her chin and she shivered for an entirely different reason. The smirk on his face said everything, as did the heat that flashed through his eyes.

"Perhaps we should find a safe hobby for you to enjoy, even when I am not available," he mused quietly.

"Might be best," she managed to say. Though there were many other ideas swirling in her thoughts. "Are you suggesting you aren't safe, though?"

Mc'narrd laughed softly, his fingers brushing over her face before he stepped away from her. "That depends on one's definition of 'safe'."

Alyssa laughed, suddenly feeling the tension in the room drop considerably.

"Of anyone on this ship, I suspect you are the safest one to be around," she said, meeting his gaze and holding it. "Regardless of one's definition of the word."

"Your hobby is breaking codes?" Mc'narrd asked, deliberately changing the topic. Though the amusement was still in his eyes. "You appeared... shy? Is that the correct term? When you were speaking of it."

"Ah, yes. That was the correct description," she admitted, the shyness returning. The smile on her face, though, refused to leave. Shrugging, she lifted her eyes to him defiantly. "Assassins aren't supposed to be able to do such. Yet, it was something of a hobby. If I questioned everything my handler was telling me, I would spend time breaking the encryptions of his messages. Not that I ever told him. But I think he figured it out eventually because he stopped leaving out bits and pieces of the messages he received."

"Is that typical?" Mc'narrd asked, tilting his head to the side.

Alyssa suspected it was a way to display curiosity.

"Which part? To leave out information or for an assassin to break codes?"

"Both." His head remained tilted to the side as he watched her.

"No, it is not. Assassins are typically given a dossier of their intended target. Our security clearance is relatively low. Even our handlers don't have very high security clearance. There is no need when our task is literally to remove a target. Our goal doesn't involve the secrets of a nation. Or who is doing what, when, and where. We're given blueprints of a location. Information on how many people are in a building or home. The target's preferred locations. Their favorite foods."

"General information one could acquire with enough research and time," Mc'narrd said thoughtfully. Alyssa nodded, smiling. "And yet you learned to break codes?"

She shrugged, feeling smug and guilty at the same time. "I had a knack for it. I could figure out algorithms and patterns. Alistair often teased me about it. Said it went with my talent for learning languages so easily."

Mc'narrd studied her for several long minutes and Alyssa wondered what he was thinking. "I would like to show you something. If you believe you could assist, I will arrange it."

Puzzled, Alyssa gave a nod. "Of course. As I said before, I'll help however I can."

The smirk flared to life on the commander's face once more. He turned and crossed to the computer console, settling into the chair in front of it. Cautiously, Alyssa followed him.

"How am I allowed to see this?" she asked, nodding towards the screen.

Mc'narrd chuckled. "As long as I am here, you are allowed. I'm the commander. As such, I have the ultimate say of who is allowed to see what in my presence. You would not be able to access this console without me, the Master of Security, Master of Communications, or Zh'oros." He paused a moment before adding, "Not yet, anyway."

"If ever," she murmured. At his frown, she chuckled dryly. "I am not only an alien, but your prisoner, Commander. I do not see that changing any time soon. And when it does, where will I be? On your ship? Or your planet?"

His frown deepened. Irritation showing on his face. "There is time to decide your position."

Alyssa rolled her eyes, but remained silent as his fingers flew over the surface of the interface. His movements were fluid and smooth. She found it as fascinating to watch him as it was to watch the interface. Finally, he pulled up what was obviously an intercepted message from one of IMD's battleships.

"That has multiple layers of encryption, as well as a coded message," Alyssa said after she watched it play across the screen. "The security is higher than any I'm aware of."

Before she could say anything else, the door to her room slid open. She turned to find a silver-haired being entering with a pair of K'laisians behind him. Immediately, she moved away from Mc'narrd, who was still sitting at the console.

Mc'narrd stood and she took a few steps further away, allowing the commander space.

"Commander," the silver-haired K'laisian said, stopping in the middle of her room. The pair of guards remained a respectful distance from him. "I was unaware you were here with the sergeant."

Alyssa glanced at Mc'narrd before turning her attention back to the trio in front of her. Fear gripped her and she felt her pulse rising even as her blood ran cold. Despite her emotions, she retained a calm outward appearance.

"Explain," Mc'narrd said, his tone several degrees cooler.

Alyssa took a few steps further away from him, uncertain of her position. The guards behind the one in front stiffened and she stopped moving. Her gut told her this was going to go very badly, very quickly. Keeping her hands at her sides, she focused her attention on the strangers. Mc'narrd, she hoped, she could trust.

"I was informed the console was being accessed," the male K'laisian in the front said, his eyes shifting between her and Mc'narrd. "I was not informed you were here, Commander."

"Allow me to introduce Master of Security Eldonn Ra'dett, Alyssa," Mc'narrd said, not turning his attention away from the trio. "I find it interesting that you were not informed that I was the one using the interface. Considering only a select few could ever use it, and currently, Alyssa Zelaya is not one of those beings."

"The system would also have flagged it as you the moment you entered your code," Ra'dett added, darkly. "My apologies for the intrusion."

"I am not who you should apologize to," Mc'narrd countered, his eyes narrowing on the master of security.

Ra'dett's pale face lost even more color, puzzling Alyssa.

Turning to face Mc'narrd, she took an unconscious step closer to him. Before she could open her mouth to question anything, she noticed motion from the K'laisian behind Ra'dett.

The guard to Ra'dett's right had removed something from his belt. She jerked to her left, her right hand snapping up.

Her fingers wrapped around the handle of a knife stopping its flight. The metal was cold and textured beneath her hand. Unfortunately, the blade was longer than most she'd caught, and a good three inches had embedded itself into her arm. She'd managed to stop most of it, but what was in her arm burned. It did not help that the blade was at least an inch wide where it met her skin. Silence filled the room, even as Alyssa studied the knife in her arm. Blood seeped around it before sliding down her arm in small rivulets.

"I... she was moving towards the commander," the guard stuttered when Ra'dett turned to face him.

"She's an unarmed human," Ra'dett retorted, fury filling his every word. "That is an insult to any K'laisian. Even if she were trained at hand-to-hand combat, she's maybe half the size of Commander Mc'narrd."

The dark-haired, gold-eyed guard's face grew several shades darker. From anger or embarrassment, Alyssa didn't know, choosing to remain silent. The pain was making it difficult to control her emotions and something felt very odd against her skin and she didn't think it was the knife.

The longer the silence in the room grew, the more it allowed her to debate on if anger or fear was going to win the battle. She was equally uncertain of which would be the better option.

Shrugging, she turned to the problem of the knife and decided to do something bold: she removed it and flipped it in her hand. The temptation to return the knife to its owner in the same way she'd received it was strong, but she did one better. She held it out to Mc'narrd, the blade flat in her hand. The blade had missed any major arteries, being closer to her radius bone rather than the ulna or the series of veins between them. Blood flowed from the wound, but not in a gush. Mc'narrd plucked the knife from her hand without looking at her. She, in turn, immediately pressed the free hand against the wound.

"Confine yourself to your quarters," Mc'narrd snapped, plucking the knife from her hand without looking at her. "Both of you. Until further notice." The pair of guards hesitated, their eyes wide. "Or am I to presume neither of you are under my command? And as such, you are willing to be Challenged?"

The pair turned and left the room with such speed, Alyssa gave Mc'narrd an appraising expression, despite the blood flowing down her arm. From the corner of her eyes, she saw Ra'dett turn and stride briskly to the bathroom. When he returned, he held a folded towel in his hand.

Instead of applying it himself, or even handing it to her, the master of security offered it to Mc'narrd. The commander exchanged the knife for the towel before turning to her.

"You should have left it in," he chided her. Pressing the towel to the injury, Alyssa inhaled sharply. The blood loss was starting to affect her vision and balance. He removed the towel, only to have more blood pour forth. Instead of trying to wipe it away, he pressed it tightly against the wound. "That is going to require treatment in the medical wing."

Alyssa pressed the towel against the wound, grimacing at the pain. "It isn't the first time I've been stabbed." Glancing at the towel that was darkening with her blood, she frowned. "I've endured worse."

"I'll walk with you," Ra'dett offered, his silver eyes meeting the commander's gaze. "Lieutenant Pe'rroth will need to be examined by Zh'oros."

"The guard's reasoning was rather pathetic," Alyssa murmured.

When the men looked at her, she shrugged her uninjured shoulder.

"It isn't as though I could possibly best you, Commander." she continued. "Ra'dett is not wrong. Our difference in size alone gives you the advantage. The fact I currently owe you my life also gives you a greater advantage."

Ra'dett snorted. "Let's get her to the medical wing."

Mc'narrd studied her and gave a nod. He placed a hand in the middle of her back and she sighed. Ra'dett gave her an amused look before turning and striding from the room. Alyssa followed behind him, allowing Mc'narrd to remain beside her, his hand still in the middle of her back.

As they walked, she kept her attention on following Ra'dett. The blood loss was starting to affect her, as was shock. She managed to traverse one corridor before the hallway tilted to the left. Blinking rapidly, she slowed her steps. When the hallway returned to its proper position, she quickened her pace. Until the hallway began spinning. Stopping, she leaned against the wall, turning until her back was flush against it. Tipping her head back, she stared up at the ceiling, trying to will it to stop, even as it continued to twirl around her.

"Alyssa?" Mc'narrd asked, concern in his voice.

She turned her head to face him, and saw worry in his eyes. "I'll be fine. Just give me a moment for the ship to stop spinning."

Instead of replying, Mc'narrd turned her until her injured side faced away from him before sweeping her up into his arms. She leaned her head in the crook of his neck and shoulder.

"I'm fine," she whispered.

"That is a lie," Mc'narrd replied in an even, calm tone. "You are not fine. You're suffering from blood loss."

She didn't even reply. Instead, she relaxed against him, allowing his smooth, fluid steps to lull her into a sense of safety and security. Her eyes closed and she allowed unconsciousness to claim her.

Mc'narrd knew the moment Alyssa fell unconscious. He felt her weight alter in his arms. The commander turned his attention to his master of security, who looked decidedly uneasy.

"Zh'oros?" Mc'narrd said as he strode briskly towards the lift.

"I'll meet you at the lift," the healer replied. "Her levels have evened out, but they're still high. Her blood loss is the concerning part at the moment, but it appears the nanites have slowed the wound to where the bleeding is no longer a threat."

The commander remained silent as he stepped into the lift. Ra'dett touched the interface, not speaking, either. When the doors opened, Zh'oros was waiting for them. Mc'narrd paused just outside the lift, allowing the healer to examine the wound.

"I suspect we will be in dock considerably longer the next time we visit K'lais," she said darkly. "We'll use a standard room this time. There is no need to treat her as a danger."

Turning, the healer strode down the hallway, leaving Mc'narrd and Ra'dett to follow in her wake. The door to the room was open when the men approached it, allowing Mc'narrd to cross to the bed without stopping. He gently placed Alyssa on the diagnostics bed, watching as it conformed around her.

Unlike the previous room, where the bed was made from a force field, this room had an actual bed that conformed around the patient. Even if he'd considered arguing, Zh'oros would be able to override him. The only being aboard a battlecruiser capable of overriding a commander, or giving orders to everyone, including him, was the master healer. Mc'narrd suspected Zh'oros would have overrode any objection he or Ra'dett may have made in regards to Alyssa.

Two medics entered behind him and Ra'dett, the same females who had helped treat Alyssa when they'd originally rescued the human.

"Out," Zh'oros ordered. Ra'dett darted from the room. Amusement flashed through her eyes when Mc'narrd made no move to leave. "I'll inform you when she's stabilized. We'll discuss the problems that may result from this after she's been treated."

"Such as if she will trust us," Mc'narrd murmured.

"As I said, we'll discuss it shortly. Now leave, Commander," Zh'oros ordered, looking at him pointedly.

Mc'narrd's response was skittered humming, but he acquiesced. Turning, he strode from the room, leaving Zh'oros with Alyssa and the medics. Ra'dett fell into step with him outside the room. Together, they continued to the healer's office.

The interface flashed green and the door slid open as they approached it. Ra'dett settled into the chair in the corner to the left of the door. Mc'narrd slouched in the chair opposite of the healer's desk.

"Fark, that went horribly," Ra'dett finally said. His silver eyes met Mc'narrd's gaze and held it. "My sincere apologies, sir. I'll start an investigation as to why I wasn't informed you were the one in the room." He paused before shaking his head. "I should have known she couldn't have accessed it. Or even checked myself."

"She's an alien," Mc'narrd countered. "You were doing your duty. The problem came from the guard. We won't know his true reason until Zh'oros examines him. There are several possibilities, aside from xenophobia."

Ra'dett raised his brows. "Do you think ,K'rell will attempt to use this against her?"

A cold gleam flared to life in Mc'narrd's eyes. "Comm Override. Record to my file and copy Admiral Ad'dari only." He waited for the standard acknowledgement from the interfaces in the room before continuing. "I don't want ,K'rell to hear anything else. He can try. But we both know what the result of that would be."

"What do you not want him to hear?" Ra'dett asked. "Aside from the obvious threat of being eval'ed for xenophobia."

"Admiral Ad'dari questioned who the humans have opened trade and communications with," Mc'narrd admitted. He straightened in the chair, concern for the mission overruling his worry for Alyssa. "There have been rumors about the Va'nu'ians being seen with humans on multiple trade planets."

"As mates or captives?" Ra'dett asked, leaning towards the commander. "Or captive mates? Since that is still something they do."

"Unknown. But the fact there are rumors has the admiralty concerned. Alyssa stated she has a skill for breaking codes. She confirmed the codes transmitted between the humans' battleships have layers of encryptions. And it's a coded message."

"If the Va'nu'ians have had contact with the humans, that could explain why the humans reacted as violently as they have," Ra'dett said thoughtfully. "We may trade with Va'nu, but it is an uneasy alliance. Trade is done only on designated neutral worlds."

"And we still see plenty of battles with them when we meet in space," Mc'narrd added. "It's no secret the Va'nu'ins have always wanted to reclaim K'lais for themselves."

"Is this why you were given the private briefing with Ad'dari?" Ra'dett asked, studying the commander. "And allowed so much freedom for this contact?"

Mc'narrd gave a nod. "Complete with permission to do whatever is required to open trade. To acquire the answers and ensure no war occurs between our people."

Ra'dett hummed lightly. "And yet they give you ,K'rell."

"Indeed," Mc'narrd said dryly. "There is one positive side to this." Ra'dett tipped his head to the side in question. "He cannot claim Alyssa made any threatening moves."

That brought another round of humming from the master of security. "No, no he cannot. I believe the fact she so willingly handed you the knife shocked my guards, though."

At that, Mc'narrd joined in the humming. "She would be an asset to any race."

"I cannot argue that," Ra'dett admitted.

"Comm override off," Mc'narrd said, relaxing in the chair.

The feminine voice of the interfaces acknowledged the command.

"Comms off. No recording," Ra'dett said abruptly. "Emergency contact only per Master of Security Eldonn Ra'dett."

The comms in Mc'narrd's ear went completely silent.

"Something you want to say, Eldonn?" Mc'narrd asked, reclining in the conforming chair. With the comms off, there was no need to be formal.

The master of security shrugged. A sly smile curved his lips as he spoke. "Let the policy master stew for a while."

Mc'narrd hummed loudly. "You have something you want to say. So say it."

"Do you truly believe she can help, 'Zarry? Would be willing to betray her people? Her race?"

"Yes, I do," Mc'narrd said quietly.

"What do you plan on doing if certain beings on this 'cruiser decide to Match you with her?" Mc'narrd raised a brow at the question. Ra'dett hummed loudly. "There is an obvious attraction between you both, Commander. Dairra and I both have noticed it. As has Ash."

"You all have too much free time, if that's all you talk about," Mc'narrd countered. Ra'dett's humming grew even louder. "We do not even know-"

"You're avoiding the question, It'zarry," Ra'dett replied, amused. "Matching is a time-honored tradition of our people. As you have said, she'd be an asset to any race. Including our own. And, to be perfectly honest, we saved her life. She belongs to K'lais, now."

"That is not how it works," Mc'narrd argued dryly. "K'lais no longer claims life debts. She can make her own decisions when the time comes."

"Of course," Ra'dett replied, still amused. Which annoyed Mc'narrd.

The last thing he needed was his crew trying to Match him with Alyssa. True, K'laisians did so when they saw a couple who had a physical attraction that could evolve into something more. But that did not mean he needed his crew to intrude into his personal life. Or do so with the human woman they'd rescued.

Silence fell over the pair as they awaited Zh'oros. With the comms off, Mc'narrd couldn't even listen to what was occurring on his ship. Though the break was nice. Ra'dett didn't seem to mind it, either.

Eventually, the door slid open and Zh'oros entered the office. Humming was not what Mc'narrd expected. From Ra'dett's frown, he suspected the master of security didn't expect it, either.

"You both look positively grim," Zh'oros commented, thoroughly amused. "Our human is resting peacefully. Asleep. Not unconscious."

"How is her mental state? Or do we know yet?" Mc'narrd asked, ignoring the healer's amused expression.

"She was uncertain as to what she did to cause such a violent reaction," Zh'oros admitted. "Concerned she'd done something wrong, but otherwise she's doing well."

"Do you believe she'll continue to trust us?" Ra'dett asked, his eyes flicking to Mc'narrd before returning to Zh'oros.

"Seeing as you have effectively silenced my office, Eldonn, I feel no concern in replying," Zh'oros said, smirking. "She has not stopped trusting the commander. As to anyone else? I believe it would be best if you allowed her out of her room for exercise and to socialize with a select few. Her restlessness will not abate. As such, it will affect her mental well being, as well as her physical health.

I would suggest my medical staff to begin with, as they are more thoroughly evaluated than the rest of the crew, it seems."

"When will she be released?" Mc'narrd asked, refusing to show his pleasure at the healer's comment.

"I would prefer she remain in the room for observation until tomorrow," Zh'oros stated, leaning back in her chair. "We are unaware of how humans react to blood loss, how fast it is replenished, or even how their bodies react to being in shock. She is also not your typical human. As such, it is difficult to gauge how she is reacting to anything. Including pain."

"Not unlike many of our own race," Mc'narrd commented, trying to stop a smirk from forming.

"Like those in command?" Zh'oros asked, raising a brow.

Both men glanced at each other, then grinned at the healer, though neither spoke for several moments. Humming filled the room after several heartbeats.

Finally, Mc'narrd asked, "Do you believe, if she's willing, it would be acceptable for her to work alongside our own people?"

"For her mental health, I would think it would be better than leaving her in solitude for long periods," Zh'oros finally said. Her gaze shifted to Ra'dett. "She would be under supervision, but Alyssa is someone accustomed to working. Prolonged bouts of inactivity *will be* detrimental to her mental health. It is part of my service to care for the psychological health of a patient, as much as their physical health. I will advise against leaving her in solitude. Even if the room is more luxurious."

Ra'dett sighed, but held his hands up in supplication. "I will not argue with you, Master Healer Zh'oros." A mischievous smile flashed across his face. "Healers are at the top of my list of beings to *not* anger."

"Even above your commander?" Mc'narrd drew the words out, his eyes narrowed at the master of security.

Ra'dett's grin broadened. "Even above a policy master and commander."

Zh'oros hummed and Mc'narrd joined in a heartbeat later.

A light flashed on the healer's interface. She touched it and the diagnostic readouts above Alyssa's bed floated in the air above the interface.

"It appears our human sleeps as lightly as you, Commander," Zh'oros grumbled. "If you wish to speak to her, now would be a good time." Lifting her gold eyes from the interface, they locked with Mc'narrd's silver ones. A twinkle brightened them as she asked, "Is the human our guest… or captive?"

"That is for her to decide," Mc'narrd allowed, a smile flashing across his face.

Zh'oros and Ra'dett exchanged amused expressions. Humming lightly, he left the pair in the room.

"Comms to normal," Mc'narrd said once he was outside the office. "Override per Commander It'zarry Mc'narrd."

A series of chirps filled his ear and he sighed as the usual din of noise returned. He would have preferred having the silence when he spoke to Alyssa, but that would have raised even more questions. Eventually, he would be able to have silence with her, but she'd have to earn it first.

Chapter Nine

When Alyssa woke later, the room was empty. Examining her arm, she discovered the suit had been repaired. Either that, or she'd been dressed in another uniform. Staring at the sleeve, she noticed movement. Looking closer, she saw there was something in the suit itself moving and her eyes widened. It appeared as though it were cleaning itself. But… that was impossible right?

Plucking at it with her other hand, the movement didn't stop. Yet, it felt like fabric. Very odd, alien fabric. But what else was to be expected by such a sophisticated alien race?

The door slid open and she paused in her examination of the suit she wore to find the commander stepping inside the room. Concern filled her and she wondered if the offer of the quarters was being revoked. If she would be sent to their version of a brig or left in her current room as a prisoner.

"Fascinating, isn't it?" Mc'narrd commented. She furrowed her brow, tipping her head to the side. He chuckled and she realized it was something K'laisians did, also. It brought a smile to her own face. "The bio suit. I suspect you're wondering about it."

Giving him a slow nod, she remained silent. When he didn't continue, she sighed, the smile fading slightly. "Earth doesn't have anything even remotely like it."

"That is not surprising. Nanites are something K'lais has developed over the centuries. Few other worlds have them. Fewer still have them at such an advanced level," he said, resuming his position at the foot of her bed. His eyes swept upward for a brief moment before turning back to her. "You are not in trouble, Alyssa."

"Nanites," she repeated, glancing at the bio suit before looking back at him. She knew of the tech, but had never seen anything as sophisticated as the clothing she wore. "What do they do?"

"For K'laisians, they provide healing and care of a body," Mc'narrd answered. The pleasant smile didn't fade from his lips, even as he watched her closely. "As we have never met a human before, we were uncertain how they would react to you. But it appears they are adapting to your physiology with little difficulty. They also repair the bio suit you wear when it's damaged, as well as removing foreign particles."

"Like blood?" she asked, glancing at her sleeve again. There was no hiding her unease at the strange tech, but it wasn't as though she had anything else to wear.

"The nanites are harmless, Alyssa," he said in a gentle tone. "How are you feeling?"

At the strange question, she looked up at him. Searching his face, she found genuine concern.

"As though I don't know anything about, well… anything," she replied honestly. Why lie to them? It wasn't as though it would get her anywhere but in more trouble. And she did not want to die, regardless of what her own race wanted. "What do you plan on doing with me?"

He frowned, tipping his own head to the side. "I'm afraid I do not understand what you're asking. I… *we* wish for you to help us with opening trade with your race. With humans. That has not changed."

"But… what about…" she trailed off gesturing towards her now-healed arm.

Mc'narrd shook his head slowly. "That was a mistake on our part. The actions of the lieutenant involved are being investigated. I assure you, Alyssa; you did nothing wrong." He paused, his silver eyes boring into hers. "Do your own people never make mistakes?"

Alyssa laughed, though there was no humor to it. "It would be a lie if I said 'yes'. You know better than that, as do I. Mistakes happen frequently. Between those from the same planet, and even more among those of different planets."

"Then it is settled. It was a mistake on our part. When you're released, you return to the same quarters as before," Mc'narrd stated simply.

"Thank you," she said quietly. "May I ask you a question?"

The smirk appeared on his face and for some reason, that expression made her relax more than the smile. She needed help just for that alone. The commander gave a very human-style nod, bowing his head slightly before raising it again. And she knew then he was behaving in such a manner in an attempt to make her more comfortable with him. Amusing, considering where her mind kept wanting to drift.

"You showed me that transmission for a reason. Why? Obviously it wasn't to have me tell you what I suspect you already knew."

"Obviously," he parroted.

"Are you teasing me?" she asked, trying to not laugh.

Laughter confirmed it, even as he gave another bow of his head.

"Very good," he allowed, the smile broadening on his lips. "As for the recording, we have intercepted multiple transmissions being sent to and from multiple ships in this sector. There are three that we know of, involved in the communications."

"That you know of?" Alyssa asked, her brow furrowing. "What do you mean by that? Do you suspect there's another?"

"You're very astute," Mc'narrd commented. She suspected it was approval she heard in his voice. "That is exactly what we believe. The third battleship involved is sending and receiving messages outside the range of our sensors."

"I wouldn't advise going searching for it," Alyssa said without thinking. At his raised brows, she blushed. "I'm not a battle strategist, but I do love playing chess. It's a game of strategy. Where the goal is to 'checkmate' your opponents 'king'. You use various pieces that are allowed only certain moves on a checkered board of alternating colors. 'Checkmate' means you can 'capture' the king. That it can't move anywhere without being caught. I'm certain you can find it on anything you've intercepted from Earth." She paused before adding slyly, "Or even any of your allies who also trade with Earth."

Mc'narrd laughed and it was one of pure amusement. She couldn't stop the smile that curved her lips. This time it met her eyes. When the laughter faded, the amusement remained in his eyes, as did the smile on his lips.

"I've heard of the game," he admitted, his silver eyes twinkling with mirth. "And we are not going in search of those answers at this time. The question has arisen if you would be willing to work with my crew in an attempt to decipher the code, since you are familiar with Earth's codes already."

"I would need access to a console. And I'd need someone willing to train me on it," she said bluntly. She shrugged, wincing at the movement. Shooting her arm a glower, she considered the fact that maybe her arm wasn't completely healed, after all. Looking back at the admiral, she found him watching her. "I'm not entirely certain how I'd do it using your technology. It's so… different."

"I will ensure you are working with beings willing to help," Mc'narrd promised.

He crossed to the side of her bed. Almost cautiously, he ran his hands over her arm. She winced as his fingers ran over the injured muscles. Glancing above the bed, his fingers danced up her arm again, shifting and turning it. She watched in fascination.

"How does a commander know so much about injuries?" she asked.

Mc'narrd chuckled as he ran his fingers over her arm a final time and it felt more like a caress than anything else. When his eyes met hers, she felt her pulse jump at the spark of heat she saw for a brief moment.

"It is not uncommon to sustain injuries during Duels," he answered. "I suspect everyone receives such at least once in their lifetimes. Those who are Champions, incur even more than most others."

"As I said before, it isn't the first time I've been stabbed. My profession was not without dangers." Alyssa gave a slight shrug. She couldn't stop herself from asking, "So what is your… diagnosis, sir?"

She did manage to not tease him about playing doctor, though. That would probably have brought about far too many questions that she did not want to answer.

"You'll need physical therapy to keep it from stiffening up. I'll arrange for you to have use of the gym, also." The smirk reappeared as he spoke.

He was definitely doing it for her benefit, she decided. His eyes shifted to something above her bed.

"You need to rest, Alyssa," he said gently as he looked back at her.

"I am resting," she quipped. "I'm not sleeping, but I am resting."

His laugh did more to help her relax than the smirk. And she didn't care if he was doing it solely for her benefit. Stifling a yawn, she chuckled.

"When will I be released?" she asked after a few moments of silence filled the room.

"Not until after you sleep," he retorted. At her frown he laughed again.

"Not funny," she muttered, refusing to give into the smile that was pulling at her lips.

"Tomorrow," he admitted, chuckling. "I will see you tomorrow."

When he turned to go, Alyssa reached out, touching his hand with hers. He paused and turned back to her, a question on his face.

"Stay?" Lifting her eyes to his, she threw all caution to the wind and asked, "Talk with me until I sleep?"

Warmth swept across his face as he gave a slow nod. Sliding her hand into his, he moved closer to the bed. "What would you like to talk about?"

She slid over slightly, allowing him space to sit on the edge. He paused a moment, before perching almost gingerly on the edge of the bed.

"Tell me about K'lais," she suggested. "You know so much about my world, but I know so little about yours."

Delight and approval filled the commander's eyes. What she was now considering his trademark smirk appeared and he began telling her about his world. Staring up at him, she felt as though she could listen to his dulcet voice forever. The smile remained on her lips, even as sleep slowly claimed her.

Chapter Ten

Sliding from the edge of the bed, Mc'narrd eased away from Alyssa. He remained there a few moments watching her to ensure she didn't wake up. At least, that's the excuse he told himself. Finally, he turned and strode from the room. Once outside, he found Zh'oros waiting for him.

"What?" he asked calmly. "Do you believe she would have slept so easily if I'd refused such a simple request?"

"Doubtful," Zh'oros replied, she tipped her head towards the direction of her office. "Be careful with her, 'Zarry." At his sharp look, she hummed lightly. "Not for concern of physical harm."

"Ah," was his only reply.

"Even if you do not suffer from an emotional attachment, that does not mean she would not." Zh'oros glanced at him from the corner of her eyes. "Despite your comments of 'later', there *will* eventually *be* a later. None of us know if High Command would allow a human to remain on board as personnel. As such, the probability of her being left on K'lais is strong."

Mc'narrd's jaw clenched at the thought, but he shoved it away. "K'lais has always welcomed other races as citizens, provided they follow our laws and rules. Other races are allowed on space-going vessels, even those that are military." The amusement on Zh'oros' face did little to help him. "Anything else?"

"Yes," Zh'oros replied. "Don't forget I have to care about *your* health as well as hers."

"First Officer Ac'kyll," Mc'narrd said, meeting Zh'oros' gaze and refusing to comment.

"Sir?" Ac'kyll said over the comm.

"Gather the command crew in the usual meeting room," Mc'narrd replied. "I'm on my way there now with Zh'oros. We have a few things to discuss and plan."

"Yes, sir. Ac'kyll out," the first officer replied.

"I'm certain ,K'rell will object," Mc'narrd said with a sigh. "Which is why I need you there to reinforce what we know."

"That she needs to find her place among our people," Zh'oros suggested, smiling. "Or the fact for her mental well-being, she needs a task that will keep her out of trouble?"

"Both," Mc'narrd said, humming. "Mostly the latter, though."

Zh'oros hummed. "Let's get the meeting over with. Then we can share a drink while we decide who best to assign to the task."

"Stars, that is the best idea I've heard yet," Mc'narrd said with a sigh.

Turning, the pair headed for the lift, arguing good-naturedly over what drink would be best for the task. As well as placing bets on how long it would take ,K'rell to object. They both knew the policy master did not monitor the comms. Preferring to do everything 'in person' instead of using the ease of the comms.

By the time Mc'narrd and Zh'oros arrived at the meeting room, everyone else was already there. Including Policy Master ‚K'rell. The policy master noticed Zh'oros staring at him until he shifted over one seat so he was not in the one closest to Mc'narrd's position at the end of the table. As master healer, Zh'oros could request any position at the table and be granted it. Including the chair at the end of the table opposite Mc'narrd.

As the entire command crew was aware, she preferred the seats on either side of the commander. Since Mc'narrd preferred being near the door, Zh'oros always chose the seat which placed her back to the door. It allowed the healer the ability to leave quickly and easily if an emergency arose requiring her presence in the medical wing.

The fact ‚K'rell had picked the one she typically preferred revealed his arrogance.

"I think we can dismiss repeating our objectives yet again," Mc'narrd began once he and Zh'oros were seated. ‚K'rell's face remained neutral, but the commander noted annoyance flashed through his eyes. "Ra'dett, you've been informed of the sergeant's physical requirements. Will there be a problem with you escorting her to the gym on a set schedule?"

The healer touched the interface before her, her attention focused on the screen. She didn't look up as Mc'narrd turned to the master of security. Mc'narrd was aware Zh'oros could monitor any being's bio suit's readouts from any interface. She took her position as master healer seriously. More so than many other healer's he had met.

"No, sir," Ra'dett replied. "Until the investigation is concluded and we've received Master Healer Zh'oros' evaluation on Lieutenant Pe'rroth, I will escort her personally."

"The evaluations have already begun with Pe'rroth," Zh'oros interjected. Her eyes not leaving the interface. "I have spoken to Pe'rroth briefly. The initial evaluations reveal Pe'rroth acted out of jealousy towards the sergeant being in her current quarters. I will wait until all evaluations have been concluded before deciding on if he should be grounded to planetside. He's cooperating willingly with the healers. Until now, he has shown no signs of any illnesses. He is also showing not only remorse towards the harm caused, but also the jealousy he exhibited."

Her gold eyes glanced up briefly to meet Mc'narrd's gaze. The slight twitch of her head indicated a negative sign. He gave a slight nod.

After years of working together, and even more years as friends, they had developed a form of silent communication. The negative indication meant she wasn't planning on sending Pe'rroth planetside upon their return. If she wasn't concerned, he suspected there wasn't anything pointing towards xenophobia, racism, or similar. Jealousy and fear were common emotions exhibited by every being and ones that could require treatment. Nothing that would require a discharge from the military. Or even to cause someone to be grounded upon their return to the planet.

"I do not agree," ,K'rell objected immediately.

"The nature of your objection?" Mc'narrd requested.

"There is no conclusive evidence, as yet, that the human is a direct threat to Mc'narrd or any other crew member," ‚K'rell began confidently.

As the ship's policy master, he would have access to all reports made and security details. So there was no question that he would have been aware of any such data. Especially, Mc'narrd pondered, if he was eagerly waiting for any reason to further question the decision to have the woman aboard.

‚K'rell continued, his smugness growing. "Therefore, Pe'rroth had no sane motivation for his actions against the human. In order for him to have attacked, he had to be convinced that it was to save someone or some theology we K'laisians hold. Yes? Yes. So that points to obsessive thoughts, followed by obsessive behavior, culminating in him throwing a bladed weapon with intent at the human." He looked smugly between the assembled crew and concluded with, "Obsession is not a foundation for a healthy mind."

Mc'narrd somehow managed to keep from laughing. The policy master's decision to use a quote directly from the thesis written by Zh'oros herself was foolhardy. Although he was confident, ‚K'rell considered it the crowning part of his answer.

"Could you recite the rest of my dissertation, ‚K'rell? I confess to not memorizing it once it accorded me the position of Master Healer for this vessel," rejoined Zh'oros.

‚K'rell opened his mouth, but it hung lifeless and silent for several moments.

"Very well," Zh'oros continued. "The bulk of the paragraphs before and after that particular line, and I'm so honored that you like it so, detailed where the levels of concern in regards to how we obsess should be obtained. For example, we, that is, everyone at this table, obsess over some small details in our respective existences. They partially define who we are, individually. But is the level to which you, ,K'rell, hover and swoop down upon any action that occurs aboard this ship, the same as a crew member who decides action must be taken against a perceived threat? Especially if that perception is proven incorrect?"

"I would hope not," Mc'narrd intervened. "Since that would imply that every incorrect notion ever put forth by a policy master, be it ,K'rell or another, is that of a being who is in an unhealthy state of mind."

The visible skin of ,K'rell became instantly, observably darker.

"Just so," agreed Zh'oros. "So we have to measure the level of the behavior as well as the frequency that it is acted upon before deciding if there is an unhealthy crew member. Which is still, unless I have missed a command update, the responsibility of the healers. I do thank you for your insight, ,K'rell, and will carry it with me as I do my evaluations."

,K'rell managed to croak, "You are welcome." His eyes remained overly wide and darted amongst the other crew at the table.

Mc'narrd made a command decision to put the policy master out of his self-imposed misery.

"Moving on," Mc'narrd announced. "The next topic: Sergeant Zelaya has offered to assist in deciphering the encryptions used by the humans' battleships. As well as aiding in decoding them. It has come to light that she has done so in the past and has a talent in doing such."

"These are confirmed facts? Or claims from," ,K'rell paused before saying, "Sergeant Zelaya."

Mc'narrd suspected he had to consciously use her name instead of 'the human'.

"How would she confirm the facts?" Ar'ath countered, her humming skittering. "Perhaps by requesting a report from her former employers?"

"He is doing his job," Mc'narrd answered, while giving a nod towards ,K'rell. "She has requested the opportunity to show her skills before we entrust her with anything of a confidential or upper security nature."

"Zelaya needs some activity to occupy and engage her mind," added Zh'oros. "While I cannot be the one to give clearance for her specific request? I do recommend we find something of a similar nature for the sake of her health."

"I can find old ciphers that were difficult to solve in the past. Ones that have since been declassified," offered ,K'rell. "Let her put her skills toward those, and we can see the results."

Mc'narrd nodded again.

"An excellent suggestion, from both of you," he stated. "How soon can you acquire them?"

"Within a week," ,K'rell said, lifting his chin defiantly.

"Make it three days," Mc'narrd replied calmly.

"I have-"

"This mission takes precedence over all else, Master ,K'rell. You will have a set within three days." Mc'narrd's tone remained even, though his eyes bore into ,K'rell, almost daring him to argue.

There was a significant pause before ,K'rell gave a single nod in acknowledgement.

Mc'narrd looked across the faces of his crew.

"Are there any other topics or updates that need to be brought before the table?"

"Who do you propose to instruct Sergeant Zelaya on the use of a console?" Ra'dett asked. "The interfaces she has used currently will not be sufficient for the task we're placing before her."

Mc'narrd's attention shifted to Ar'ath. "Will you be up for the task, Master Ar'ath? Or have someone we can trust the task to?"

Ar'ath smirked. "I'm confident I can handle the task of instructing her, especially if she already has some knowledge of what she's doing."

Studying the Master of Communications, Mc'narrd had a suspicious feeling the conversations would not pertain solely to using the interface. Dairra Ar'ath was the daughter of esteemed scientists who traveled the galaxies studying the lifeforms on the planets. She also had multiple sisters. The latter was of more concern to Mc'narrd than the former, mostly because he was well-versed in what women often discussed when together.

"I have no doubt you'll be capable of training her," Mc'narrd commented, keeping his reservations to himself. "If Zelaya proves she has a skill at decryption and decoding, we'll continue forward with allowing her to assist with the encrypted, coded messages from the humans' ships. Are we in agreement?"

,K'rell didn't appear thrilled with the situation, but he remained silent while the rest of the command staff gave their acknowledgements.

"Dismissed," Mc'narrd said, leaning back in the chair.

As usual, ,K'rell stood and swept from the room with all the grace of a winter storm. Once the door slid shut behind him, there was skittered humming from most of the beings in the room.

"How long do you believe it will take the lady to go through the older codes?" Ra'dett asked, humming lightly.

"If she's as skilled as she claims? Maybe a day or two, depending on how many he locates," Ar'ath commented. The smirk blossomed into a wide grin as Mc'narrd raised a brow. "Unlike our esteemed policy master, I do listen in on the conversations of the ship."

Mc'narrd hummed deeply. "Very well. Do you have any concerns or questions regarding your new student?"

"I intend to approach her as if teaching a child. Once my initial conclusions are made, I shall adapt to her style of learning. Unless you have a different path to suggest," replied Ar'ath.

"Then proceed on that path, as shall we all," concluded Mc'narrd. "Anything else?"

There was a general murmur of dissent. Mc'narrd stood, signally an end to the after-meeting meeting. Zh'oros followed suit, as did the rest of the command crew. As the healer left, Mc'narrd followed after her.

"About that drink," Mc'narrd commented. Zh'oros glanced at him. "Your stock or mine?"

Zh'oros hummed, even as she smiled at the commander. "Mine, this time. You can replace whatever we drain after we return home."

Mc'narrd's humming joined hers as they traversed the corridors for the healer's quarters, thankful to have such a close friend on his battlecruiser.

Chapter Eleven

The next morning, the door to her medical room slid open to reveal Zh'oros. Though Alyssa was disappointed in it not being the commander, she understood he couldn't be around her all the time.

"I'm here to escort you back to your quarters," the healer said pleasantly.

"Thank you," Alyssa replied as she stood in a single fluid motion. Though it wasn't nearly as smooth or liquid as the K'laisians movements. A face she envied greatly.

The healer gave her a smile and gestured towards the hallway. There were no guards near them, a fact that surprised Alyssa.

"What surprises you?" Zh'oros asked kindly as they traversed the corridor.

"The fact there are no guards," Alyssa replied honestly.

Zh'oros' hum was light and amusement shone on her face. "As Master Healer onboard, none would dare argue my orders. As such, I am able to dismiss whoever I choose. You are not a threat. For your mental wellbeing, I dismissed the guards." The healer glanced at her from the corner of her eyes. "Or am I incorrect and you do plan on attacking me and others onboard this vessel?"

Alyssa laughed, shaking her head. "No, Master Zh'oros. Did I get the title correct?" Zh'oros gave a nod and Alyssa grinned. "Oh, good. I have no intentions or desire to attack anyone. On Earth, doctors… healers… do not have such command abilities. Thank you for explaining it to me."

"You're welcome," Zh'oros replied as they stepped onto the lift.

The healer touched an interface on the wall and the door slid shut. Alyssa glanced at the other woman, but remained silent.. When the doors opened again, she had to force her jaw from dropping. They were on a completely different level of the ship, and she hadn't even felt the lift move. The first time she'd wondered if it was an anomaly. Or due to her being recently healed. Perhaps even distracted by the commander and her unease at being escorted through the ship.

This removed all questions and doubts about it.

Talk about superior technology, she thought.

There was little to say as Alyssa considered the advanced technology of the K'laisians. She couldn't help but wonder if the technology would frighten her fellow humans or find it as fascinating as she did.

Once Zh'oros left, Alyssa was left with the same question as before she was injured: How to pass the time without growing too bored. She gave the console a wistful look. Mc'narrd had shown her the transmissions and her fingers itched at the opportunity to crack that code. But, without him there, she had no chance of doing it.

And so, she turned to the sofa and the one thing she did have: the tablet with the reading material. Flopping onto the sofa, she powered it up. There was still plenty of reading material for her to go over and a lot about the K'laisians to learn. Including their language.

Maybe there was a way for her to learn the language if she couldn't spend her day doing other challenging tasks. Like breaking codes. Or teasing the commander.

When a soft chime sounded in her room, she looked up, startled. It rang again, and she realized someone was at her door.

Taking a chance, she asked, "Who is it?"

"Commander Mc'narrd."

Well. That was different, she thought, amused by the formality. He was more than welcome to enter whenever he wanted.

"Um, enter?" she said, turning to face the door.

Much to her amazement, the door slid open to reveal the commander and another of his crew. Mc'narrd strode into the room with the casual ease of someone accustomed to entering the room. Unlike the other woman who entered with hesitation.

Wasn't that interesting? Alyssa thought. *Why would she be hesitant? So far, no one else has been.*

Instead of focusing on the woman's beauty, Alyssa studied the other woman's features. Sharper than the others she'd met so far, the woman's eyes were a softer shade of silver with speckles of gold in their depths. Her silver hair didn't show any difference, but her skin wasn't as pale as Mc'narrd. Maybe by two shades, but it was still slightly darker. The new woman was also an inch or so shorter than the other K'laisians she'd encountered.

"Satisfied?" the newcomer asked after several moments.

There was no malice in the woman's voice, but it wasn't completely warm either.

"I'm still trying to learn what sets all of you apart," Alyssa replied as she set down the tablet and stood in a single fluid motion. "I meant no disrespect or insult."

Amusement lit the woman's eyes.

Alyssa turned to the commander, who had remained silent during the exchange.

"I'd like you to meet Master of Communications Ar'ath," Mc'narrd said simply. "She is here to instruct you on how to use the console."

"Once you've learned its use, you'll be given the opportunity to decipher a variety of older transmissions," Ar'ath continued. A slight smile tugged at her lips. "Prove your skills and you'll be given the opportunity to do more."

Alyssa's eyes shifted between the pair, a smile on her face. "Thank you."

"You do not appear to mind having to prove yourself," Ar'ath commented.

Laughing, Alyssa shook her head, ignoring the frown that appeared on the communication master's face.

"No, Master Ar'ath, I do not. In fact, it is something I've been doing since I was very, very young. It is actually… refreshing to know that there are some similarities between us, after all," Alyssa replied.

"Is that normal for your race?" Mc'narrd asked.

"It depends, to be honest," Alyssa said, turning her attention to him. "Humans have a very odd social structure. A great many positions, titles, and such are inherited. I was an orphan, and a female. As such, I had to prove my worth, skills, and knowledge constantly until I earned a position of renown. There are many who do not have to do the same. They're born into a position, are given it for one reason or another, or earn it through money or fame."

"Such is not the way of K'laisians," Ar'ath said thoughtfully.

"Everything is earned on K'lais," Mc'narrd agreed.

The two K'laisians glanced at each other and exchanged amused expressions. Alyssa felt jealousy flare, then shoved it away. She had no right to feel such. No matter how much she liked the commander, he was K'laisian. Regardless of how much he might tease her and show an attraction, she was still an alien. Nor could she compare to the beauty of those around her.

"So, if I learn to use the console, and prove myself, I'll be able to do more?" Alyssa asked.

"Prove yourself skilled, and you may find yourself with a new position," Mc'narrd teased.

Alyssa bit her lip and looked down, knowing her cheeks were warming. Humming came from the other woman. Alyssa snapped her eyes up to her, the heat growing. Mc'narrd chuckled, but didn't say anything more. Ar'ath appeared amused, even as her silver eyes shifted briefly to Mc'narrd before looking back to her.

"I think we will be fine, Commander," Ar'ath said, still humming. She gestured towards the console. "Shall we?"

"Yes, please," Alyssa said, thankful for the reprieve from the other woman.

Mc'narrd hummed, then laughed like a human. Alyssa couldn't decide which she preferred and chose to remain silent, instead.

"Then I will leave you two ladies alone," he announced. Without another word, he turned and strode from the room.

Once the door slid shut behind him, Alyssa turned around to find Ar'ath watching her curiously. She raised her brows in question.

"Do you like him?" the communications master asked.

It sounded like an innocent question, but Alyssa suspected there was depth to it.

"Yes," Alyssa replied slowly. "He's very unique."

The amusement only grew on the woman's face and in her silver eyes. "He's a well-liked commander."

"I have no doubt," Alyssa murmured, forcing herself to not look back at the door.

Ar'ath hummed more and crossed to the console. As she stood in front of the console, she frowned. Turning, she located another chair and moved it beside the first one. Sitting beside the console, she gestured for Alyssa to sit on the other one.

"He likes you," Ar'ath commented as Alyssa sat in the chair. When Alyssa looked at her, Ar'ath smiled gently. "He does not tease a great many people, Alyssa."

"Despite being so good at it, that should be a crime," Alyssa joked, then paused and stared at the screen. "I'm sorry. That... I should not have said that."

Instead of being angry, Ar'ath hummed deeply. "No, no need to apologize! That... that was amusing."

"Perhaps I should warn you I do enjoy teasing people I like," Alyssa admitted, grinning at the communications master. "I wasn't able to do it a lot... before now. But it is a habit of mine. And joking is a common habit amongst humans."

"Another thing humans and K'laisians have in common," Ar'ath reassured her. Something flashed through the woman's eyes, but Alyssa couldn't figure out what it was. "To the task at hand..."

Alyssa turned towards the screen, nodding. She was eager to learn how to use the console. The conversation quickly shifted to the first lesson and Alyssa quickly realized it wasn't that different from Earth's interfaces and computers. Faster, better, and more intuitive, perhaps. More advanced definitely. But the basics were the same.

As with every other challenge placed before her, Alyssa was determined to excel at this task, also.

By the time Ar'ath's lesson was finished for the day, Alyssa was operating the console with confidence. The communications master appeared pleased with how quickly Alyssa picked up on the technology.

"Same time tomorrow?" Ar'ath asked, standing in the center of the room.

"I'm looking forward to it," Alyssa replied cheerfully. She tipped her head to the side. "I do have a question before you leave."

Ar'ath tilted her head to the side. When they realized what they were doing, both women laughed in their respective manners. "What is your question, Lady?"

Realizing the word was meant as a title, Alyssa didn't bristle. In fact, she discovered she didn't mind it.

"Will you help me learn your language?"

The woman stared at her while blinking several times. A brilliant smile slid across her face. "I'd be delighted. You will need to learn the language, regardless, since most everything is written in K'laisian, especially in our military."

"I'm not sure how helpful it is, but I can speak every language of Earth's allies," Alyssa added, grinning. "Someone long ago suggested my talent with linguistics was why I could pick up decoding and such so easily. I can find patterns and similarities in languages and learn them quickly. That I do the same with codes and such."

"It's certainly a possibility," Ar'ath admitted. "It is part of why I was able to acquire my current position." The woman's smile brightened. "I look forward to spending more time with you, Alyssa."

"I'm looking forward to the same," Alyssa replied. Taking a chance, she bowed slightly to the woman.

Ar'ath blinked at her a few times, before returning the gesture. "You're learning our ways quickly."

"I'm trying," Alyssa admitted.

With a nod, Ar'ath turned and headed for the door. The door slid open to reveal the Master of Security standing there.

Alyssa stiffened, her unease returning. Though there were no guards with him, it did nothing to ease her concerns. As he stepped into the room, Ar'ath nodded to him. When the communications master followed his eyes, she paused in her steps.

"Is there a problem?" Ar'ath asked, her silver eyes shifting between the pair.

"That depends," Alyssa said in a voice far calmer than she felt.

"On?" Ar'ath prompted.

"On why he is here," Alyssa replied, her eyes not leaving Ra'dett.

"Ah," Ar'ath said, understanding flashing across her face.

She touched Ra'dett gently on his hand and Ra'dett glanced at her. Something passed between them and Alyssa saw Master Ra'dett's body relax. His fingers brushed hers and Alyssa wondered if the brief interaction between them meant something more personal.

"Master Zh'oros has informed us all that you require exercise and physical therapy," Master Ra'dett said easily. His eyes met hers. "And I would like to personally apologize for my lieutenant's actions."

"He's lucky he wasn't demoted," Ar'ath commented, her eyes shifting to Alyssa. "You will be safe with Master Ra'dett, Alyssa. In fact, of all the beings on the ship, aside from the healers, the command staff are those evaluated the most thoroughly."

"I'm sorry, but I do not understand what that means," Alyssa said, glancing briefly at Ar'ath. "But I'm willing to forgive the misunderstanding."

"All beings who are on space-faring vessels are given psychological evaluations," Ar'ath explained. At Ra'dett's sharp look, she rolled her eyes. "If she is to live among our people, she needs to know how our military works. What she will need to do to remain onboard."

Alyssa smiled at the interaction. The more she was around the K'laisians, the more she realized they did share similarities with humans.

"The military uses psychological evaluations to determine a being's security clearance," Ra'dett said, though he didn't sound happy about admitting it. "It determines if a being is allowed to go off planet, their positions, and more. Master Healers on battlecruisers are trained to treat and recognize all manners and types of illnesses. What we consider illnesses, anyway."

"Such as xenophobia, racism, racial superiority, and more," Ar'ath added. "The command crew are given more thorough evaluations than others due to being placed in command. Our security clearances require it."

"I have so much to learn," Alyssa finally said. The pair hummed and Alyssa smiled at them. "Thank you for telling me that, Master Ar'ath. As strange as this may sound, that does help alleviate concerns I have." The woman gave a nod and smile, then turned and left. Her fingers brushed against Ra'dett's hand a final time. "You mentioned a gym, Master Ra'dett?"

The master of security gave her a smile and gestured towards the door. "I did indeed, lady. And I will be escorting you there daily after your time with Master Ar'ath is over."

"After sitting for so long, I am going to need it," Alyssa said with a laugh. At his puzzled expression, she explained. "An old habit, I'm afraid. If I spent long hours sitting at a desk, I would find some way to exercise afterwards."

"Then I'm pleased we are able to give you some sense of normalcy," he said pleasantly.

Alyssa kept watch on him as they traveled the corridors. Even as she memorized the path they took. His silver eyes were unreadable and he wore his equally silver hair braided away from his face and tucked behind his pointed ears. But most of it fell free down his back. Lithe, trim, elegant. The same symbol Mc'narrd wore curved around his left shoulder. So far, everyone she'd interacted with, aside from the medical personnel, wore the same emblem. All of them were command staff, also.

As they approached a pair of double doors, Alyssa noted there was nothing beside the door. Unlike most of the doors they'd passed. She guessed it was the gym. When they entered, she discovered she was correct. Though it didn't look like any gym she was accustomed to seeing. Mats covered the entire gym floor. To her right were multiple doors. As beings entered and exited the doors, she noticed a couple had some sort of strange equipment in it. To the far left were more doors, though she couldn't tell what was behind those doors from where she stood.

"Welcome to our gym," Ra'dett said needlessly. He allowed her a few moments to process everything before continuing forward towards a trio of beings wearing the silver-white bio suits of medics. "I'll be here the entire time."

Alyssa glanced at him and couldn't resist teasing, "So I need to make sure I keep you safe while I'm here?"

In response, Ra'dett gave her a wide smile and a humm loud enough to make him vibrate.

"By the seas, I think we may get along," he observed as his laughter ebbed.

Her steps considerably lighter, they continued toward the trio of medics.

Chapter Twelve

For the next several days, Alyssa kept a pleasant schedule between Ar'ath and Ra'dett.

Breakfast was shared with the communications master. Who seemed intent on introducing Alyssa to a variety of fruits, pastries, juice, and either human coffee or the K'laisian equivalent called jakka. As they ate, Alyssa learned more about how to use the console. Then how to decode and decipher the older transmissions using said console.

Her time after Ar'arth was spent with the master of security and the medics in the gym. Often with Alyssa quizzing them about the rules and laws of the K'laisians. Despite the fact most of what he told her was found in the texts she'd been given, her questions brought more in-depth answers. A few times the first officer joined them in the gym.

As Alyssa finished the last of the older transmissions on her fifth day with the communications master, she turned to Ar'ath.

"Now, can I have something more difficult?" Alyssa all but begged.

Ar'ath hummed deeply. "I'll inform the commander and have him examine the results. I suspect tomorrow you will be doing just that."

"Oh, good. Those might have been fun to do, they were also far too easy," Alyssa commented. "I'm used to having a challenge." The communications master gave her a puzzled expression. "I meant: I'm accustomed to something more difficult. I'm guessing 'challenge' has a different meaning to you."

"It's typically meant as formal declaration preceding a Duel," Ar'ath stated, studying Alyssa. "Do not use that word freely among K'laisians."

Alyssa gave a nod. She'd read about Duels and Challenges, but hadn't realized the word wasn't used for anything else.

"I did not realize it was only used for such. I'll try to remember to not use it for anything else," Alyssa promised.

The communications master smiled, and departed, leaving Ra'dett to escort Alyssa to the gym. As Alyssa and he continued their discussion of K'laisians laws, the conversation trailed off as they entered the gym.

Puzzled by the sudden silence of the security master, Alyssa followed his gaze to the center of the gym. Unlike the previous days, there were a pair of female crewmen in the center of the floor. First Officer Ac'kyll was standing between the pair. Her features were grim. There were more K'laisians in the gym this time, all of them standing against the walls. The conversations were in whispers.

Alyssa spotted several medics, none of them the ones she'd been interacting with, and Master Healer Zh'oros. They were all standing in a group closest to a set of doors that led into a room she knew held medical supplies.

"*Ke'desh!*" Master Ra'dett spat out.

"What's wrong?" Alyssa asked, her eyes darting between Ra'dett and the trio on the floor. Whatever he'd said was obviously a swear word, but not one the translator was able to change into English.

"A Duel," he replied, irritation in his voice. "I should have been notified." He sighed, muttered a few more words under his breath, then said, "Come on."

Alyssa followed the master of security, thankful that he wasn't leading her out of the gym. This was an opportunity for her to learn first-hand about Duels. She felt like a kid about to watch a martial arts match.

"Master Zh'oros," Ra'dett said to the healer. "Would you be willing to watch over the lady while I tend to duties?"

Zh'oros smiled and there was a twinkle in her eyes as he spoke. "Of course, Master Ra'dett. She will be safe with us."

"Of that, I have zero doubt," Ra'dett replied. At Alyssa's questioning look, he explained. "Master Healers are the only ones who can give orders to even the commander of a ship. None would dare gainsay Master Zh'oros."

With that, he turned and stalked across the gym to where First Officer Ac'kyll and the other two crewmen were standing. Both crewmen held swords in their hands, glowering darkly at each other, though neither were saying a word.

"Are swords the standard issue weapons for Duels?" Alyssa asked.

The other medics coughed and kept their heads turned away from Alyssa. She guessed they were trying to be polite and not laugh in her face.

"No, Alyssa, they are not," Zh'oros replied kindly. "Though swords are perhaps the easiest weapon to master, they aren't the only ones used."

"Master Zh'oros is very skilled with the reknir," one of the medics said.

"What is a reknir?"

"They are similar to your hand axes, with dual blades. A shaft splits the blades and there is a barbed point that rises six to eight inches above the blades," another medic said. "They're nasty things. When the barbs penetrate, they tear going in and also rip when they're pulled out. So the victim is dealt twice the amount of damage, unlike a sword or another bladed object."

"To add to it, our esteemed Master Healer can use two at a time, with the same ease others use swords or fighting sticks," the first medic stated. "I am Healer La'crou. This is Healer Ta'ladon and Healer Ac'thyt."

Each gave a slight bow as their names were spoken. Alyssa gave them the same bow in return. They stared at her for a few seconds before smiling. When she turned back to Zh'oros, she noticed the other woman watching with a curious expression.

"I presume they were supposed to inform Master Ra'dett prior to the Duel?" Alyssa asked, turning back to the subject at hand.

"That is the typical procedure, but they approached First Officer Ac'kyll instead of going through the usual channels," Healer La'crou replied. "Medical was informed due to the nature of Duels."

Alyssa watched the group in the middle of the gym as a decision was made for the Duel.

"It seems you will be granted a viewing of your first Duel," Zh'oros stated as Ac'kyll relinquished her position to Ra'dett. "Though any of the senior crewmen can oversee a Duel, it's usually officiated by either the commander or Security Master Ra'dett."

That was something to remember. Alyssa tucked that tidbit of information away for future use.

Ac'kyll crossed to where Alyssa, Zh'oros, and the other healers were standing. She gave Alyssa a nod before turning to face the trio in the middle of the gym.

"Neither is going to yield to the other," she stated in a low voice.

"Fools." Zh'oros didn't bother hiding her disgust or to lower her voice. "What is the complaint today? Dessert wasn't up to their liking?"

That caused the other medics' hums to be skittered and quiet in a manner that reminded Alyssa of a human snickering. Ac'kyll scowled, though she kept her eyes focused straight ahead of her.

"The usual stupidity of one insulting the other. The claim of neither obeying orders, despite the fact both are of equal rank," Ac'kyll stated darkly. "I'm surprised they didn't add in one had better quarters than the other."

"That's it?" Alyssa asked in surprise. "They're Challenging each other over something as trivial as that?" At the nods of the K'laisians, Alyssa shook her head. "Is that common?"

"No," Zh'oros stated, ignoring the first officer's frown. "It seems there is something else annoying our otherwise intelligent crew."

"Oh," Alyssa said softly. Guilt flashed through her. She couldn't help but wonder what other problems were occurring due to her being onboard the alien vessel. "Is my presence truly that horrible?"

"Not at all, Lady," Ta'ladon said gently. "It is the fact Commander Mc'narrd's orders do not allow them to interrogate you at every opportunity. They are divided about your people. Half believe humans should be negotiated with to open trade. The other half are arguing for the destruction of the race that attacked our people out of what they view as fear and arrogance. Almost all want to know why you were sent out to be killed by your own people."

"How do you know that?" Ac'kyll demanded. Her eyes narrowed upon the healer.

Ta'ladon smiled slightly, not the least bit intimidated. A fact Alyssa noted. It seemed healers held high positions amongst the K'laisians. More so than any human doctor or nurse.

"The crew talk to each other. Patients complain to their healers. And I have friends on both sides of the equation. The human asked. For her mental health, she needs to know what is happening around her," Ta'ladon answered, the smile not fading.

"Isn't that why neither you nor Security Master Ra'dett is forcing her to leave while a Challenge is happening?" Ac'thyt asked. "If the lady is to live among our people, she will need to know what is being said about her and around her. She isn't a child, Ac'kyll. Stop treating her as one."

"Not my choice," Ac'kyll muttered. "We'll discuss this later. They're about to begin."

The gym had fallen silent except for the movement of feet against the floor.

Chapter Thirteen

The pair on the floor kept Alyssa's attention.

Both wore their uniforms with their dark hair pulled back in a single braid that draped down their backs. Neither wore armor or protection of any sort, and both held their weapons with confidence. Neither wore the symbol Alyssa was beginning to associate with the command crew. What resembled a closed rosebud with blade-like petals sweeping up and narrowing until the tips touched together at the top. The petals formed a circle around the odd bud while being inside another simple gold colored circle.

Security Master Ra'dett stood between the pair. From somewhere he had procured a sword. The blade was held out at shoulder height, the flat of the weapon's blade facing the pair as they stood on each side of him.

"A Challenge has been issued by Madsa Vorsha Ir'toro of Engineering." He gestured to the woman to his right, who nodded. He then continued speaking, gesturing towards the other woman. "Ir'toro has Challenged Madsa Theris Ad'umi of Science," Master Ra'dett said in a loud, clear voice. "Both are crew members of the *Laedschot*, under the command of It'zarry Mc'narrd. The Duel is overseen by the Master of Security, Eldonn Ra'dett."

Laedschot. So that was the name of the ship she was on, Alyssa mused. One more bit of information to add to her growing list.

"Madsa?" Alyssa asked quietly.

Ac'kyll murmured, "A… specialist of their job."

"They are not generally career military," Zh'oros added in a voice barely above a whisper. "Though the latter does happen, they are never in the line of command."

Giving a nod, Alyssa fell silent, once again giving the Duelists her entire attention.

The two women raised their weapons in salute to each other before snapping their blades down and to the side. Each adopted a classic defensive position, their feet shoulder-width apart, their weaponless arms to their sides and back. Mirror images of each other, their eyes didn't leave each other's faces.

"Do you believe it will come to death blows?" Zh'oros murmured to Ac'kyll.

"Let's hope not," Ac'kyll stated in an equally quiet voice.

Alyssa glanced from one to the other before asking, "Why is that? I thought Duels could be to the death. Are they not allowed onboard?"

"Commander Mc'narrd does not object to Duels onboard. He does object to Duels to the death," Ac'kyll explained. "Many of our military commanders do not object, but Commander Mc'narrd prefers bringing back all his crew."

"If you want to Duel to the death, he prefers it be done planetside," Zh'oros added.

"Unfortunately, that does not always happen," Ac'thyt said, leaning against the wall and crossing his arms. "Sometimes injuries are too severe. Other times the Challenger does not care."

"What does Commander Mc'narrd do when that happens?" Alyssa asked as Ac'thyt finished speaking.

"Nothing," Ac'kyll replied simply. "Duels are a way of our life. Until Military High Command places a ban on

Duels to the death on space vessels, they will continue onboard."

Ra'dett shouted, "Let the Duel commence!"

He swept the blade down as he slid back several paces. He continued moving away from the Duelists, even as they raised their weapons.

Alyssa straightened as she watched the women. They touched swords in a greeting of some sort before moving back. After two more heartbeats they lunged forward, their blades meeting, their blades crossed in an 'x'.

Ir'toro swept her blade down and around, before slicing towards her opponent from the left. Ad'umi blocked it. The clang of metal against metal rang out in the otherwise silent gym. The snarl on Ir'toro's face didn't change as she pushed Ad'umi's blade away and began a series of swift back-and-forth strikes before sweeping her blade straight down, aiming for Ad'umi's head. Ad'umi blocked the attack and spun beneath the blades in a faster-than-humanly possible dexterous move while pushing her opponent's sword back.

The woman quickly went on the offensive, swinging her blade in a blurring figure eight before bringing the blade in for a series of quick strikes. Each time Ir'toro lost ground, moving backward with each strike.

There was no question in Alyssa's mind that these two women had been taught from an early age how to wield their blades. Each strike was aimed at the torso or head. The strikes were quick and concise, with no theatrics involved.

A duel is meant to be fast, Alyssa remembered being told by a former instructor. *There is no room for fancy spins or twirls.*

Save that for the stage and the theater. When you want to put on a show for pleasure.

"First blood!" someone called out.

Alyssa glanced at Zh'oros who was shaking her head. Looking back to the dueling pair, she noticed a small silver trail on Ir'toro's arm. It wasn't large, but it was enough to be seen.

Ir'toro spun around, putting distance between her and Ad'umi. She kept out of arm's reach of her opponent as they circled each other.

At some cue unseen by Alyssa, Ir'toro attacked Ad'umi once again. Her sword was a blur of thrusts and parries. Ad'umi met each strike, turning Ir'toro's blade away in quick succession. Finally, as their weapons' blades crossed again, Ir'toro took a step to the side, and turned Ad'umi's blade around in a tight circle. Ad'umi's blade was pushed away and Ir'toro stepped forward, bringing her blade back in a fast slice.

The weapon cut into Ad'umi's thigh before she could block the strike or move away. As the woman screamed from the pain, Ir'toro pulled back and slammed the pommel of her weapon between Ad'umi's eyes. The woman crumpled into a bleeding heap.

Ir'toro lifted her weapon in a salute, before snapping it down to her side. She turned to Master Ra'dett and bowed.

"Madsa Ir'toro wins by unconsciousness of her opponent," Ra'dett proclaimed in a neutral tone. "It will be recorded and entered into the database onboard and transferred planetside upon our return to K'lais."

"Not a killing blow, at least," Ac'kyll muttered. "You and your team are up, Zh'oros."

"Indeed," Zh'oros replied dryly, even as she was striding towards the unconscious woman.

"A delight meeting you, Lady Alyssa," La'crou said with a nod of his head. The other healers nodded as well.

"The pleasure was mine," Alyssa replied with a smile.

La'crou hurried to catch up with Zh'oros while the other two vanished into the medical room.

Alyssa ignored the departure of the Duel's audience, her attention on Zh'oros and La'crou as they began attending to Ad'umi. She noticed movement at her side, but didn't give it a second thought. First Officer Ac'kyll was still beside her, and Master Ra'dett was moving towards them with a scowl firmly in place.

"What is *she* doing here?" a new voice demanded.

Alyssa didn't groan. Not, exactly. There was always someone who ruined the fun. Apparently the behavior extended to the K'laisians, also. She also didn't stop herself from speaking. It should have been safe enough, with First Office Ac'kyll beside her and Master Ra'dett approaching.

"I'm allowed here with an escort. And you are?" she asked, turning to the annoying K'laisian.

The K'laisian had a fixed scowl and hard frown lines on his face. She suspected they were there even when he wasn't glowering. Around the same height as the other K'laisians, his dark hair was pulled back into a tight ponytail. His skin tone was a dark olive.

Probably to match his constant frown, she mused.

"I am ,K'rell, the master of policies aboard this vessel," ,K'rell stated as he lifted his chin imperiously. Gold eyes tried to stare her down. He gave a sniff before turning on the first officer. "This is improper! She could have escaped!"

"Escape? To where?" Alyssa retorted. "I'm on a spacecraft. My own people want me dead, and I have no clue where we are in the universe, anyway. Since I have no desire to commit suicide by way of an oxygen less, endless vacuum, I don't think 'escaping' is going to happen."

Ac'kyll coughed slightly, and Alyssa noticed the woman's lips twitching.

,K'rell frowned harder. "This goes against all security protocols onboard. Choosing to ignore that list of infractions, the presence of an alien during a Duel? Was there a consent taken to ensure the crew did not consider themselves or our social norm from being violated?"

"Violated?" Alyssa blurted to avoid laughing. "I was standing. No one was touched or even spoken to without initiating contact. Or does 'violation' mean something else under this ship's policies?"

"Who authorized this? Zh'oros, are you prepared to clear your schedule to give any affected crew members adequate time for your council?" The loud mouth was going on as if she hadn't spoken a word.

"Last I checked, it was Commander Mc'narrd who gave orders on this vessel," Alyssa retorted, her eyes narrowing as she studied him.

Cold, furious gold eyes stared at her in disdain or disgust. Alyssa wasn't certain which emotion was shining in his eyes. He was ten pounds lighter than most she'd seen, which gave him something of a scrawny appearance.

"You are most certainly not the commander," she observed, "Not only do you lack his manners and quick wit, but also his good looks."

There was a spattering of humming from around her, the senior officers, and the K'laisian Alyssa now viewed as a very pompous ass. Apparently, the other K'laisians found her comment amusing.

,K'rell the Pompous Ass spluttered as his face turned a dark shade bordering on what she suspected was a dangerous black hue. On a human, he would probably have been turning purple.

She kept a smirk from forming at her success of winning round one of the verbal tête-a-tête.

"Perhaps I should escort you back to your quarters," the smooth voice of the commander said from behind Alyssa.

That tone, Alyssa decided, could coax her into doing anything. When Mc'narrd had arrived, she didn't know, but the fury on ,K'rell's face made her thankful he was there.

"We will discuss this later," ,K'rell said.

It sounded a lot like an order to her.

"Careful, ,K'rell," Mc'narrd said in a warning tone. "Despite your position, you do *not* give orders to *me*. We will discuss this later, rest assured. Perhaps when your temper has waned."

Without another word, Mc'narrd placed a hand on Alyssa's shoulder, turned her towards the door, and ushered her from the gym.

She could feel a pair of eyes burning into her back. There was zero question in her mind that whoever ,K'rell was, he was not well liked. He was also now an enemy among her alien captors. Captors she had begun to consider to be companions.

"That was not wise," Commander Mc'narrd chided Alyssa once they were back in her quarters. ",K'rell has a lot of pull with High Command. Be thankful we are not within easy communication with our planet."

"Is any of what I said a lie?" Alyssa asked.

"No," he replied slowly. "Though I cannot speak of who is more 'good looking'."

"Then he revealed his rudeness and insubordination to his commanding officer." Her lips curved into a mischievous grin as she added, "I assure you, Commander, you are far more attractive than any other being I have met."

The commander stepped closer to Alyssa, and she felt a shiver race down her spine. Not one of fear, either. She felt her own feet moving closer to him until she was looking up into his eyes.

"Are you not concerned about having an enemy when you are a captive?" Mc'narrd asked, a smile curving the corners of his lips.

"I'd be more concerned if you were the enemy," Alyssa admitted.

As Mc'narrd's eyes captured her own, she felt her body come alive. Her nerves sang in excitement. Her heart beat wildly, yet she felt breathless. As though she'd taken a punch to the solar plexus and had all the air knocked from her lungs. Warmth spread across her body, heating her from the inside out.

No man had ever made Alyssa feel this way. But then, Alyssa had to admit the fact this particular man was not human, and he held her fate in his hands.

Hands that were now lightly gripping her shoulders and sliding down her arms. Hesitantly, she settled her hands on his waist. For the first time touching a K'laisian. For the first time, in far too long, touching a man in an intimate way without the objective of killing him later.

Mc'narrd's eyes searched hers as he lowered his lips. They hovered inches above hers, and he seemed to be waiting. Possibly for permission to continue or a refusal.

Refusal was the last thing on Alyssa's mind. In fact, she was fairly certain sanity had departed where he was concerned the moment she had set eyes on him.

Rising on her toes to close the distance between them, she pressed her lips against his and gave into her lust. Part of her mind questioned if this was just another ploy. Another way to manipulate her. But the larger part truly did not give one damn. She hadn't seen him in the past several days. Absence, it seemed, did make the heart grow fonder.

Or, at the very least, lustier.

She was an exile from her people, among an alien race who she was starting to trust. And if the man who curled her toes with just one look wanted to manipulate her in this way? Well, she might as well enjoy the ride.

Her initiative was the answer Mc'narrd had apparently been waiting for, because strong arms wrapped around her. He pulled her closer, deepening the kiss. She shifted slightly, her own hands sliding around him until there wasn't even room for air between their bodies.

Alyssa melted against his chest, marveling at the sweetness of the kiss compared to the hardness of the commander's body. She didn't know how long the kiss lasted, but at some point he pulled back slowly, their lips parting.

His eyes were bright as she stared into them. Moving slightly, she raised her hand to his face, her fingers trailing along his cheek before curling into his silken silver strands. Her smile grew as she discovered his hair was truly as soft and silken as it appeared.

Mc'narrd reached up, grabbed her by the wrist, and gently disentangled her fingers. He kissed her wrist at the pulse point, and she melted even more.

Someone, she thought with a smile, *has been doing his homework.*

"That was not a wise idea," he finally said as he lowered her wrist.

"No. No, actually, I think it was a great idea," she countered. "Definitely a good way to broaden relations between our people. An excellent method to study each other's biology."

The commander chuckled. "You do know how to convince yourself."

"It's a gift. I admit it," Alyssa teased. She tipped her head to the side slightly. "Just don't tell me you regret it."

"No, Alyssa," the commander said gently. "I do not regret it at all."

Chapter Fourteen

The sparkle in Alyssa's eyes was everything Mc'narrd needed to know that he was in deep, deep trouble. "Then why do you say it was a bad idea?" Alyssa asked, refusing to give up.

The woman was tenacious, he had to admit it.

Beautiful. Witty. Determined. And stubborn.

Traits that even his own people claimed and admired. Though none of his fellow K'laisians had ever tempted him the way this human did. There were few women onboard the *Laedschot* who had not tried to seduce him in one way or another. Even the females on K'lais were attracted to him.

Or to his position and growing status within their society. The stronger, and more capable the person, the more attractive that person becomes to the opposite gender. Though, most who learned he was career military had little interest in pursuing a long-term relationship with him. Most K'laisians preferred remaining planetside, which was why most of those who went off planet took mates who were also military-driven in their life goals. Few enjoyed having a mate who was off planet more often than they were planetside.

"It was a bad idea because I am the commander of the ship," Mc'narrd replied, easing Alyssa back a few steps. She frowned but didn't object. Yet. He suspected that would come later. "How would your people react if the situations were reversed?"

"Oh, that's easy," she replied glibly. Her eyes sparkled with what he was coming to understand as mischief. "The human of the pair would be encouraged to continue the relationship, even to the point of bedding the alien. It's easier to manipulate someone who is emotionally and physically attached to another."

The comment certainly brought several images, and ideas, to Mc'narrd's thoughts. He wondered if they occurred to the woman before him, also.

Alyssa paused before adding thoughtfully, "Though I suspect the human would not be the captain of the ship. That would give the alien the chance to manipulate someone with power. The human would probably also be someone the military considered 'disposable'. In case the alien killed the human. Or threatened to kill them."

"That's a rather harsh assessment of your people," Mc'narrd stated, hoping to draw out why she gave such a critical view of her own kind.

Alyssa sighed, the warmth fading slightly from her features. "Humans aren't the nicest beings. You already know that. My superiors sent me out here to die, remember? I have little reason to not tell the truth about what they would do."

He couldn't argue her reasoning, nor could anyone who would hear this part of the recording. "That is fair. But how do I know you won't try to manipulate me?"

Alyssa laughed, her eyes twinkling with merriment as she gestured at him. "I cannot see anyone ever manipulating you, Commander."

"Why?" he asked, honestly curious.

He'd had many people try, but so far none had succeeded. Well, none that he knew of, anyway.

"Sir, you have the ability to see through people's bullshit. Umm, that is, their lies, trickery, and foolishness," Alyssa stated. She shifted her weight to her left side as she spoke, seemingly at ease with him and the conversation. "You read people's expressions and their body language with ease. Whether that is common for K'laisians or unique to you, I don't know. But you do it. You have a presence about you that says you're in charge. You can be foreboding, and I suspect fearsome when needed. You are most certainly intimidating when you want to be."

"Is that all?" he asked, unable to contain the smirk.

Alyssa was perceptive and didn't pull punches when she spoke. In fact, she had no trouble speaking her mind at all.

"Oh, I'm sure there will be more the longer I am able to get to know you," Alyssa replied. "As I said, I cannot see you ever being manipulated by anyone. Not unless you allowed them to do it."

"You're very outspoken," he commented. "Was that allowed in your position as an assassin? Or are you enjoying the sudden freedom of not having to worry about angering your superiors?"

"Maybe I'm hoping you're planning on taking over so I can give you that list," Alyssa countered.

Mc'narrd hummed laughter, knowing she was teasing him. That alone made him like her even more. Few of his own people would dare tease him the way she did. Not since he had taken command of his own vessel. Only his closest friends, his senior crew, and comrades from his days prior to becoming a commander teased him the way she did.

"I don't doubt you want to get vengeance on those who sent you out to die. Though, perhaps that is why you have such feelings towards me? Hmm? I am the one who saved you from death, and so you feel indebted to me?" Mc'narrd countered.

What he presumed was indignation flared in Alyssa's eyes as she glowered at him.

"I am eternally thankful to you and your crew for saving my life, but I owe no one my body. Yes, I am attracted to you, but it has nothing to do with you saving me. It has everything to do with you being a handsome man who is confident in his position. Someone who I doubt I could ever best at anything."

"Someone who would be a challenge to you?" he suggested.

It was part of why he had yet to find someone to take as a mate. A long-term partner. Being part of space travel and often battling against space-going adversaries was only one reason. The other main reason being it was difficult to find a woman who wouldn't buckle and concede because of his position as a commander. He wanted someone willing to fight with whatever tools they had at hand, may it be wits, words, or weapons.

"Exactly," Alyssa said with a sigh. "You appeal in a way no other man I've met has. The fact you're extremely handsome is the cherry on top, as the human saying goes."

"Then we have more in common than you may have originally thought." He paused before adding, "You also didn't answer the question."

Her pursed lips and glower was enough to know she was trying to avoid it, too.

"Fine. I was not as outspoken during my employment at my former job," she admitted. "That sort of thing would have, ironically, gotten me killed sooner. So being able to voice my opinion without fearing death? So far, it has its appeal." A slight smile returned to her lips. "Don't believe I didn't want to say what I thought. I did. But I enjoyed living, so I found ways to say what I wanted using softer, kinder words."

"You seem very adept at insults, though," he replied. "Was that part of your training? Or a skill you sharpened over the years?"

Alyssa laughed as she crossed to her bed and settled onto the mattress. He found it amusing she chose the bed, which happened to be in an adjoining room off the main living section. He had little choice but to follow her, remaining just outside the bedchambers. A safe distance from her and the temptation the bed offered.

Watching Alyssa move reminded Mc'narrd that she wasn't K'laisian. His people's movements were fluid, almost liquid. She was graceful, but there was a weight to her steps. A stiffness to her body that K'laisians did not have.

"That I had in spades before entering the government program. It was merely sharpened and honed into a useful weapon at the academy. It's come in handy," she said, meeting his gaze.

As far as he knew, she hadn't been taught from practically birth how to fight with weapons, and she had made an enemy by insulting ,K'rell. For now, none could Challenge her since she was technically still a prisoner. That would change unless he took steps to prevent it and prepare her for a life on his world. That did not mean ,K'rell wouldn't demand retribution. Or push even harder to be allowed to speak with her.

If anyone could antagonize Alyssa and prove humans were dangerous, it would be ,K'rell. The man was insufferable. Skilled at his job, yes, but that didn't stop ,K'rell from being disliked by the majority of the crew. From the moment the policy master had joined his ship, the man had antagonized the *Laedschot's* crew. New members and those of the lowest ranking were particular favorites for ,K'rell to target.

Fortunately, the crew knew how to outmaneuver the policy master and did so with polite ease. To the point where the policy master could not argue or demand retribution.

Mc'narrd knew if ,K'rell had his say, Alyssa would be sent planetside. Left to fend for herself and carve a life out without help from their people. The thought of her on K'lais without him felt like a punch to the gut. Watching as the light played along her features, highlighting the different shades in her blonde hair, Mc'narrd was more determined than ever to make sure she was able to remain on his ship.

If she wanted. And going by the ferocity of their shared kiss, he had no doubt she wanted him as much as he wanted her. With luck, it wasn't a short-term, lust-filled desire.

",K'rell's position on this vessel isn't small. He reports everything directly to Military High Command," Mc'narrd said, feeling a need to explain.

Sighing, he closed the distance between them and settled on the bed beside her. Perhaps a dangerous place to be, but he discovered he disliked having distance between them. She turned to face him, curiosity showing in every feature.

Pausing for a moment, he said, "End recording. Privacy Code Tachu Jil." When the comm beeped twice in his ear, he spoke again. "Being in command has its privileges. One being I can stop recordings whenever I want, especially within my quarters... and these." Before she could say something, he rushed forward with his explanation. ",K'rell reports to High Command. As such, he is slightly above the first officer, but still below me in the command chain. Policy Masters are placed on the ships to ensure the objectives and orders from High Command are followed. Not all policy masters are as... stringent in their duties as ,K'rell."

"So, he can give orders to anyone but you and the healers," Alyssa guessed.

Mc'narrd nodded, pleased at how quickly she caught on. She would do well with his people. Even as a member of his crew.

"And you just insulted his position, intelligence, and cut him in the vanity department." She shrugged. He sighed, though at the same time he was amused at her dismissal of having such a powerful enemy. "Eventually, I will not be able to demand that no one Challenge you to a Duel, Alyssa."

"You should be more concerned about him," Alyssa stated.

"Just remember, when the time comes, you can choose a Champion," Mc'narrd said, realizing there was no way to convince her to be more wary. "Are all humans as stubborn and foolish as you?"

"Probably not," Alyssa said thoughtfully. "Are all K'laisians willing to risk a reprimand from their superiors by taking equally foolish risks?"

He started, uncertain of where that question came from. "What do you mean?"

"You turned the recordings off while alone in your female prisoner's room," Alyssa replied with a smug smile. "You did not tell the cameras of the room to turn off. So ,K'rell, if he were watching or demanding the recordings, will know you are in here alone with your personal camera off. Why, Commander, we could be doing anything!"

Mc'narrd laughed in the way humans did. It was a sound he'd discovered she loved hearing from him. "There are no cameras in this room or mine. Another bonus of being the commander of a vessel. In truth, they are rarely used even in general quarters. As for the recording? ,K'rell can do as he pleases. Until we return, he can't go crying to High Command. As long as I return successful, nothing he does can be twisted to change the fact that I succeeded despite the efforts of the humans."

"So, no cameras in here?" Alyssa asked, looking around the room.

Curious as to what she had planned, he shook his head slowly.

"Good. That's good," Alyssa mused.

Faster than he would have thought possible, she slid into his lap and wrapped herself around him, dragging him down to the bed. Her lips were pressed against his. Her hands slid through his hair.

Rolling her over, he pinned her to the bed as he chuckled. She wiggled against him, her legs trying to pull him closer to her.

"I know, I know. It's a bad idea," she said, her eyes dancing with laughter. "We humans have a saying: just because it's a bad idea, doesn't mean it won't be a good time."

"You are absolutely incorrigible," Mc'narrd stated before brushing his lips across hers.

The comm buzzed in his ear followed by Zh'oros's voice. "Is everything well, Commander?"

There were times when wearing the comms at all were annoying. This was most certainly one of them. Alyssa gave him a pout. He groaned as he pushed away from the bed, disentangling himself from her.

"Commander?" Zh'oros repeated.

"Everything is fine, Zh'oros," he said, moving away from the bed and the woman laying on it, her elbows propping her up. A question on her face and desire in her eyes.

The sound of humming filled his ear. He hid a glower and his irritation.

"Ah. Conducting an interrogation? Questioning our, *ahem*, 'prisoner' for more information?" More humming came through the comm in his ear. "That would explain the drastic shift in the readings from her bio suit."

"How is Ad'umi?" Mc'narrd asked, changing topics.

"Oh, she'll live. She'll be in the medbay for a while, but she'll survive her injuries," Zh'oros said dismissively. "Zh'oros out."

"Sometimes I hate these things," Mc'narrd grumbled, tapping his ear. "Before I leave, allow me to warn you of one more thing." Alyssa nodded, and he smiled. "The bio suit you are wearing sends your body's readings to the medbay. Only Master Healer Zh'oros has access to your readings, though. Unfortunately, they are constantly monitored. Anytime your readings are elevated to a questionable level, Zh'oros is alerted."

Alyssa's brows furrowed as she pursed her lips in thought. When she realized what he was saying, her eyes widened, and her jaw dropped. What could only have been dismay and embarrassment filled her every feature. She flopped back on the bed, slapping her hands over her face.

"Oh, gods above and below," she bemoaned. "So anyone who goes over those readouts will know how I feel about you. That's not the least bit embarrassing."

"Why would you feel embarrassed? Are you ashamed of your feelings?"

"No!" Her response was fast and insistent. "But it's not exactly something humans are accustomed to, either!" Her face was quickly turning red. On her, he found it sweet and attractive. She continued, hands still on her face. "Humans prefer to keep those feelings private until both parties are willing to make them known to others. Even then, they don't want everyone to know when they feel such strong emotions."

"Ah, then I shall leave you to adjust to the information I've just given you," Mc'narrd said.

Knowing he shouldn't, but not being able to stop himself, he crossed to the bed with soundless steps. He knew he surprised her when she jerked slightly as he moved her hands away from her face.

His lips captured hers as he kissed her breathless. Brushing his fingers along her ears, from tip to lobe, they trailed along her cheek to the center of her jaw.

"If you promise to behave, I will visit you more often," he murmured.

Without another word, he turned and left.

Yes, he'd allowed his emotions and desires to get the best of him. Yes, it was foolish and could cost him a great deal.

But there was a nagging sensation telling him that Alyssa was important. Trust could be built through many avenues.

The question was: Would he survive the encounter? And if he did, would he come out on top?

Chapter Fifteen

"Commander Mc'narrd!" ,K'rell called from behind Mc'narrd as he r strode through the corridor. "Commander, we need to talk!"

"If you are going to whine like a petulant child about an alien embarrassing you, please schedule a meeting time," Commander Mc'narrd replied evenly. "The fact that she managed such a feat with ease merely points out the fact you are not an ambassador."

,K'rell's steps faltered before picking up and matching his own. Mc'narrd hid a smile at that fact.

"She is being given too much freedom," ,K'rell snapped. "You have given Security Master Ra'dett, Master of Communications Ar'ath, and First Officer Ac'kyll the ability to speak with her. She converses openly with the healers and Zh'oros. Yet I am still refused permission to speak to the human."

"Nor is that going to change any time soon," Mc'narrd stated.

He stopped and turned on the policy master. A fluid movement ,K'rell had not expected. The policy master stumbled to a quick stop.

"If Sergeant Zelaya was able to anger you with such ease while in the presence of First Officer Ac'kyll and others, then she will be able to do it again."

"I can handle an insolent being," ,K'rell retorted. "It has been a part of my job for decades. You said we all would be given permission to speak and interact with the human."

"The human has a name," Mc'narrd said, trying to not grit his teeth.

How ,K'rell had managed to become a policy master for any military vessel was beyond him. The man had zero social skills. Nor did he know how to not anger anyone, including his superiors.

"You also seem infatuated with her," ,K'rell commented. "Are you certain you can continue this mission when you so obviously wish to bed the human?"

Mc'narrd raised a brow, refusing to allow ,K'rell to goad him. "Is that the best you can do, ,K'rell? I know what my orders are regarding this mission. I was privately briefed prior to our departure." He paused, narrowing his eyes as he stared down the policy master. His tone became several degrees colder as he asked, "Do you remember what *your* orders are?" ,K'rell swallowed several times before nodding once. "Good. You're dismissed."

The policy master turned and stalked away. Mc'narrd sighed, shook his head, then continued down the corridor.

"First Officer Ac'kyll," he said as he strode towards the lift.

"Yes, Commander?" she replied over the comm.

"Has there been any further update on the reaction from the humans to the lack of response from the destruction of Sergeant Zelaya's ship?"

"None that we can decode yet," Master Ar'ath replied over the comm. "Are we still going to move forward with allowing Alyssa to attempt to break the codes and encryptions?"

Once the doors to the lift opened, he stepped onto the bridge. As usual, the crew turned, saluted, and returned to their stations. His first officer rose from his command chair, which she was currently occupying, even as he crossed to Ar'ath, who was at her console.

She turned in her chair to look up at him. "Security and linguistics still have had no success, and they're equally curious as to if she can succeed where we have not."

"We will have to have a contingency plan in place, if she is unable, " Ac'kyll spoke up as she neared the pair.

"I'm certain ,K'rell will find even more objections to Alyssa assisting," Ra'dett stated dryly. "But this would be a chance for her to prove which side she will be on. Especially towards those who may question her motives. It will solidify her position towards us and against Earth." All of them looked at Ra'dett at the same time. The security master tipped his head back and forth in a shrug. "You did leave your comm on, sir."

Mc'narrd remained silent. It was difficult to keep a smug smile from his face, but he managed it. He felt no shame in his actions, especially since Alyssa had been a willing participant. To the point of instigating the kiss.

The military kept those with xenophobic tendencies off their military ships due to the very nature of their missions. He was thankful that his crew were not xenophobic and showed little concern with his interactions with their human passenger.

"She also made valid points," Ra'dett continued, ignorant of his thoughts. "So far, the lady hasn't changed her story. Either she's a skilled liar to the point where she can fool a bio suit, as well as you, Commander, or she's being honest. If she's willing to do as she claims, this will be the perfect opportunity to find out."

"Unless any of you see a reason for it, we'll move forward without calling a meeting," Mc'narrd stated. The other three glanced at each other, before shaking their heads. "Very well, then. Call up a replacement, Ar'ath. See if Alyssa would be willing to begin work on the transmissions from the Earth ships. The sooner we have those codes broken, the better. Find out if she knows any frequencies and such that we do not currently possess."

Ar'ath gave a quick nod and turned towards her interface.

"You think she can do it?" Ac'kyll asked as the communications master turned towards the interface.

Mc'narrd nodded as he headed for his command chair. Ac'kyll and Ra'dett followed beside him. "I believe she has a better chance of doing so, even if she ends up requiring assistance from our own departments."

"You don't believe the crew will feel 'violated' by having to work with an alien?" Ra'dett asked, a smirk flashing across his face as he spoke.

"If anything, I suspect they'll find it to be the opportunity they've wanted to interact with her," Mc'narrd admitted. "Humans are not the only humanoid race we interact with or allow on our ships."

"Not even close," Ac'kyll agreed. "And our crew is one of the best in the fleet."

"We'll give Alyssa two days. If she doesn't make progress of any sort in that time, we reconvene to decide on our next steps in regards to the humans," Mc'narrd declared.

The pair gave a nod as he settled into his chair. Removing the interface at the side of his command chair, he began scrolling through the reports. Ac'kyll and Ra'dett drifted back to their own stations. The usual discussions rose among his command crew. Questions asked, answers given. Conversations turning to their daily life among the stars.

There were duties to be done. Either Alyssa would have the knowledge and be willing to share it or not. There was little to achieve by dwelling on the subject or the woman. No matter how much he might want to do so.

Chapter Sixteen

After Mc'narrd left, Alyssa sat on the bed staring at the door for several long minutes. Knowing her bio suit recorded every fluctuation of her body was both embarrassing and comforting. It wasn't that different from her old suit. Though she doubted the monitors on her old military suit recorded nearly as much as the one she now wore. Her old suit certainly didn't remove waste products from her body.

Nor had her old suit contained nanites. She still wasn't certain how she felt about that fact.

Eyeing the console, she sighed deeply. She really wanted to try her hand at cracking the code Mc'narrd had shown her. But she had to be patient and hope it was still an option. After all, Policy Master Jackass did not command the ship. That honor went to Mc'narrd. Who really knew how to kiss a woman.

No, no, no. That was not something her mind should dwell upon. And yet, her fingers were brushing over her lips even as she remembered the kiss they'd shared.

When had she turned into a love-sick teenager? Actually, had she ever been a love-sick teenager?

Chiding herself, she retrieved her tablet and powered it up. There was still plenty of reading material for her to go over and a lot about the K'laisians to learn. Settling into a chair, she decided to start reading about their history instead of picking up on their current political and economic climate. And it was definitely safer than researching their biologies.

When a soft chime sounded in her room, she looked up, startled. It rang again, and she realized someone was at her door.

Taking a chance, she asked, "Who is it?"

A voice filled the room, one she did not recognize. "Master of Communications Ar'ath."

That sounded promising, Alyssa thought. Maybe she hadn't ruined her chances, after all.

Aloud, she said, "Enter."

Ar'ath smiled at Alyssa and did as bid, crossing to where Alyssa sat.

"You've been granted permission to attempt to break the encryption and coded transmissions from the Earth ships," Ar'ath said without preamble.

Something about Ar'ath's posture had Alyssa pausing. "There's more, though."

Ar'ath gave a nod.

"May I?" she asked, gesturing towards the viewscreen.

"Yes, absolutely." Alyssa nodded. "I'm afraid I still haven't been given permission to use it."

There was a flash of smugness on Ar'ath's face as she spoke a series of commands so quickly, Alyssa wished she had a recorder.

The viewscreen came to life, showing the sector of space they were currently occupying. "This is the sector we're currently in." She spoke another set of rapid-fire commands, and the view shifted. "This is the sector where we found you."

Alyssa nodded as she stared at the viewscreen. She would have enjoyed the view more if she didn't have painful memories of that particular sector. Just staring at the stars in that area made her shoulder hurt. She rubbed it unconsciously. Maybe the communications master would show her how to change the view, she wondered.

The action brought a concerned expression to the other woman's face. A fact Alyssa found comforting.

"Are you well?" Ar'ath asked, gesturing towards Alyssa's shoulder.

"I'm fine, I think," Ayssa replied, smiling slightly. "The reminder of… what happened made my shoulder ache. Almost like a phantom pain. That is, a pain that is psychological and not physical."

Ar'ath lifted her chin before dropping it. The K'laisian version of a nod. "Many of our people suffer similarly. Perhaps Master Zh'oros can assist you in the same manner she assists our people."

Alyssa must have worn a doubtful expression because Ar'ath's humming was skittered. Their version of chuckling, Alyssa supposed.

"Our healers are well versed in both psychological and physical illnesses," Ar'arth reminded her. "Seeking medical aid, regardless of if it is physical or psychological, is encouraged. It is a sign of strength to seek aid, not refuse it, among our people."

"That is definitely far better than how humans act," Alyssa admitted. "I suspect that it is a great benefit on your ships."

Ar'ath gave another nod. "It is. If you desire to speak to her about it, just speak her title and name." She paused, before adding, "Though, I suppose you would require a comm for that to occur."

"I would appreciate any assistance Master Zh'oros could give, if it will help," Alyssa said. "As for the comm? I will wait for that privilege. In the meantime, I can mention it during my next visit to the gym and the healers I see there." She paused, before adding, "My apologies for changing the topic. Why were you showing me the sectors?"

"You are aware we have intercepted communications from Earth to ships in this sector and cannot decode the transmissions." Alyssa gave a nod as she spoke another command. The communications appeared on the viewscreen. "Do you recognize any of this?"

"Before I answer that, can you tell me how you are able to do that?" Alyssa finally asked. Her curiosity, Alyssa was certain, would eventually doom her. "Can you pull that up on any viewscreen? Or only specific ones?"

Ar'ath stared at her for several moments, her head tilted to one side. "I am the Master of Communications. I can access anything related to communications on almost any viewscreen. You gave me permission to use the one here. Otherwise I would not have been able to access it."

"Wait… you mean you had to be given verbal permission to use this viewscreen?" Alyssa asked. She was missing something important, but didn't know what she was missing. "Why?"

"These quarters–" Ar'ath began, then stopped abruptly. She sighed. "I'll explain if you answer my question first."

When the K'laisians jaw tightened, Alyssa suspected there was a conversation going on through some sort of communicator that she couldn't hear.

"That is the same code I used to contact my handler prior to my last assignment. It is not the same one the commander showed me earlier, though," Alyssa replied. She wondered if the earbud Mc'narrd had shown her was also a communicator. It would certainly explain a great deal. She brushed the thought aside and asked, "Why didn't you just ask for all the codes and frequencies I know to begin with?"

"Would you have given them without an explanation?" Ar'ath countered.

"Actually, yes," she replied, wondering if they would ever trust her. "Look, I know none of you have a reason to believe anything I say. It's probably a smart thing, if you know any other race that has dealt with humans. I doubt my race has a good reputation of any sort."

"That is a fair assessment and accurate guess," Ar'ath admitted. "But you are not 'all humans'. Just as those onboard this ship are not 'all K'laisians'."

"So you probably are questioning where I fall among the human race," Alyssa stated. "I can give you all the codes I know, including the outdated ones, as well as every frequency I'm aware of. You may already be aware of them or not, I don't know."

"Why would you do that?" Ar'ath asked, crossing her legs as she leaned back in the chair.

"Because I have no reason not to," Alyssa replied flippantly. At the other woman's frown, she smiled. "Several reasons, I guess. First and foremost: I'm on your ship. If my people decide to attack, I'd rather you be prepared. Especially if I want to ensure I survive the encounter. Secondly, Admiral Lynchen and the rest of the IMD admiralty expected me to die. Okay, that isn't entirely accurate. They didn't just expect it, they *wanted* my death. My loyalty to them died with that ship."

Alyssa swallowed hard, knowing she spoke treason. Knowing her people would already believe she'd betrayed her race if the aliens hadn't killed her.

"Wouldn't that be considered treason among your people?" Ar'ath asked. Alyssa nodded stiffly. "Yet you speak it easily?"

"Fluently, actually," Alyssa replied with another nod.

She paused, trying to find the right words to explain her reasoning. Ar'ath remained silent, giving Alyssa time to compose her thoughts and words.

"As I said, I have no reason to remain loyal to those who tried to kill me. They would have succeeded if the crew of this ship hadn't intervened. As much as I would like to stick a knife between the ribs of the ones who ordered my termination by way of an exploding ship? I'd rather see them fail at whatever plan they have towards Commander Mc'narrd and your people."

"Would you be so willing if your people had not tried to kill you?" Ar'ath asked.

Alyssa shrugged. "I don't know. I suspect that if they hadn't sent someone to die, they would not be trying to claim this ship is an enemy to be attacked. They would have sent an envoy of dignitaries to open communications."

"How did your people open trade with the other races?" Ar'ath asked after a few moments.

Again, Alyssa suspected Ar'ath was receiving orders through a comm link. Considering she couldn't see it, it reaffirmed her thought about the earbud the commander showed her.

"I only know what I have been taught," Alyssa replied. "My people made first contact with each race, then sent a diplomatic mission to open trade and negotiations with each race. Since my particular skill set had nothing to do with politics, negotiations, or similar, I'm afraid I wasn't told more than what was on our history holos."

"Is that normal for your people?"

"To not be told a lot? Or to gloss over everything?" Alyssa asked with a smile.

"Both," Ar'ath said, returning the smile.

"That and more," Alyssa confessed. "I imagine there is a lot more that occurred during those initial meetings than what is told to the general population. It would be considered 'classified' information. My clearance was different, so I didn't have access to any of that."

The communications master didn't say anything, which gave Alyssa time to collect her thoughts. Her eyes drifted to the viewscreen in time to see bits of her former ship float by in the eternal empty vacuum that was space. She suppressed a shiver at what could have happened to her.

Forcing her eyes away from the screen, she met Ar'ath's eyes. There was something in her gaze that gave Alyssa pause. It wasn't malice, but she couldn't figure out what it was, either. She'd have to discern it later.

"Is there a way I can input the needed code onto the viewscreen?" Alyssa finally asked.

Ar'ath gave a single nod. "How would you do it with your people?"

"You want me to recite all of it?" Alyssa asked. The K'laisian nodded. Shaking her head, Alyssa sighed. In a dubious tone, she said, "Comm data, input code: Jackal's Fire, frequency eight-one-eight point three, channel Alpha Two. Decode and decrypt."

The voice of someone Alyssa didn't recognize filled the room. "Captain Landry of the *ESS Valiant*, this is Admiral Dalton of IMD. Have you received a new transmission from the Valkyrie's homing device?"

Another man's voice came from the viewscreen. "Captain Landry here, Admiral. We have not received any signal yet. It seems to be jumping around. Uncertain if it is a mistake or if the aliens retrieved it after the ship exploded."

"Find out, Landry. Confer with Captains Snyder, Meyers, and Cortez. Be prepared to put Operation Manticore into effect. Dalton out."

Alyssa frowned. "Those are four of the IMD's best captains and the heaviest hitters the IMD has in this quadrant. In fact, Cortez was supposed to be in Hoag's, not even near here."

"How are you aware of the movements of these ships?" Ar'ath asked. She pulled a small, hand-sized interface from a side holster. "You can use this to input the codes and frequencies and anything else you think we should have and can use."

Alyssa accepted the device and studied it as she replied to Ar'ath. "I only know because of the last contract I had. I overheard the captain, Spivey, talking to his first officer about Cortez's position. The ships I know because it's general knowledge in the IMD."

"Your assistance will be greatly useful," Ar'ath said.

Alyssa glanced up at the K'laisian woman. "Will you explain your earlier statement? About these quarters?"

"Ah, that," Ar'ath said, shifting in the chair. Alyssa wondered if she was uneasy. "These quarters are typically reserved for the mate of the ship's commander. Often, that person is not part of the military, and so he or she is outside the usual structure on the ship. Those who are in the military, are career military in their chosen field. Usually not in the line of command, though it does happen. Due to the fact the mate isn't always under anyone's true command, that being is granted complete privacy. Although, strictly speaking, these quarters are also the commander's."

Alyssa paused in the middle of entering the information she knew. She felt her eyes growing wide at the woman's comment.

The commander's mate. No wonder the K'laisians were so… unhappy. It probably had nothing to do with her race, but her current location on the commander's ship AND because the commander was affectionate towards her.

"As the Commander's mate, that being has the same security clearance as the commander of the ship. Due to the security clearance differences, the cabins are completely private. None would dare enter without permission, including the commander. The only ones who can override the door's security is the master of security and master healer of the ship," Ar'ath concluded.

Bloody hell. She hadn't been given just any protection. She'd been given the commander's personal protection and put in quarters where she was absolutely safe. Even from the commander, himself.

Not that she wanted to be "safe" from him.

"Thank you for telling me that," Alyssa said after a few long heavy moments of silence. She added, holding up the interface, "This shouldn't take long."

In fact, it took less time than Alyssa had originally believed. Once she'd finished listing off all the information she knew about the codes, frequencies, and channels, she included the names of the admiralty she knew. That, in turn, was followed by what she knew about the command structure of the IMD and the battle cruisers and starships she was familiar with.

Handing the interface back, she said, "I hope that helps. Though I do not know what 'Manticore' is or what it has to do with the battle cruisers Dalton mentioned."

"That was only a small portion of the communications we received. With what you've given us, we will hopefully have those answers and more," Master Ar'ath said.

Alyssa thought she was trying to sound reassuring, but something about Manticore kept bothering her. She tried smiling at the woman, but didn't quite manage it.

"Can I try to break the encryption on the other transmissions now?" Alyssa all but begged. "I really want to see if I can manage that."

Ar'ath tipped her head to the side, an amused smile on her face. "You are very eager to do so. Is that normal for humans?"

Alyssa laughed and shook her head. "Only among those who enjoy a challenge or dare. I've always loved testing myself. And there is no better word to describe what you've offered me: a challenge to see if I'm able to accomplish that task." Her smile grew sly as she added, "Besides, I want to know what my government is hiding, also. There's a reason they wanted me dead, and I'd love to know what it was."

Humming was the response from the K'laisian communications master. "That is fair. Shall we?"

Alyssa nodded, watched as Master Ar'ath stood in a single fluid motion, reattaching the interface in the same movement. "If you want to pull up any of the views directly outside the ship, you can do so by simply requesting it. There isn't anything classified, and many of us enjoy the sight."

"Can we alter it to what is currently outside?" Alyssa asked, preferring anything to seeing bits of her former ship floating in space.

Ar'ath nodded and spoke the words so the view altered once again. Alyssa felt relief flood over her as they crossed to the console. Sitting in front of the screen, Alyssa touched the smooth surface. Maneuvering her way through the interface, she discovered all the information she'd given Ar'ath was now part of the database.

As was the transmission Mc'narrd had shown her. She played it through three times, watching the information scroll across the screen. Touching the surface, she lowered the speed and began the transmission again.

Ignoring everything around her, Alyssa focused on what was in front of her. Slowly, she began spotting the patterns in the encryption. With painstaking care, she began to unweave the encryption, finding bits and pieces that were familiar. The technology of the K'laisians made the process of deciphering the encryption so much easier. All she had to do was add in what she recognized and the program ran through every possible combination that could coincide with it. Slowly, Alyssa figured out half of the encryption.

"One more quarter and the program can finish it," Ar'ath said from beside Alyssa.

Alyssa started. She'd actually forgotten the woman was still sitting beside her. In fact, she wasn't even entirely certain how much time had passed since she'd begun deciphering the code. Leaning back in the chair, she realized her body was stiff. Her fingers ached as she stretched them.

Ar'ath, though, appeared as though the time sitting still hadn't affected her at all.

"You've been at this for ten hours, Alyssa," Ar'ath said gently. "You could take a break."

"Another five and I'll have three-quarters finished," Alyssa said, stretching languidly in the chair. She rolled her shoulders and bent forward. Ten hours was nothing to her. In fact, after spending days on end having nothing interesting to do, she was finally starting to feel more like her old self. "I hate stopping in the middle of a project."

The K'laisian woman hummed, shook her head, and leaned back in the chair. "I may suggest you be kept onboard simply for your tenacity at such projects."

Alyssa paused, her hand half-way to the screen as she looked at the communications master. "I'm sorry?"

"There are some onboard who are relentless, but most do not spend fifteen hours straight working on a project," Ar'ath said in amusement.

"I'm sorry," Alyssa said honestly. "If you wish to stop for the day, we can. It's just… this is the first time I've actually been encouraged to break a code. And the thought of learning why the admiralty wanted me dead is…"

"Important?" Ar'ath suggested. "Too tempting to leave as an unknown?"

"Both, I guess," Alyssa admitted, unable to locate the words that fit her feelings. "Are you certain you do not want to stop? I don't want this to affect your day tomorrow."

"I've been given leniency where this is concerned," Ar'ath replied dismissively. "Let's finish it to where the interface can finish the deciphering. You'll still need to work on decoding the message, which can be completed tomorrow."

"Actually, from what I've seen, the code appears based on a different language," Alyssa admitted. "It isn't one I'm familiar with or have seen before. It reminds me of yours, to be honest."

Ar'ath grew still and Alyssa looked at her warily.

"Let's finish this tonight," Ar'arth said simply, her tone not changing.

Alyssa gave a slow nod and turned back to her task. She hadn't paused to eat a meal and she was starting to wish she had. But food could wait.

Five hours later, Alyssa sat in front of the interface awaiting the decryption of the rest of the message. Ra'dett had arrived as they awaited the last part and he'd brought food and beverages with him.

Ar'ath and Alyssa sat in front of the console with Ra'dett standing behind them. All three were silent as they ate. Alyssa's body was reminding her why sitting hunched forward at a console for fifteen hours, at least, was not a wise idea. But she didn't regret it.

"If any of the transmissions mention why they wanted me dead, will you tell me?" she asked, breaking the silence.

"We will," Ra'dett promised.

As the decrypted message flashed onto the screen, Alyssa smiled slightly.

"Good to know I haven't lost my touch," she murmured. Even if it had taken longer than she'd expected. Having the codes and frequencies she technically wasn't supposed to know had been helpful. "And here we go."

Touching the screen, she brought up the message.

"Ra'dett," Ar'ath said quietly. "We need the commander."

Alyssa turned to Ar'ath, who wore a grim expression. "You recognize that? It's not an actual code?"

"It's a code, but it isn't from Earth," Ar'ath stated.

"Then… who?" Alyssa demanded. "It isn't anyone I know of, and as I've said before: I've encountered every race humans have encountered. If it's a planet we trade with, I've… been there. We'll just say I've been there."

"Except for one," Ra'dett stated calmly. "You've never once encountered anyone who appeared as us? Or any ship?"

Alyssa shook her head. "No. And believe me, I would remember someone who is as perfect as you." The pair of K'laisians stared at her, their eyes blinking. Alyssa shrugged. "What? You all appear perfect compared to a human or the other races I've encountered. You're also the only humanoid ones I've ever encountered."

"If one is on the humans' ships, it wouldn't be impossible to find one who appears as a human," Ar'ath suggested. "I doubt he or she would be visible to most. They'd choose a spy who could blend in easier. Perhaps even surgically alter their appearance."

"Would one of you please tell me who or what you're talking about?" Alyssa demanded.

"The language is Va'nu'ian, Alyssa," Ra'dett replied in a cool tone. "They are bitter enemies of K'lais. They appear similar to us, though they are not nearly as… civilized. And there is one on each of the three ships we've intercepted these coded messages from. Only a Va'nu'ian would be able to use those codes. Unlike other races, they are very… proprietary of their information. *Especially* their codes."

"Manticore," Alyssa said quietly. "Man-eater. A hybrid creature of ancient myth and legend."

Ra'dett gave her a curious look, but remained silent. "I'll inform Commander Mc'narrd. Thank you, Alyssa, for assisting us with breaking the encryption."

Without another word, the master of security turned and left the room.

"Manticores, in ancient Earth legends, were vicious creatures. Hybrid animals that had a lion's body, a human's face, and a scorpion's tail that ended in a ball of spikes. They were said to prey on humans," Alyssa said, feeling dread well up in her. "And the IMD has some sort of operation named after them. That involves a race that just happens to be your enemies."

"We've dealt with Va'nu'ians before, Alyssa," Ar'ath said, reassuringly. When Alyssa glanced at her, the communications master gave her a gentle smile. "If your people believe you are dead, they don't know we've been able to decrypt the messages. Nor would the Va'nu'ians believe a human could manage such. This is the edge we may need to keep all of us safe."

"I hope so," Alyssa said, her eyes shifting back to the screen. "I just wish I knew what they meant by 'Operation Manticore'."

"Give us time and we'll find out," Ar'ath said firmly. When she stood, Alyssa followed her lead. "I think you will find things to shift once I return with this information and it's verified." She paused, a sly smile curving her lips. "Comms off, Lady Alyssa's quarters, order from Master of Communications."

A feminine computerized voice spoke, "Comms off per Master of Communications Ar'eth."

"May I give you a suggestion?"

Alyssa nodded, curious. Ar'ath gave a nod, glancing towards the door briefly, she turned her attention back to Alyssa. "Ear tips. They're very… sensitive."

Alyssa's brow furrowed in confusion. The master of communications brushed back her silver hair to reveal the pointed tips of her ears. She tapped them.

"Think about it. Just don't mention who told you. Comms on," she said before turning and departing the room.

Alyssa watched after her, still confused, even as the computer spoke again. Then it suddenly dawned on her.

Ear tips are sensitive. At least to a K'laisian. Coming from a woman, spoken in complete privacy, Alyssa suspected it was more in a romantic fashion than a physical weakness. She grabbed her tablet and flipped through the subjects until she came to K'laisian biology. After a quick search using various keywords, she finally found what Ar'ath was talking about.

Why the master of communications gave her that suggestion, she didn't know. But she was thankful. She also hoped Master Ar'ath didn't get into trouble for turning the comms off, even briefly.

Now she just needed the opportunity to test it.

Chapter Seventeen

"**S**atisfied?" Mc'narrd asked ‚K'rell and Master Ra'dett as he turned away from the viewscreen. He'd been standing on the upper deck in front of the large viewscreen so he could oversee his bridge crew. They all had been listening to the conversation on a top clearance frequency. None said anything when Ar'ath paused the comms briefly. Alyssa had shown she wasn't a threat, otherwise, the human would have remained in the brig.

"I am," Master Ra'dett stated. "Between the frequencies she gave and spending most of a day decrypting the transmissions, it has allowed us to decode all the current communications." He paused as he continued to skim over the reports. "If anything, I would say she was being humble about her skills at code breaking. Even Master Ar'ath was impressed with her tenacity and abilities."

"Master Ar'ath should not have turned off the comms while in the human's quarters." ‚K'rell's nose wrinkled in a very unbecoming manner. "I am still not convinced of the human. Her people are shown to be suicidal. They manipulate every race they encounter. We have it on record of how they interact with the Xoutians. And now we learn they have a secret treaty with the Va'nu'ians. We do not even know how long the Va'nu'ians and humans have been in contact. Though it would explain why the humans attacked us outright!"

"We will continue this in Room Three," Mc'narrd stated. "Call up your reliefs, and meet me there. Master Ar'ath, meet us in the briefing room."

"Yes, sir," she replied.

"Master Li'kox, you have the conn," Mc'narrd stated.

"Yes, sir!" The Master of Weapons gave Mc'narrd a salute before moving to the command chair.

Mc'narrd didn't wait for anyone as he departed the bridge. Unfortunately, ,K'rell fell into step beside him as he left for the briefing room.

"I have been researching the human position of 'assassin'," ,K'rell began, his voice sharp as he clipped the ends of each word. "Assassins kill for money. They don't care for anything but wealth and the luxuries it affords. They are cold beings with shallow feelings."

The last comment from the policy master made Mc'narrd snort. He kept the smile from showing on his face, but only barely. He knew one assassin who did care and had very warm feelings.

"I am aware of what an assassin's job is, ,K'rell," Mc'narrd stated. "It isn't an alien concept. We've encountered similar beings on other planets. The Va'nu'ians are crueler and far more vicious than the humans could ever attempt to be."

"That changes nothing. We do not have a Va'nu'ian onboard, but we do have a human who is *insubordinate*. None of us know what her motives are or if she will turn against us at the first opportunity!" ,K'rell retorted, his voice growing sharper and higher as he spoke.

Mc'narrd didn't pause in his steps as he asked, "Are you certain this isn't because an alien female dared to insult you? To speak in a way no crewmember would dare?"

,K'rell's eyes narrowed at Mc'narrd, but he didn't say anything for several long moments.

"That has nothing to do with my position," he finally said. "Until we know the motives behind the humans, including your pet, I will not alter my position."

"That is your choice," Mc'narrd stated in a calmer tone than he felt.

If ,K'rell wanted to call Alyssa his 'pet', so be it. It made Mc'narrd question what ,K'rell had been viewing from Earth. He had used the phrase to test Alyssa. Nothing more. ,K'rell, though, definitely knew how to irritate him. He couldn't get rid of the obnoxious fool, but could take some enjoyment in seeing ,K'rell forced to accept the actual commander's decisions.

For perhaps the millionth time, Mc'narrd was thankful policy masters could not give orders to the commanders of ships. Otherwise, he would most certainly have Challenged ,K'rell long before now.

Thankfully, Room Three was in close proximity to the bridge, so it didn't take long for them to arrive. ,K'rell settled into his usual chair and began tapping away at his console. Mc'narrd took the time to read over the decoded communications.

As he scrolled through the transcribed communications, the requested crew filed into the room. Being the last to arrive, the door slid shut after Ar'ath took her seat.

"Thanks to Master Ar'ath and Sergeant Zelaya, we now have the required information to decode and decrypt the communications from Earth to their ships in this sector," Mc'narrd said once everyone had time to settle into their chairs. He tapped his screen a few times and brought up a schematic of the sector showing their ship as well as the four mentioned in the snippet Alyssa had helped decode.

"These are the current positions of Earth's vessels. Battleships are what Sergeant Zelaya called them."

Mc'narrd gestured to Master Ra'dett who nodded to his commander before continuing. "The humans have sent four ships into the sector, all equipped with high-power weaponry." He paused, a brief smirk flashing across his face. "Well, what they consider 'high-power', anyway. Regardless, they've referenced 'Manticore' several times and we can only assume, by their movements, it's an offensive-based operation meant to attack those they consider an enemy."

He paused, allowing his words to settle before glancing at Mc'narrd, who gave a slight nod. The information needed to be spoken and placed on record. The fact it confirmed what High Command had sent him to discover did not please Mc'narrd. But they now had an edge neither Earth's military or the Va'nu'ians were aware of.

"The most troublesome information comes from the code used. The encrypted messages were sent in Va'nu'ian. Sergeant Zelaya is unaware of any being who remotely appears K'laisian on the ships she has traveled on. As such, it appears the Earth government is keeping their relations with the Va'nu'ians secret. Even from their own people."

"Does the human know anything about this 'Manticore'?" ,K'rell asked, looking up from his console.

"No," Master Ar'ath stated. "She appeared to me to be concerned about it, though."

"Is that a professional opinion?" ,K'rell asked in a snide tone.

Not taking his bait, Ar'ath replied, "No. It comes from being one of four girls in a family that traveled the systems extensively."

,K'rell blinked several times. Mc'narrd suspected it was due to the fact he forgot Master Ar'ath's family were respected scientists. They traveled the systems researching the biologics on other planets. Her grandparents were retired career military and were now politicians on their home world.

"Moving on," Ra'dett stated, when the silence continued. "We have not been sending transmissions as we change our positions since our last meeting. The humans have stated they are actively searching for the transmitting device we obtained from Zelaya's body and ship."

"I'm not seeing any mention of the woman in any of these transmissions. Only to the destroyed ship," Ac'kyll stated in disgust. "That does go to show she isn't considered of importance to them."

"There has been one single mention," Master Ar'ath interjected. "Though it came from Earth and was sent to the closest planets. Instructions in the transmission demanded it be relayed to every colony, ally, and ship within their federation."

"Go on," Mc'narrd said. He already knew what had been sent, but he wanted it said to the rest of his crew. It would place it on record and be sent to High Command with the rest of the recording of the meeting.

"They're claiming we deliberately destroyed the ship after it was disabled due to a mechanical malfunction." She didn't bother hiding her disgust of the situation.

"I suppose a bomb could be considered a 'mechanical malfunction," Ra'dett said, though there was no mistaking the derisive tone.

Ar'ath gave a few taps of her screen and the hologram image of the sector darkened. The transcribed section she referenced overlaid it in brighter colors. "The military of Earth is urging extreme caution and to avoid the sector the *Ramshead* was lost in. They state that Sergeant Zelaya volunteered for the mission to open communications with us, an unknown alien race. Her ship suffered a malfunction and instead of assisting, we simply destroyed it."

,K'rell leaned back in his chair, a smug expression on his face. "So, who do we believe? The human? Or her masters?"

"The ship had explosives planted on it. Yes, that would certainly 'disable' a ship, but it could have easily killed the person onboard," Ac'kyll stated without blinking. "Or are you willing to ignore the facts that our own people have established? The evidence showing that the humans deliberately destroyed their own ship and didn't care about who was onboard it?"

,K'rell frowned, but remained silent. Mc'narrd made a mental note to add a recommendation in her file.

"Do we know why the humans are so adamant about showing us as coldhearted, merciless killers?" Ac'kyll asked, turning her attention to the communications master.

"Nothing," Ar'ath replied. "There has been nothing mentioned anywhere. In fact, nothing the humans are doing relates to how they behaved upon their first contact with the Xoutians."

"If the Va'nu'ians are involved, the question arises as to what they have told the humans of Earth," Ra'dett stated. "We are all aware of our tenuous truce with the Va'nu'ians. Despite being very distantly related to us, they still harbor an ancient anger towards K'lais. As such, it is known they would be willing to do anything to reclaim their ancient home planet, our current home world of K'lais."

"How did they respond to the other races? Specifically their technology?" ,K'rell asked, not looking up from his console.

,K'rell's fingers flew over the keys, his eyes on the display.

Mc'narrd wondered what the policy master was leading up to. He turned his attention to his crew. They, in turn, looked at each other before looking back at him. All of them shrugged.

"That is a question we would need to ask Sergeant Zelaya," Mc'narrd stated.

,K'rell raised only his eyes to meet Mc'narrd's even gaze. "Then perhaps we should ask the human."

"Master Healer Zh'oros, please bring Sergeant Zelaya to Room Three," Mc'narrd stated.

"We will be there within seven minutes," Zh'oros replied.

,K'rell gave a nod before turning his attention back to his console.

"What else have you learned from the communications to and from Earth, Master Ar'ath?" Mc'narrd asked. "We will wait for Master Healer Zh'oros and Sergeant Zelaya before continuing with ,K'rell's line of questions."

Master Ar'ath turned back to the hologram. "With Alyssa's assistance, we've been able to decode and decrypt almost every transmission within the past decade or so."

Mc'narrd gave the floor to his communications master and master of security. There was no question they deliberately used her name to annoy the policy master. And he had no reason to object. Despite that fact, he only gave them half his attention. It wouldn't take the entire seven minutes, and he wanted to hear the interaction between the healer and Alyssa.

The knock on the door pulled Alyssa away from the tablet she'd been reading since Master Ar'ath left. The viewscreen showed the sector outside the ship. A much better view than the reminder of how she ended up on the *Laedschot.*

The current view was of a sector she was unfamiliar with and it piqued her fascination and curiosity. She appreciated having something other than a blank screen to watch, even if she had no way of learning more about her current location in the galaxies. She'd have to question one of the K'laisians at a later time.

"Come," she called absentmindedly.

It was only after the door opened she realized how comfortable she was becoming in the room and on the ship. Or maybe it was simply because she was so absorbed in what she was reading?

"You appear comfortable," Zh'oros said, giving voice to Alyssa's inner musings.

Alyssa looked up at the healer. "Is mind reading a talent of your people?"

Zh'oros hummed. "Not off planet." Her humming grew at Alyssa's startled expression. "It is a rare Gift, but it has been found among our people."

"Why not off planet?" Alyssa asked. She hadn't reached that part of her self-appointed studies.

"The Gifts K'laisians are born with cannot be used anywhere but on the planet. Those who go off our planet are highly skilled in combat and strategy, among other things. Nor is just anyone able to go off planet in the military." She paused in speaking, before adding, "Do not believe that the Gifts of those who go off planet are minor. Often that is not the case."

"Is there anything available for me to read on that?" Alyssa asked, tempted to ask what about her and Mc'narrd's Gifts.

"I'll bring you a disc with that information," Zh'oros promised. Alyssa thought she heard approval in the woman's voice, but wasn't certain. "For now, I've been requested to escort you… somewhere."

"Where?" Alyssa asked, slowly standing.

The healer's smile didn't fade. "To a meeting with the other senior crew. We have new questions about your people."

That could mean a lot of things, Alyssa thought.

There were certainly an endless number of questions she had about the K'laisians. She wouldn't be surprised if they had as many, if not more, about the humans. Especially now that it was known her people had a truce of sorts with the K'laisians enemies.

"I'll answer them to the best of my ability," she replied easily.

As tempted as she was to ask why the master healer was so at ease when she entered her quarters, Alyssa didn't ask. For now, her attention was on the corridors they were traveling and trying to memorize the route. When they reached a lift, she followed Zh'oros into it with only a little trepidation.

Zh'oros touched the wall and then waited. Alyssa glanced at the other woman, but remained silent. As before, she couldn't detect the lift moving, even when she concentrated on trying to do so. When the doors opened, Zh'oros led her through another set of hallways.

Within five minutes, Zh'oros was stepping to the side and gesturing for her to enter a medium-sized room. A table was centered in the room with chairs around it. The setting reminded Alyssa of a dinner table with a head, someone opposite, and the guests at each side. Her eyes breezed over the crew before returning to the holo floating above the surface of the table.

It, at least, was familiar. Even if it was higher tech than her own people's methods. The colors were similar, but this display was larger, and the table's surface wasn't black. Nor did it have lenses allowing the holo to be projected upward into the air instead of on a viewscreen.

Currently, there was a transcription of what she recognized as communications from Earth. Behind the transcript was an image of several ships, positions of planets, and small labels written in what she now understood to be the K'laisian language.

"Thank you for joining us," Mc'narrd said, rising from his position at the head of the table. He gestured towards an empty chair. "Please, have a seat."

Glancing around at the faces of the other K'laisians, she noticed that even ,K'rell appeared pleased she had joined them. With only a nod, she settled into the chair, which shifted to conform to her body. Suppressing the desire to jump out of the chair, she tried to relax, but found it difficult.

"Are you well?" Zh'oros asked, as she sat in her own chair. She began touching the console in front of her as she spoke.

Alyssa was intrigued with the fact the console screens appeared to float in front of each K'laisian. Though the screens were not completely opaque, she couldn't see anything on them. They reminded her of a two-way mirror, where one side was reflective, but you could see through it from the opposite side.

"I still am not accustomed to a chair that changes to fit me." To change the topic away from her, she asked, "What questions did you have for me?"

Mc'narrd gestured to ,K'rell, who spoke. "I was wanting to know how your people responded to the other races? To their technology, to be specific."

Alyssa opened her mouth to answer, then closed it. After a few moments, she finally answered him. "Please keep in mind that I was not a part of any of the first contacts. Nor did I interact with those who did." ,K'rell gave a nod, so she continued. "From what I have read, and heard, we – that is, humans– have enjoyed the advances other races have offered. There has not been any outright hostility towards either the technology or races. At least, none that I've been aware of."

"Why do you say that? None that you are aware of?" Ra'dett asked.

"Though I am not a direct member of the military, I sometimes had to appear to be one. My transport between assignments were on military cruisers, or on rare occasions, science vessels. Because of that, I often heard anything from admiration to hatred and bigotry towards the other races. Despite the personal opinion towards a particular race, there were no derogatory comments towards the technology." Alyssa met Mc'narrd's eyes and kept them. "When you eventually open negotiations for trade with humans, I am certain you will find many who will be anything but pleasant and complimentary towards your race."

"Yet you proclaim to harbor neither bigotry, racism, xenophobia, or any other negative reactions towards other races," ,K'rell demanded.

"I was an orphan, Master ,K'rell," Alyssa replied, refusing to be goaded.

She shoved her feelings down just as she had since childhood. Ever since she learned people felt empowered by receiving an emotional reaction. Glancing around the table, she noticed curiosity and encouragement from the rest of the crew. They were beings she'd grown to like, so she continued. For them, if for no other reason.

"Orphans are often left to survive with only their wits, luck, and the ability to grow up fast in the streets. Where theft is the way of life. Or, if they are lucky, they are allowed into a so-called home. There, they are given food, shelter, and the ability to attend school. But anything else, such as love or affection?" She shook her head. "Those things aren't found. I was lucky. I had a skill set my government wanted. I had no family, so there was no one to object to anything the government did. Or to look for me if I died in the learning process."

"That sounds like a very cold, harsh environment," Ar'ath stated. "Children are the future. As such, they should be given homes and the chance at opportunities to help society. The same comforts as those born of blood."

"In case you haven't noticed, Master Ar'ath, humans aren't exactly the most compassionate race," Alyssa said gently, trying to hide the pain she felt as memories threatened to bubble up.

Her life in the orphanage hadn't been the most pleasant. There had been a reason the government placed her in the program for training assassins. It hadn't been because she was a good thief.

Alyssa turned her attention back to ,K'rell.

"I have seen the depravity of my own people, Master ,K'rell. I have been looked down upon and hated simply because I was an orphan. I try to be better than those people, To treat another race in the same way I was treated is not something I could be proud of."

Turning her attention to the holo, she noticed Zh'oros making a slight movement. Mc'narrd gave a nearly imperceptible nod before looking down at his console. She doubted they meant for her to notice, but she'd always been vigilant. That trait hadn't atrophied since her rescue. Something had obviously passed between the two, but she didn't know what.

,K'rell studied her for several long moments. Finally, he asked, "What about their opinions of the aesthetics of the other races' technology?"

That gave Alyssa pause. It also allowed her the ability to shove her childhood memories back behind the doors that were slowly starting to creak open. With the memories went the pain.

"As far as I know, the appearances of the other races' technology and the humans' is fairly close. There aren't a lot of design differences." She glanced towards Mc'narrd. "The images of your ship, Commander, were the first I've ever seen that are sleek and smooth. Not clunky or with sharp corners, if you'll pardon the term." She paused before asking, "Are all your ships as elegant and similarly shaped as yours?"

Mc'narrd smirked. "Most, yes. Those that are battlecruisers have similar designs. I suspect all our vessels would be considered 'elegant' and more efficiently designed than those your race lays claim to."

"Have your people encountered any other race that is humanoid?" ,K'rell interrupted.

Shaking her head, Alyssa said, "Not that I'm aware of, and I've assassinated beings of every race we deal with. That I know of, anyway. Admittedly, I also was not aware my own race had communications with Va'nu'ians. So I suppose there could be others, as well."

"The humans, Commander, turned their weapons on us after we hailed their first ship," ,K'rell stated.

Mc'narrd glanced at Masters Ar'ath and Ra'dett. Alyssa suspected it was for confirmation, since both gave a single nod. The commander frowned.

"What are you thinking, ,K'rell?" Mc'narrd asked.

The policy master touched the top of his console, and it lowered until it was flat with the table surface. Alyssa watched with fascination as it seemed to meld with the table.

"The humans have claimed to have not met another humanoid race. The closest would be, possibly, the Xoutians. Though I'm only guessing at that fact. The first ship we encountered, we hailed them, complete with video.

Did I get that correct, Sergeant?" he asked, looking at Alyssa.

She nodded, equally curious as to where he was going.

He returned the nod before turning back to the commander. "We used video and after the humans saw us, they grew defensive and aggressive. They then opened fire on our ship. Thankfully, our defenses are far superior to anything they possess. When they refused to stand down, we were forced to return fire. Since then, they have stated we are a dangerous enemy and to be avoided at all cost."

"You're merely recounting things we are already aware of," Ra'dett stated in a neutral tone. "Please get to the point."

,K'rell's eyes narrowed at the security master, but if he was annoyed, Alyssa couldn't hear it when he began speaking again. "The humans have shown themselves to be vain creatures. Their past is riddled with evidence of that. They turned aggressive upon seeing a race with superior technology. Sergeant Zelaya has shown she finds our race to be superior in appearance to the humans." He paused, before adding, "At least compared to her."

"Considering how vain humans can be?" Alyssa said, ignoring the jab. "It wouldn't be surprising if whoever you hailed felt inferior to you. Between the technology, ship's design, and your appearances? There's a good chance that the captain you spoke to had a sudden inferiority attack. But are you insinuating that's enough for war?"

There was a gleam in Mc'narrd's eyes that left Alyssa suddenly feeling uncertain of her fate, but she shoved that feeling away. The beings, these K'laisians, had promised to make sure she survived. Master Ac'kyll even hinted that she might eventually be able to have a family. That one may be willing to take her as a lover… a mate. Considering Commander Mc'narrd's behavior earlier, she was holding that hope close to her chest, terrified it was nothing but a lie. All the while hoping for more.

Just as she had as a child, she couldn't allow her fears and insecurities to rule her.

"So to sum this up," ,K'rell began, and Alyssa did not like his smug tone. At least, that's what she would have called it if he were a human. "The humans have lied about dealing with a race similar to ours. They are, the facts show, plotting active military engagements. The race they have allied themselves with is an enemy of ours. As a result, we have a race, her race, who would rather call us the enemy and begin attempting to trap us rather than open communications and work *with* us."

"That is certainly one way to view it," Alyssa said, refusing to allow ,K'rell to have the upper hand. "Until now, you haven't had a human to speak to them. One who they have claimed is dead."

"She isn't wrong," Master Ar'ath stated, speaking up. "The transmissions sent to the public mentions her name and has her image alongside the transcript."

"Perhaps they will claim I've been 'brainwashed', but they cannot refuse the fact that I was not killed. Or that I am alive and well aboard your ship," Alyssa added. "I am willing to do what it takes to help end this attack and open communications between my people and yours."

"Do you have any suggestions on how to do so?" Ac'kyll asked.

"For starters, if the IMD is planning a pincer move of any sort, I would suggest bringing in more ships," Alyssa stated, turning to the first officer. "I would be very wary of any signals that appear to be for distress. That is a common method used by the IMD to lure in enemies prior to attacking them. Until you have backup, I would also advise not answering any hailing calls, either."

Mc'narrd leaned back in his chair, a pleased expression on his features. Alyssa deliberately looked at the holo in front of her instead of him. It was safer for her. Possibly safer for him, too, since she didn't know how any of his crew felt about his interest in her.

"It seems that despite your declaration of not knowing your military, you know their methods well," Ra'dett said, watching her closely. "How do we know you aren't lying about any of this?"

"I don't have to know the minds of a military strategist to know how to bait someone. Or to know what has been done with other races, or each other. Even before humans began space explorations," Alyssa replied, sounding calmer than she felt. When would the suspicions end? Or would they? "Humans have been using those tactics for centuries. Probably since the first of my kind figured out how to make weapons and had a reason to fight against each other."

"It isn't uncommon in other races, either," First Officer Ac'kyll stated easily. "Baiting the enemy is a common method used by all races, including our own."

"Regardless," ,K'rell said before anyone else could speak. "We have already broken our primary objective, including compromising our own security."

He looked pointedly at Alyssa. She clenched her jaw but remained silent, refusing to give any other outward sign that she wanted to throttle him. Instead, she gave him a wink and blew him a kiss, minus raising her hand. ,K'rell's features darkened. Alyssa smiled sweetly.

From the various humming sounds around the table, she surmised the others were amused by her response to his goading.

"By the humans turning against us, we have lost the ability to hide ourselves. It is entirely possible they are now claiming we are the vicious, bloodthirsty race. That our goal is to start a war to take over Earth and lay waste to their allies," ,K'rell continued. "It won't be long before they discover our routes and move to intercept any and all vessels belonging to our people!"

"That would depend on how long those races can keep their mouths shut. Or even believe what the IMD is claiming," Alyssa stated calmly. When he jerked around towards her she added, "My guess is you have had trade with the Xoutians for years or decades. Possibly with others on the outermost edges of our current territories. There may even be other races we have not made contact with yet."

She looked at Mc'narrd who gave a nod in confirmation.

"I do not know what your orders were to begin with, but it was inevitable that everything would be FUBAR once my people decided you were an enemy. For whatever stupid reason they may have had."

"What does 'FUBAR' mean?" Master Ar'ath asked, leaning forward slightly. "It's been used in other transmissions, but Communications and Linguistics have yet to figure out its meaning."

"Um… it's a term to mean a situation has gone very, very badly." She decided to give them the phrase not using the word 'fucked' because that would just bring on more questions she really didn't want to answer. Again. "It stands for: fouled up beyond all recognition'."

"Interesting," Master Ar'ath replied, immediately touching her console.

Alyssa guessed it was to make notes on what she'd just been told.

"Are you saying there was no changing the current course of actions?" First Officer Ac'kyll asked. "There was nothing we could have done differently at the first interaction with the humans?"

"I don't know the answer to that, because I wasn't there. Nor am I familiar with the humans involved," Alyssa replied. "But considering what has occurred? I would say you had to react defensively after they made their decision to call you the bad guy. That is, the enemy. Now you have to decide if you want to use me to achieve your goal. Or return to your home planet empty-handed and hope the humans don't attack your trade ships. Or allow the Va'nu'ians to encourage an out-right war with your planet."

"What do you mean by 'use you'?" ,K'rell asked. "Why would the humans listen to someone who they thought was dead? You, yourself, say the humans wouldn't welcome you back. That they would call you a traitor to your own kind."

"You could use me when you next talk to a human battlecruiser," Alyssa replied evenly. "Or to record a message to Earth's public and private sectors. Not the military sector, though I'm certain they would listen."

"What sort of message?" Mc'narrd asked, making a slashing motion with his hand towards ,K'rell.

"The military claims I'm dead and you killed me. I can appeal to the private sector, telling them of the bomb the military placed on my ship. Stating that I was meant to die and not by your hands. I have enough knowledge about the military that I can appeal to conspiracy theorists. If it's worded the right way, the citizens of Earth and colonies will be demanding negotiations with you while at the same time wanting to know why the IMD tried to kill one of Earth's citizens." She paused, then smiled ruefully. "Remember, the only ones who know I was an assassin are the military. My record doesn't say 'assassin'. It states I was part of Military Affairs and Inventory."

"That is certainly something for us to consider. We will confer and discuss all that you've told us before choosing the best method with which to proceed," Commander Mc'narrd declared. "You may return to your quarters. Thank you for answering our questions."

Alyssa glanced from the commander to the holo then back to him as she stood. "If there is anything else I can do, please let me know."

"I'll escort you," Zh'oros said, also standing.

There was no missing the fact the healer didn't wait for a dismissal from the commander. She merely stood and met Alyssa at the door before anyone else could move. Even ,K'rell didn't say anything to the healer.

Once outside the door, Zh'oros said, "Well, that didn't go badly."

"No," Alyssa admitted. "It didn't seem that way to me, either."

The return to her quarters was done in silence, though Alyssa couldn't help but wonder what was being said in the meeting. Somehow, she doubted ‚K'rell was saying anything good about her or humans in general.

"Instead of continuing on your diatribe against the sergeant and her race, we will turn to the current problem," Mc'narrd said, stopping ‚K'rell before he could speak. "As I have stated before, I was personally and privately briefed on this mission. If Admiral Ad'dari did not give you the same, then that is for you to discuss with the admiralty upon our return."

‚K'rell fell silent, seemingly quelled for the moment.

"In regards to the security of the ship, the human has not even attempted to leave her quarters. Though there are guards stationed in the corridor outside them, she has not even looked outside her door. If she were a K'laisian, I would believe she was following the typical guesting rules. Regardless, the ship's security is not in peril," Ra'dett stated. "To change subjects: is there a way we can use the relay beacon to watch and acquire surveillance on the humans?"

"The human suggested we not answer any distress signals," ‚K'rell mused. "But what if we were to have her send one, instead?"

"Go on," Mc'narrd said when ‚K'rell didn't say anything else. Despite the man's insufferable and contentious behavior, he wasn't without useful suggestions and insight.

"What if we were to go to an area far from where the human's ships are currently, in a line of sorts from where her ship exploded, and have her send a distress signal? Have the transmission sent on whatever frequencies she would have used had her original ship not exploded?" He paused, a sly smile curving his lips. "Perhaps even make it obvious it's from an alien vessel?"

"What would that do, aside from drawing the humans' attention to us even more? Possibly even the Va'nu'ians…" Ar'ath trailed off.

If they could draw out proof of the Va'nu'ians, it could only be used to their benefit. Mc'narrd was pleased she came to the same conclusion he did and voiced it for them all.

Ar'ath dismissed the transcripts still scrolling above the table, bringing the diagram of the sector back to the fore. "Are you suggesting we attempt to engage the humans? Or time their response to a distress signal?"

"In a way," ,K'rell replied. "We would leave parts of debris, or even one of our pods, where the signal came from. That way we can watch from a safe distance, while cloaked, and record their actions. If our Va'nu'ian enemies show themselves, all the better. For us."

"If we leave a pod, it would certainly allow us to see what they will do upon learning Alyssa is still alive," Ac'kyll said thoughtfully. "Is there a way to make it appear as though there is a lifeform aboard the pod?"

"I'm certain if we approach Science and Engineering, they will come up with a suitable solution, at least for a short span of time," Ra'dett replied. He turned to Ar'ath. "You'll have to confer with the sergeant and record something believable."

Mc'narrd watched the policy master as his crew discussed ,K'rell's suggested idea. ,K'rell sat with a smug expression on his face.

"Since this is your idea, ,K'rell, I'm leaving you to ensure everything is put into place. Confer with Navigation and Weapons as to the trajectory and position for the false distress signal." He turned to Ar'ath. "Ensure that Communications and Science can completely scan and record everything the humans do. You may also want to add cameras to the outside of the pod to get a view from the front of the humans' ships." He paused before adding, "Do not disable any of the usual recorders and trackers left when a pod is destroyed. We want a complete recording returning to the closest K'laisian ships, as well as our allies."

"Standard procedures?" First Officer Ac'kyll asked.

Mc'narrd nodded. "If the humans end up attacking instead of attempting a rescue, I want it known. Not hidden."

"It is good to see you are finally following standard policy and procedures," ,K'rell muttered. "I was starting to think you had forgotten how to do it."

"As I said before: I was privately briefed," Mc'narrd said easily.

Though he had to admit, at least to himself, there had been no discussion about taking an alien aboard his ship and placing her in her current quarters. Nor did he want to discuss how Alyssa affected him on a very personal level.

,K'rell didn't say anything, but Mc'narrd could see he was dwelling on every action that had been taken up to this point. Shaking away the possibility of High Command siding with ‚K'rell on what he'd done, Mc'narrd stood, signaling an end to the meeting.

"You all have tasks to complete before we can begin engaging with the humans once again," Mc'narrd stated. "Dismissed."

‚K'rell, as usual, was the first to dart from the room. Ra'dett and Ar'ath left while discussing their parts in the plan. Ac'kyll studied Mc'narrd as she moved towards the door.

"Will you also be doing as the lady suggested and seeing if there are any other battleships in the area?" she asked as they stepped outside the meeting room.

"I believe it would be wise, yes," Mc'narrd replied. "Not simply because the sergeant suggested it, either. Her people are growing more chaotic and unpredictable. If they are planning on a serious attack against us, a second ship would be beneficial. More would be preferable, but two should be enough against their clunky ships. It would also give a Va'nu'ian destroyer second thoughts about attempting to attack us."

"What of the recordings of her room?" Ac'kyll asked after a few moments had passed. "She has proven she is no threat to us, despite what ‚K'rell may declare."

"Confer with Ra'dett, but unless he has a logical reason? They end," Mc'narrd stated. It was a risk, but Alyssa had earned the privacy. "Leave the restrictions on the console and interfaces. But the recordings end now."

"I'll inform Ra'dett. The true question we all have is what you plan to do about Alyssa?" Ac'kyll asked as they headed back to the bridge. "Despite being an alien race, she is a strong woman. She would make a good addition to our race."

"Let's get through this mission before we start planning out her future," Mc'narrd said, sidestepping the subject. "The end of this mission will play a large part in what fate has in store for her."

His first officer didn't reply, for which Mc'narrd was thankful. The last thing he needed was someone trying to arrange things between him and Alyssa Zelaya.

It was common among their people to arrange relationships. To connect one K'laisian with another in the hopes a strong relationship or bond formed. Ashyna was a very astute woman, and he knew she was aware of his feelings towards Alyssa. There was no denying the entire command crew was aware of the fact Alyssa was attracted to him. Or that the feelings were mutual.

But until their mission ended, there were too many variables and too many things could go wrong. He would have to simply wait and hope that whatever feelings Alyssa had for him didn't dwindle. Or vanish completely.

Chapter Eighteen

"*Mayday! Mayday! Mayday!*"

Alyssa's voice rang out across the *Laedschot's* bridge, broadcasted from one of the K'laisian pods.

"*This is Sergeant Zelaya of Earth's IMD. I am in sector Delpi Two Dash One and am in need of immediate aid! Request immediate assistance and extraction! I repeat; I am in need of immediate aid! This is a Code Chrysalis. I repeat, Code Chrysalis!*"

Alyssa stood beside Mc'narrd as he sat in his command chair on the bridge. Master of Security Ra'dett stood on her other side. Both chaperone and guard. Not that she was going to move from her spot. Her feet were rooted in place, and she was thankful she was able to grip a portion of the command chair.

She had practiced her script with both Master Ar'ath and Ra'dett before recording it two days prior. Now she was watching the K'laisians' plan being put into action. They had taken a vial of her blood and some hair, enough to fool any scanner the human's possessed. A dummy had been made and placed onboard, complete with a mechanical heart that beat in a pace similar to hers, and projected other biological readings that matched hers closely.

At the moment, she was apprehensive.

"You do know that I can't promise my people will even respond," she said, trying to hide her emotions.

"We are aware," Mc'narrd replied, not looking at her. "Nothing in life is ever a guarantee."

"Picking up transmissions between approaching human vessels, Commander," Master Ar'ath said from above and behind them.

"On speakers," Mc'narrd commanded.

"ESS Watcher, Colossus, *and* Zephyr, *this is Captain Landry of the* ESS Valiant. *Are you picking up the signal?"* *Landry's voice said.*

"Valiant, this is Captain Cortez of the ESS Zephyr. *We are receiving the signal and are approaching with shields up and weapons ready."*

The other two captains reported, also stating the same.

"Private Channel eight-oh-one-point-twenty-two," Landy stated. A few seconds later, after the other three captains reported in, Landry said, "Orders direct from Admiral Lynchen are to silence Zelaya. To clarify: under no circumstances is the target to be given the opportunity to communicate further."

Alyssa stiffened and swallowed hard. She felt as though the temperature of the room had dropped several degrees. Her grip tightened on the command chair, her short fingernails digging into the material.

Yes, she knew she'd been sent to die, but it still hurt to hear it. To know that her fellow humans would follow these orders without a second thought.

And yet assassins are still considered cold-blooded psychopaths, she thought.

"What's the possibility of any others having picked up her distress call?" Captain Meyers asked. "If any others appear before us, that could cause problems."

"We destroy them, as well. Lay the blame on the aliens," Cortez retorted. She laughed. "No one will believe we killed one of our own, let alone destroyed any civilian or ally craft that got in the way."

"You are recording everything, right?" Alyssa asked, already knowing the answer.

"Recording and making duplicates for our records as well as placing it in separate files to send to our allies, should it become necessary," Mc'narrd replied in a cold tone. "How far away are our 'friends', Master Is'roda?"

The K'laisian replied, "They should arrive within five of their minutes. Putting them on the viewscreen now."

The viewscreen currently showed the elongated oval pod that currently held a dummy in the pilot's seat. Debris had been scattered around the pod. Pieces of scrap metal and similar. Some, she'd been told, had been parts of her former ship. There were some pieces of asteroid mixed in, as well. The view was shifted so the pod and debris were in the center of the screen, though much smaller than previously. Now the four approaching battleships were shown, moving inward, directly between each point of the ship.

To approach at the four main sides— bow, stern, starboard, and port— would have been predictable, Alyssa guessed, so they approached in the dead center of the sides.

The main objective for the faux distress signal had been to learn how the humans would react to learning she was still alive. That had been answered by the declaration that she was wanted dead at all costs. The secondary objective was to see how they would treat other debris near the pod that appeared to hold her. It appeared that question was going to be answered quickly.

"I'm getting the distinct impression that my death this time won't be appearing in any broadcasts outside military channels," Alyssa said quietly.

"Why does this bother you?" ,K'rell asked, approaching on the opposite side of Mc'narrd. "You were an assassin. Wasn't your job to kill in cold blood?"

"Because I don't even know why they want me dead," Alyssa replied, trying to figure it out herself. "This is… different. I don't know. I can't explain it."

"Four ships against one person who did what she was hired to do. Her government trained her to do that one task from her childhood. She followed the orders she was given or risked being killed for insubordination," Ra'dett said without emotion. "Four ships were ordered to destroy someone who sent a distress call. Yes, it may be their job, but they're also discussing destroying an ally simply because that hypothetical ally is willing to help someone in distress. Someone who did nothing more than their job."

"Not only discussing it, but amused by the fact they suspect no one would believe they would kill an ally in cold blood," Master Ar'ath added, disgust evident in her voice.

As they spoke, the four ships dropped out of hyperspace around the pod.

"Scanning now," Captain Landry said.

"Oh, thank the gods, you're here!" Alyssa's pre-recorded voice rang out.

The K'laisians' viewscreen showed the false heart had sped up. Their scanners were showing the android body as being excited.

"Thank you for coming!"

A few moments later, Landry spoke again. "Scanning complete. Records show Sergeant Alyssa Zelaya is onboard. Open fire."

Without even attempting to contact the pod, they opened fire on it.

When the flares of light stopped, there was nothing left in the center of the battleships. The pod, the debris, even the pieces of the asteroid were just gone. Annihilated completely.

Alyssa inhaled sharply, thankful for the ability to brace herself with the commander's chair.

"Good thing I never tried escaping," she said, trying for levity and failing miserably. This was going to give her nightmares for years to come. She was certain of it.

"Indeed," Mc'narrd said as the four ships jumped back into hyperspace and left the area. "It appears they have confirmed your fears of not being welcomed back."

"Yeah, it does," Alyssa said quietly.

She closed her eyes, refusing to allow herself to become an overly emotional female. When she felt a hand on her arm, she opened her eyes open to find Ra'dett looking at her.

"Are you well?" Master Ra'dett asked gently. "Witnessing such hostility towards you by your own people is… disturbing, and must be difficult to deal with."

"I will be fine, eventually," Alyssa replied. She realized she had no interest in lying. At some point, she'd lost the desire to even consider it as an option with these beings. That telling the truth was refreshing, especially knowing there would be no shame or humiliation to be had from anyone. Not to mention, her bio suit would give it away, anyway. "And yes, it is hard. Any sliver of hope I may have held about returning to Earth has been destroyed in the same way the pod was."

"How do you humans normally respond to such hostility, be it given or received?" Ra'dett asked.

"Some drink alcoholic beverages. Or break down and cry or scream. Some become violent. Others withdraw into themselves," Alyssa replied, recalling what she'd seen, heard, and done herself. "Personally? I prefer drinking myself into oblivion."

"What do you mean by that?" Ra'dett asked, tipping his head to the side.

"Sorry. It means that I would rather drink alcoholic beverages until I collapse into a deep slumber," Alyssa explained, offering a smile and failing. "You are familiar with our alcoholic drinks, yes?"

"Oh, indeed," ,K'rell replied. "One of the things races love trading, above all else, are beverages. The stronger the beverage, the better. The Xoutians introduced us to your planet's liquors once you began trading and selling it to them."

"Do you have a preference?" Mc'narrd asked, finally looking up at her.

Whatever he was thinking or feeling was hidden from her, as well as his crew. The only emotion she could detect was curiosity and concern. The same two emotions she received from Ra'dett.

"Gin, actually," Alyssa replied with a small smile. "Usually mixed with other liquors or beverages. My favorite drink is called a Nebula. It's a green, sweet, slightly tangy beverage."

"Perhaps we can locate something for you to enjoy," Master Ra'dett suggested thoughtfully.

"Indeed." Mc'narrd glanced at Ra'dett before looking back to her. "A way to thank you for your help in this experiment."

"Thank you," Alyssa replied, trying to sound happier than she felt. "I'm glad I was able to help."

Mc'narrd gave a nod before turning back to the viewscreen. Ra'dett gently turned and followed him from the bridge. When the lift opened, she didn't notice Ra'dett hadn't stopped the lift on the same level as her quarters. When she paused mid step, the security master gave her a smile.

"I'm escorting you to our dining area," he explained. "I'll take full responsibility for the deviation, but it is where we can acquire your preferred drink of choice."

"You keep liquor onboard in your mess deck?" When Ra'dett gave her a puzzled look, she sighed. One day she'd remember to use their terms, not hers. "Where you eat. The dining area. Humans refer to it as a cafeteria, mess hall, or mess deck depending on the location and vessel. Though on the fancier cruise ships, they're called 'dining halls'."

"Interesting," Ra'dett said. "Your language is very confusing."

"Yeah, I know," Alyssa said with a sigh. "It's even confusing to my own people."

Ra'dett hummed loudly, then stopped abruptly. "My apologies. I meant no offense."

"Oh, none taken!" Alyssa replied, giving him an actual smile. "It really is amusing when you think about it."

Ra'dett hummed again, making Alyssa laugh as well. When he began walking again, she fell into step beside him. The rest of the walk to the dining area was spent talking about their respective languages. A distraction as welcomed as the promised liquor.

Sometime later, Ra'dett escorted Alyssa back to her quarters. A couple other security officers walked with them, though not because they were needed. Master Ra'dett had introduced her to them, and they had enjoyed talking freely. They shared knowledge of their races and between the comradery and gin, Alyssa felt relaxed.

The shared laughter and conversations reminded her of better times among her people. When titles and jobs were ignored in exchange for a pleasant time. She'd always treasured those moments, and she found herself enjoying the moment with the K'laisians.

Just as she did with her fellow humans, she knew she'd treasure the gift Ra'dett had given her: a chance to mingle without expectations of anything other than an enjoyable time.

After thanking Master Ra'dett a final time, she stretched out on the sofa opposite the viewscreen. Leaning down, she pulled off her boots before picking up her tablet. Instead of looking for something more interesting, she continued reading about the history of the K'laisians. Slowly her eyes drifted shut and sleep overtook her.

But her sleep was not pleasant.

Dreams of holding a block of thermal plastique that exploded in her hand, sending her out into the giant vacuum of space, kept causing her to jerk awake. When those images were not plaguing her sleep, she was seeing herself sitting in the cockpit of a ship begging for help. Only to have Admiral Lynchen smiling at her and a voice saying "fire."

No matter how much she tossed and turned, she couldn't prevent those images from invading her dreams. Finally, she gave up. Glaring at the viewscreen, she grabbed her tablet and looked towards the door connecting her room with Commander Mc'narrd's quarters.

Out of pure desperation, and the hope a change of scenery would help, she crossed to the connecting door.

"Open," she said.

The door, much to her surprise and relief, slid open to reveal the commander's quarters. Drawing a deep breath, she squared her shoulders and stepped into his domain. Refusing to allow herself to turn and dash back into her quarters, she forced one foot in front of the other until she was standing in front of a large chair. A table sat beside it. Both were in front of a large blank viewscreen.

Not seeing anywhere else she could curl up, and not brave enough to search for his bed, she settled in the chair with the tablet. Inhaling deeply, she allowed a smile to form.

The chair smelled like the commander.

With that thought, she began reading the tablet again. She didn't think about what might happen if Mc'narrd found her in his quarters. The desire for peace, perhaps even peaceful sleep, was far too great.

Her eyes drifted shut before she finished the second sentence. The interface fell from her fingers and she curled into a small ball, her head resting on the arm of the chair.

Chapter Nineteen

There was much to glean from the recordings before another meeting could be called.

Mc'narrd knew that all too well. It was standard procedure for each department involved to go over the recordings and scans first. They had to view every angle and clean up the audio and video before individuals from each department could put everything together into a cohesive report.

That took time. His crew may have been one of the best, but even they required time to do their jobs.

Mc'narrd tended to his daily duties as commander, checking in on the various departments on his ship and tending to the usual matters. Including checking whatever transmissions had finally been relayed to his ship.

Thankfully, none of that took more than a few hours. Efficiency was something his people excelled at when given the freedom to work at their own pace and style. Mc'narrd believed in allowing his people enough freedom to find a method that worked best for each being. Provided it didn't cause a distraction or slow down the speed of completing their appointed tasks.

High Command acknowledged that Mc'narrd's methods were unorthodox in some ways, but they couldn't dismiss the results. So, they allowed him leeway and he had yet to fail in a mission. Although if he couldn't find a solution to end the humans' antagonistic behavior, this mission might be his first failure. The thought did not sit well with him.

Finishing his daily tasks, he released command to his first officer and departed the bridge. Ac'kyll gave him a curious look before settling into the command chair and taking over. Typically he remained long after he completed his duties.

This time, his concern was on a blonde-haired human who had just witnessed her own people's complete annihilation of what could have been her. He was thankful Ra'dett had shown compassion towards Alyssa. It gave promise towards a possible future with her on his ship.

Pausing in front of Alyssa's door, he shook his head slightly before continuing around the corner to his door. He could check on her after speaking to Zh'oros about her health and how best to ensure she remained well. The door slid open and he stepped inside, only to find a sleeping Alyssa curled up in his chair.

Her chest rose and fell in gentle, even motions. The skin around her eyes was darker than usual. When his first thought was concern that she might have come here because she was uncomfortable sleeping in her own quarters, Mc'narrd had to pause.

His first thought should have been if anything had been disturbed. If there were any signs of treachery or attempts at sabotage. Something that would foreshadow deception by the technically unknown being in his favorite chair.

Even data collection could be considered spying, although he had nothing here that required security clearance or rank to see. His personal terminal was keyed to his specific DNA in seven measures.

None of those points, which ,K'rell would be first to list as proper procedure, had come to his mind until he'd forced them. His concern was for her well-being and the pleasure he took in the sight of her.

With silent steps, he moved closer, watching for anything to show her waking from her slumber. But she did not awaken. She continued sleeping, though every so often a muscle would twitch or an extremity would jerk. Yet, somehow her eyes remained closed and her chest rose and fell in the slow, steady rhythm of a sleeping being.

Perhaps, he thought as he retrieved her data interface, *she is having difficulty sleeping peacefully.*

Sliding his thumb over the surface, the screen lit up, showing the last thing she was doing. He felt his pulse jump at the fact it was information on his people's history. With a few touches, he discovered the only thing she had been doing was reading. No attempts to access anything aside from the reading material she'd been provided had occurred. He turned the interface's screen off once more before placing it on the table. He had just straightened when her body jerked again, and she whimpered softly in her sleep.

The sound caused his heart to ache. Without thinking, he knelt beside the chair and gently brushed her cheek with the tips of his fingers. Feather light, they trailed from the middle of her forehead, along her hairline, to the tips of her rounded ears. At her soft sigh, and without changing the delicate touch, he continued tracing the curve of her ear to her jawline. He didn't stop until his fingers reached the middle of her chin.

Slowly, her eyes fluttered open to meet his gaze. He went to move his hand, but was stopped when she wrapped her fingers around his wrist, holding him in place. Her soft lips curved upward and parted slightly.

The temptation to kiss them was strong, but he didn't lean forward. He did run a finger along her bottom lip, though. He did not, however, expect her to capture his finger with her mouth, nipping the tip before drawing it into between her lips.

Her breath was hot as she ran her tongue over his skin.

A low moan escaped him at the touch. Apparently, the lady had ideas for a conversation that did not involve words. And he'd be hoxed if the idea didn't appeal to him.

"Trouble sleeping?" he asked, hoping to gather his wits before he gave into the temptation curled up in front of him.

Temptation that was staring at him with heavy, heated eyes, and who hadn't released his finger yet. With a final nip and caress, she let him slide his finger from between her lips.

"Unfortunately," she said in a sultry, low voice.

He suspected she didn't even realize how her tone had changed. Though his body certainly knew. It was all he could do to not shift at the growing discomfort.

"Is there anything I can do to help?" he asked.

Perhaps it was a poor choice of words, but at the moment, he couldn't manage to think about propriety, policy, or anything remotely akin to protocols.

Releasing his wrist, she reached over and ran a finger along the tip of his ears. He couldn't stop the shiver that coursed through his body at the touch. Someone must have told her about how sensitive their ear tips were, and he was half tempted to ask who it was so he could thank them. After a moment, he had a suspicion of the who, but the thought was fleeting.

"Oh, I can think of a few things," she murmured, delight and an intense desire shining in her eyes. Leaning forward she brushed her lips across his before whispering in his ear. "The question is: how much do you wish to help?"

Then her lips found the tip of his ear, and she nipped it gently before pulling it into her mouth and giving it the same sensual treatment as she had his finger.

Groaning, he pulled her from the chair and into his arms, rescuing his ear from her tongue. His lips crushed hers in a soul-searing kiss. A soft moan escaped from her lips, even as she wrapped her arms around him, her fingers tangling in his hair.

When she pulled back, breathless, he lifted her in his arms.

"I think this is a discussion for somewhere else," he replied, his eyes not leaving hers. She giggled, an endearing sound that he hadn't heard her give anyone else. His body responded to it, and he pulled her closer against his chest. He brushed his lips across hers again as he carried her into his bedchamber.

Instead of laying her on his bed, a fact he didn't enjoy, he lowered her to her feet. The question in her eyes pulled at his heart once more. He toyed with the collar of her suit, running his finger from one side of her neck to the other.

"Was there a different conversation you wish to have?" he teased. "Or should certain things be... dismissed for a complete coverage of topics?" He paused, some sense finally shoving itself into his brain. "Do you truly wish to continue, Alyssa? There is no shame if you wish to stop."

"I believe I would have to Challenge you if you did not continue," she replied, the smile still on her lips.

His hum was low and deep. This was the first time he'd brought a woman into his quarters. And the woman before him was by far more enchanting and captivating than any other he'd met.

She inhaled sharply, letting it out in a jagged breath as his fingers paused at the seam of her bio suit.

If Zh'oros were watching, Mc'narrd had no doubt the healer would realize where Alyssa was and what they were doing.

"No one will worry if the suit stops… broadcasting?" Alyssa asked. She didn't sound concerned.

"No," Mc'narrd murmured. "Not when you are in my quarters."

"What about the comms? Don't they always record what's being said?"

"Not within the privacy of your quarters or mine. Not unless they're told to record or certain words are spoken. We are not without a desire for privacy," Mc'narrd explained, his smile not wavering.

Ra'dett had agreed with him and Ac'kyll. The recordings had been ended without further discussion. Alyssa posed no threat to the security of the ship, and so privacy had been returned to her quarters. Not that he was going to inform her that it hadn't always been that way.

Within his quarters? They had never been there to begin with. Once he'd relinquished command, his comm stopped recording the moment he entered his quarters.

"Oh. Good," she said, the grin on her lips broadening.

With that, she reached over to his suit and found the seam at his collar. This night would be seared in his memory for the rest of his life and he suspected the same would be felt by her.

Chapter Twenty

Mc'narrd watched Alyssa sleep, curled up beside him with an arm draped across his chest. Her head rested on his shoulder, her golden hair a messy tumble around her shoulders. Her breathing was even and deep. Instead of twitching and jerking, her body was still, and she moved very little as she slept deeply. Peacefully.

After their mating, they had cuddled together before partaking of a sonic shower together, where another round had commenced. Finally, exhausted, they had collapsed back onto the bed where Alyssa had snuggled up beside him. She had fallen asleep wrapped around him, and he hadn't objected in the slightest.

Her face was serene, and she appeared far more youthful as she slept. He should have been concerned. He should have questioned her motives. Worried about how this would affect her actions. How his own people would react, if they discovered he had been intimate with the human.

Xenophobia was not something the military allowed, but vestiges managed to burrow its way into even the most hardened person at times. It was part of why healers constantly debriefed and examined those who went off planet. Before and after they departed their world. Those who showed more than an 'acceptable' amount were removed from going off planet, or not allowed to begin with.

Mc'narrd knew that the 'acceptable' amount was very miniscule. Less than one percent, if one had to give it a number. Perhaps that was why he hadn't allowed his attraction for this woman to override any sense of caution. Or, well, any sense for that matter. He didn't care what species or race a being was; he looked at their character, their personalities, in order to decide if they were friend or foe. Ally or enemy. Help or hindrance.

That ability had allowed him to climb the ranks and gain his own battlecruiser.

Now it seemed he'd allowed an alien being to slide beneath his defenses. At least he didn't need to worry about their encounter being recorded. Had it taken place in her quarters before the audio recordings had ended, he would have needed to input the proper commands for recordings to end.

Normally, none would record what was being said within her quarters, but he had allowed it to be put into place due to the situation. Possibly even an enemy. He was thankful his Master of Security and First Officer had agreed to end the recordings.

Of course, they probably also suspected such an event would occur. Which was probably why his first officer had mentioned it. His command crew were astute, intelligent beings. Mc'narrd did not, and would not, include ,K'rell among his command staff. Policy masters were not command staff and he'd yet to meet one he enjoyed.

For a moment, he wondered if he should tell her it hadn't always been that way.

No, he decided, brushing a finger up her arm. That would cause more problems than he wanted to handle at the moment. She had earned her privacy. Especially since she had yet to do anything to raise questions of her intentions among his crew. Her motives had not changed and they had to prove they were better than her former employer.

Alyssa sighed in her sleep and rolled over, curling her hands around her face. Mc'narrd sighed, missing the warmth of her body. He knew this was the perfect opportunity to move away from her, but he was loath to do so. But, move away, he did. No matter how tempting the woman was, he could not put her above his duties. Leaning over, he lightly kissed her cheek before running his fingers a final time through her hair.

Retrieving a robe from his closet, he slid it on before returning to his favorite chair. There he retrieved his data interface from the desk drawer. It lit up as he touched the screen. While Alyssa slept, he began reading over the data they'd retrieved from the humans' battleships.

Several hours later, he felt fingers sliding through his hair. He looked up, startled, to find Alyssa standing beside him in all her naked glory. Her eyes were sleepy, but the smile on her lips was anything but tired.

"Are you well?" he asked, looking up at her.

"You left me," she said, twining her fingers through his hair.

Mc'narrd smiled, his finger touching a corner of the screen. He didn't have to look down to know it had turned off. He slid an arm around her waist, guiding her around to stand before him even as he placed his interface on the table with his other hand. He tugged her into his lap.

She settled against him willingly.

"You appear tired. Perhaps you should return to the bed so you can sleep and be rested," he said, wrapping her in his arms.

She settled her head against his shoulder. "I will if you join me."

Chuckling, he stood with her in his arms. Not a difficult feat considering her light frame.

"I will join you for a while if you promise to sleep, even should I leave again."

A pout formed on her lips, but she nodded, her eyes already drifting shut once again. Kissing her on the head, he carried her back to the bed where he joined her. She snuggled up against him, and he sighed. It would only be a few more hours before he had to return to his position as commander. He would have to return to the bridge, yet he didn't feel a need to order her back to her quarters.

As she slept once again, he considered his next move in regards to the humans. Their complete destruction of the pod confirmed one decision. One he would put into place once he was certain she was in a deep sleep. Anything else he would need to confer with his crew on.

Chapter Twenty-One

When Alyssa awoke, Mc'narrd had left. Where he had been on the bed was cool to the touch. She wasn't certain when he'd left. Part of her was disappointed, but the realistic part knew he couldn't stay with her until she awoke.

He was, after all, the commander of the ship. He had duties to the ship and his crew. She knew about duties all too well. Duty had been her saving grace for years. Her life, if she wanted to be honest.

The commander was career military. He wouldn't be happy planetside. At least not anywhere in the near future. The stars were in his heart and part of his soul. She could understand it since she loved being onboard a ship traveling between planets. Visiting different worlds, even if she didn't get to explore any as much as she may have wanted to.

Now, it seemed she would have plenty of opportunity to eventually explore at least one planet: K'lais.

Commander Mc'narrd's home world.

Her lover's home world.

The memory of their night together had her smiling and her body warming from head to toe.

With that thought, she realized she was still in his bed. Somewhere was her bio suit. At least she didn't have to wonder where her shoes were. That made her giggle as she looked around before spotting a sleeve peeking out from under the bed. Reaching down, she pulled it out and quickly dressed.

As the suit seamed shut, she realized it felt… odd. Having the suit off for half a day made her realize that the suit shifted to conform to her body's every curve and adjusted to be the perfect temperature for her. It also didn't feel the same as the clothing she used to wear. For a brief moment, she wondered if any clothing had been rescued from her ship.

Shaking the thought away, she padded from the commander's bedroom. She couldn't call it a bunk or berth because the bed had its own small separate room and was not attached to the wall.

Maybe if the K'laisians decided to use her to send a video transmission to the citizens of Earth, she could convince them to find her some actual clothing. Otherwise it might appear as though she had been completely brainwashed by her rescuers.

Though, she was certain she could figure out how to explain her current attire. Maybe she could blame it on the bombs the military had left for her?

Retrieving her tablet, she touched the screen to make sure it was hers. When it lit up and revealed the same place she'd stopped reading, she gave a nod. Standing beside the chair, she finally took a long look around the room.

The walls held images of a foreign world. One she guessed was a city with its twisting skyscrapers and various other buildings. The smooth metal structures curved upward to meet the clouds above them. Their silvery-blue color glinted in the sunlight. Blue-green grass covered the ground. Even the trees were hues of teal. Tearing her eyes away from the cities, for each was different in architecture and design, she turned to the rest of the room. Another pair of swords were crossed on one wall, within easy reach and beside a writing desk that looked identical to the one in her quarters.

There was a smaller cabinet filled with bottles of what she guessed were liquors or some other beverage. She recognized one as Teragun Whiskey due to the distinct gold and green swirled liquid in the tear-shaped ripple-textured bottle. Glasses lined a shelf below the bottles, further indicating the other bottles were beverages of some sort.

Only the bookcase filled with a variety of small objects gave any hint that this wasn't quarters for just anyone. She couldn't find anything to hint at Mc'narrd's personality or interests.

Maybe, she thought, she just didn't know what to look for? After all, Mc'narrd wasn't a human.

Shaking her head, she left his quarters and returned to her own. Settling onto her sofa, she tried reading again, but her mind kept drifting to her night with Mc'narrd. His silken hair. His touch. How intense he was and how he ensured she received as much pleasure as possible. How he enjoyed snuggling after.

She really needed to go to the gym and do something. Spar or exercise or *something*. The knock on her door was a welcome reprieve from trying to entertain herself when she felt alive for the first time she'd awoken on the K'laisians' ship.

"Come," she called, biting her lip to keep from grinning. Her mind had spiraled into the proverbial gutter, and she knew it would be difficult to pull it back out any time soon.

Master Ra'dett stepped into her quarters. She would have expected someone to be delivering her breakfast, not the Master of Security. To add to the strangeness, he was wearing a sword. It was a strange combination of a katana and saber, complete with an intricately-curved guard that would have protected her entire hand, not just a part of it.

"Is there a problem?" she asked cautiously. Did he know about her night with the commander?

"No," he said, his lips twitching in what she suspected was a suppressed smile. "I am here to ask if you would like to have breakfast in our dining hall." He paused before adding, "Though you will have extra guards, you have been granted permission to eat outside your quarters."

Alyssa stared at him for several heartbeats. Grabbing her boots, she shoved her feet into them and stood, dropping the tablet onto the now-vacated sofa.

"I would love that," she said, a brilliant smile spreading across her face. "Thank you."

Master Ra'dett finally gave into the smile. He gave her a small bow and gestured for her to exit ahead of him. She returned the bow before stepping out ahead of him. Outside her quarters she found two other guards, both wearing weapons. Both had swords with cross guards, though each was slightly different.

"May I ask a question?" she asked as they walked through the hallways. Ra'dett nodded. "Why are you wearing a weapon today?"

Ra'dett gave her a side-long look before answering. "We were planning on sparring later. First Officer Ac'kyll stated you were interested in the Duels. Master Healer Zh'oros said it would not be a bad decision to ask if you would like to be instructed in our weaponry with the proper supervision."

"That would be greatly appreciated," Alyssa replied, breathing a sigh of relief. At his concerned expression, she smiled. "That was a purely human reaction. Something we do when we're very relieved. I am relieved to be given the opportunity to exercise more. I am not used to such a sedentary lifestyle."

"Please explain what you did previously. Perhaps we can create a better exercise regime for you," Ra'dett said.

"You're aware of my profession prior to being rescued," Alyssa began. Ra'dett gave a nod. "I spent a great deal of time in gyms between my assignments. I would do a lot of cardio. That is, aerobic exercises." When he nodded slowly, she stifled another sigh of relief. She didn't know how to explain aerobic exercise to anyone. "I would also lift weights or swim or a variety of other exercises. Often I would practice hand-to-hand fighting or train on a range."

"What sort of range?" one of the other guards asked.

"Humans have a different type of service weapon. We would practice shooting paper targets to perfect our aim," Alyssa replied, hoping she wasn't confusing the K'laisian.

"Ah. We also do that," he replied cheerfully. "Though I suspect it will be a long time before you are allowed to use one."

Alyssa laughed. "I would be concerned if you offered me one of your service weapons." She shook her head. "I would much rather prove myself and show I am not a threat by using one of your swords or similar first."

"That is very reasonable," Master Ra'dett said as they stepped into the lift. "After the morning meal, we will go to the gym. There we will introduce you to our weaponry and begin instructing you on their use."

Merely smiling and nodding, Alyssa remained silent. There was no need to inform these men she was trained in sword fighting. It was an unusual skill, but it had proven to be helpful on occasion. Most humans learned to fence. She had learned how to actually fight with a sword.

Some people preferred bladed weaponry to anything else. Sometimes those people were ones she'd been sent to kill. But there was no need to tell them that little fact. Not yet, anyway.

Chapter Twenty-Two

Breakfast in the dining hall began pleasantly in Alyssa's opinion.

Between Master Ra'dett and his two fellow security officers, she didn't feel a need to watch her back. A strange feeling, considering she'd always felt as though she needed to worry about someone attacking her from every side at any time.

For the first time, she realized how tense she'd always been. It was so strange to actually be able to relax and be at ease. Something she suspected most other humans did on a daily basis. It was a weird, but pleasant feeling. One she could certainly get accustomed to experiencing. It was odd to have found such among an alien race.

She wondered if part of the reason Ra'dett allowed her to eat in the dining hall was because there the other crew members could approach her without concern. She welcomed their questions and answered them to the best of her ability. They returned the favor.

In fact, she was now sitting with a buffet of options before her with the K'laisians arguing good-naturedly among themselves about which was the best dish. She, in turn, was willing to sample everything, trusting that they wouldn't give her something poisonous to a human.

"Are all humans so willing to share knowledge and try new things?" First Officer Ac'kyll's voice carried to her from a few feet away.

Alyssa looked up to find the woman approaching the table, an amused look on her face.

"No, not all," Alyssa admitted, smiling. "Many humans, especially those in space exploration, enjoy trying new things. Sometimes it doesn't go well, depending on what the new experience happens to be."

"Has that ever happened to you?" one of the other crew members asked before taking a sip of his quella tea.

The tea was emerald green and sweet at first but with a sour afterbite. Though it wouldn't be Alyssa's first choice of beverage, she had to admit it was good.

"Oh, yes," Alyssa admitted with a laugh. "Sometimes it's the food. Other times it's a sport or other type of entertainment." She paused, before reiterating, "Usually it's the food."

As she opened her mouth to explain, another all-too-familiar voice broke through the crowd.

The spoilsport had joined the party.

"Enjoying a meal to celebrate victory? Pleased with how you've fooled them?"

"Master ,K'rell," Alyssa said in a pleasant tone. "Are you planning on joining us? I was invited to dine here instead of in my room. This sort of just... happened."

If she'd planned on celebrating anything, it would have been the previous night with the commander. The thought made the smile on her face broaden despite the walking wet blanket.

"How amusing! Certainly, I will sit at your table," ,K'rell replied before taking the seat nearest and opposite of her. His plate had sparse rations on it, little more than a few sections of fruit and what looked like water in a metallic bottle. "You did quite well! I doubt there were many who saw through your deception."

"It was certainly good enough to fool the captains of those ships," Alyssa replied, a little confused. "Hopefully the admiralty doesn't realize it was a ruse. They may not be so willing to respond to anything else the next time. If there is a next time, that is. I guess that will depend on what the commander and the rest of the crew decide on."

"Oh yes, certainly. I am confident there will be a next time. That was the intent, was it not?"

"I did it because I was asked," Alyssa replied, glancing at Ra'dett then Ac'kyll before turning back to the jerk. "Wasn't that the intent of the experiment? To see how my people would react?"

"That's what the crew thinks, including our increasingly gullible commander." ,K'rell agreed. "But I am one that is not deceived. I wanted to verify that, despite your claims to the contrary, if there had been a pre-arranged set of codes for a rescue. And there were! You blurted them without preamble."

He leaned in conspiratorially. The eyes were an ugly hue. Barely a memory of the beautiful gold they normally were.

"Tell me, human. Since we no longer need to fool each other, what was the phrase that told them to destroy the pod? To complete your deception towards my crew?"

",K'rell, I knew that was *jiwoke* in that bottle but said nothing," Master Ra'dett interjected in a firm tone. "How much have you had today? Have you even slept?"

,K'rell kept his gaze coldly set on Alyssa as he replied. "Enough to have the steel to confront this nemesis, no matter how deeply it has fooled the rest of you."

"This 'it' has a name. If you don't want to use my name, call me 'human'. I'll answer to both," Alyssa retorted in a calmer voice than she felt. "I already explained what the codes that I used meant, but allow me to repeat them for those who were not there. 'Mayday' means the person is in trouble. It's been used for centuries on Earth. Code Chrysalis means the person is in need of extraction. That they have escaped from a situation and are in a safe place. Extraction can take place without concern about the enemy."

"I thought Chrysalis would be the word that informed them." ,K'rell sounded pleased with himself. He even offered her a salute with the bottle he had before he took a short drink from it.

"Oh, please. You obviously aren't aware that a chrysalis is the last form a caterpillar uses prior to hatching. Which is where the code came from: creatures hatch in safe environments. In other words, escaping their little shells in a safe place," Alyssa explained, refusing to stoop to his terms. "It's been used for decades by the IMD."

Though she truly wanted to tell him what a fool he was and where he could go. In great detail on how he could get there.

"Considering you said that they attempted to kill you, why should they answer a call at all? No matter what ancient relay is used?" ,K'rell pushed on, harsh humor in his voice. "They would not! No race would! So the only use of coming at all was to fool us into believing your plight!"

He held the bottle in front of her, waggling it back and forth.

"Have a drink with me before they finish their fix on our position and come with everything your fleet has!" He invited by way of a demand. "Including their Va'nu'ian allies! Who are probably waiting for their call to battle!"

"Admiral Lynchen wanted me dead. If they knew I was alive, they would want me silenced so I can't tell the entire universe they tried to kill one of their own people," Alyssa stated, resisting the urge to punch the drunk sanctimonious asshole. "Humans tend to want to keep their dead, well... dead. We have a saying: 'Dead men tell no tales'. The military has turned the saying into a motto to live by." She gave him a cold smile, her tone dropping several degrees. "I should know. I was one of the beings who ensured it happened before being sent out in the vast vacuum of space to die."

Alyssa did not miss the fact that they were drawing a crowd. More so than when she'd first arrived in the mess hall. Whether it was from the fact Policy Master ,K'rell was being loud and obnoxious or due to the subject of the conversation, she didn't know.

"Yes, yes," ,K'rell said dismissively. "And what source do we have to verify these claims? Why, your mouth and mind! Anyone who has bothered to really read the history and communications of your race's long failing attempt at civilization? It's amazing you didn't vaporize the planet around you! But you perfected lying and deception, so we can toast that accomplishment! There is no question why you have allied with our enemies! You both share those traits."

He jammed the bottle back into Alyssa's face.

"I was told, perhaps incorrectly, that the entire plan was your idea, ,K'rell," Alyssa retorted. Her eyes narrowed on the sanctimonious policy master. "Shove that bottle in my face one more time and you will regret it."

"I will never trust a single member of your hateful, spiteful, lying primate species, especially you," he declared loudly, emphasizing each word with a thrust of the bottle.

Alyssa had no problem smelling the distinctive odor of fermented matter in a liquid suspension. Especially when it was spilling against the collar of her bio suit.

"I'm afraid xenophobia is not limited to your race," Master Ra'dett began.

He was moving behind ,K'rell, and the two escorts that came with them were getting into flanking positions. Alyssa took a deep breath and told herself she just had to wait this lousy scene out. She was still silently telling herself that when ,K'rell mashed her upper lip and nose with his bottle.

"Drink, you primitive!" he demanded.

Alyssa's right fist somehow moved from next to her plate and smashed into the juncture of ,K'rell's left eye socket and the bridge of his nose. She wondered how she got to a standing position so fast after her hand had lashed out and bludgeoned the policy master's face.

"Consider yourself Challenged, asshole!" a voice roared.

Oh wait, that was her voice. She was still trying to catch up with what the hell her whole body was doing, and now her mouth had joined in on the fun.

There was a new sound in the air. It wasn't unpleasant, but nor was it the humming sound that she recognized as the K'laisians' laughter. A brief memory of an instructor showing her the ancient way of starting fire sprang to life. The pair of sticks being rubbed together, faster and faster, until a spark was made. The sound was like that.

"A Challenge has been made. A Challenge must be answered. The combatants will disperse until a place and time of meeting is arranged. I will be the Master of Ceremonies for this Challenge," First Officer Ac'kyll announced. Her voice was grim but projected easily to every corner of the dining room.

The rubbing, scraping sound grew louder. Alyssa could still only see ,K'rell, as he stumbled to get his footing, even with the offered aid of her security detail to get to his feet.

Silver blood slowly ran down from the break in the bridge of ,K'rell's nose. He was blinking rapidly, but glaring at her. She was waiting for him to make his move. He had a sword and she didn't, so she'd have to get in close as soon as he started swinging the weapon.

Arms crossed over ,K'rell's torso and yanked him back. A hand gently landed on Alyssa's shoulder. She turned to find Ac'kyll looking at her. The expression on the first officer's face was solemn but calm.

"You need to return to your quarters until summoned, Alyssa," Ac'kyll said firmly.

Giving the policy master a final glower, Alyssa followed First Officer Ac'kyll from the mess hall. ,K'rell was still glaring at her, even as he wiped his nose with a sleeve.

"The commander isn't going to be happy," Alyssa said with a heavy sigh as they stepped into the lift.

Ac'kyll gave her a strange expression as she shook her head slowly. "That is an understatement."

"Oh, well," Alyssa said with a heavy sigh. "It was fun while it lasted, I guess."

Her only response was another look and shake of the head.

She was a survivor. She would survive this and anything else placed in her path.

She hoped.

Chapter Twenty-Three

"What in all of space were you thinking?" Mc'narrd growled as he stood just within the threshold of Alyssa's door . "Challenging the policy master? Are all humans this impulsive and stupid?"

"Are all policy masters that pompous? Obnoxious? Belligerent?" Alyssa retorted, refusing to back down or rescind the Challenge. "No one else on this ship was going to Challenge his smarmy ass! I got that much out of Ac'kyll before she high-tailed it out of my quarters."

"That changes nothing!" Mc'narrd all but shouted. He clenched his hands into fists before relaxing them again. "You are an alien! You don't know enough about our culture to be doing this!"

"Do not make me Challenge *you* next, Mc'narrd," Alyssa snarled, squaring her shoulders as she lowered her head. "I was within my rights. He was insulting me. My honor. My integrity. I have every right to demand a Challenge. I'll be damned if you refuse me that right."

"You will die," Mc'narrd snapped, biting off the end of each word.

"I was dead on that ship, Commander," Alyssa said sadly, shaking her head. "You saved me, yes. But right now? If I'm not on your ship or your world? I'm a dead man walking." She shrugged. "All beings die at some point, but I will not die fighting your precious policy master."

"He's been trained from childhood. You have not."

"I began learning to fence at age ten. I was learning martial arts and how to use bladed weapons around the same time," Alyssa explained, refusing to give in. "You don't want to know how or why, and I'm not reliving that part of my past simply to pacify you. I may not have made it part of my survival in the same way as your people have, but I am not talentless or unskilled. Nor am I walking into a completely foreign arena."

Mc'narrd's jaws clenched and unclenched several times. It looked rather painful to her.

"If I were a K'laisian would you refuse me?" she finally asked after several minutes of silence.

"I would certainly be tempted," he admitted. "I cannot refuse this Duel, but I am far from pleased with you about this."

"Me!" Alyssa exclaimed. "I did nothing! I was there having a pleasant time with your crew until that asshat showed up and started a fight! You should be angry at *him*. *Not* me!"

"I will deal with him after this is over," Mc'narrd retorted.

"If he survives," Alyssa muttered.

She didn't even regret saying it, despite the fact Mc'narrd's face darkened. Not in the pleasant way she'd seen the previous night, either.

"Are you planning on killing him?" Mc'narrd asked in a quiet tone she did not trust.

"I will fight to survive. If that means killing him so I don't die? Then so be it." She met his silver eyes and held them, despite the fury she saw burning in their depths. "I have always fought to survive. And I'll be damned if I stop now. Even for you."

His jaw clenched again, but thankfully he didn't demand she not kill him. That was one promise she knew she wouldn't be able to make. Let alone keep. And Alyssa hated breaking a promise.

"You have the right to request a Champion. You could request I be your Champion."

Alyssa met his blazing silver eyes without flinching. There was no way in all the hells she was going to allow someone else to fight her battles.

"No."

"You are hereby ordered to remain within these quarters. And only these quarters until I see it feasible for you to leave. You will be escorted by a unit of guards to the gym."

With that, Mc'narrd turned and stormed from her room. A heaviness settled over Alyssa as she felt her heart breaking. It didn't shatter. Not yet. She suspected he would wait until after the Duel to complete the job.

She looked at the sword she held. He'd thrown the weapon at her when he'd first entered her quarters. She'd caught it easily. It was sheathed in leather, so she hadn't been worried about cutting herself. At least they hadn't waited until she was in the gym to give her the weapon.

Though, it wouldn't have been the first time someone had thrown her a weapon before screaming "defend yourself." For a brief moment, she wondered if any of those beings had been Va'nu'ians.

They'd certainly been vicious duelists, even if they had appeared human.

Sliding the blade from the sheath, she held it in her hand. It reminded her of a katana in length and weight. Even the blade was designed in a similar fashion. She'd be able to hold it two-handed, if needed, even with the guard wrapping around the hilt.

Holding the weapon in her right hand, she swung it around a few times. Not surprisingly, it was well-balanced and beautifully crafted.

It reminded her even more of the pair she'd seen hanging in Mc'narrd's room. Not that she was going to go through his door to find out. That was begging for problems. If the door would even open for her anymore.

Shaking the thoughts away, she turned and studied the room. If she were to win this duel, she would need a clear mind and she knew exactly how to achieve that. Moving the furniture around, she opened up a decent empty space in the main room.

Standing with her feet together, she held the weapon in her dominant hand, the blade parallel with her body. The tip was just above her head, the hilt at her waist. Her other hand was raised until the palm was parallel to the blade and directly in front of her face.

She closed her eyes and forced all conscious thoughts away.

Training returned in a rush and she slid her dominant leg back as she crouched slightly. The blade moved in fluid easy motions around her body as she went through a routine she'd been taught many long years ago. With each movement, each strike, her mind calmed, and she found her center.

No matter what happened, she refused to lose that again.

Mc'narrd stalked the corridors fuming. Nothing about the situation was good.

Though this wasn't the first time someone spoke about wanting to Challenge ,K'rell. It *was* the first time someone had actually gone through with it.

And of course it would be the alien they'd rescued. The same alien who he'd just spent a very intimate night with and who he thought would be killed. There would be no way he could even punish ,K'rell if she died during the Duel.

The lift door opened and he started, not even realizing he'd entered it. Let alone told it to go to the medbay.

Zh'oros met him in the hallway, a slightly amused expression on her face.

"Come on, let's have a drink," she said.

Mc'narrd followed his friend into her office where she pulled a bottle of Earth-produced tequila from a shelf. She poured a liberal amount into a glass and handed it to him. He tossed it back before holding it out for a refill.

"This is a mess," he grumbled as she refilled it before setting the bottle beside the commander. "The human Challenged ,K'rell to a Duel. He accepted, and there's not a *ka'deshed* thing I can do about it!"

"Are you more concerned about harm coming to the human or what it might mean if the policy master falls at her hands?" Zh'oros asked, settling into her chair. "The very fact they are going to Duel is going to have repercussions throughout our people."

"I know," Mc'narrd said before tossing back the second round of tequila. "Every ship is required to have a policy master. By her Challenging him, it means she's willing to abide by our rules, even if she has only the slightest bit of knowledge about them."

"Not only that, 'Zarry, but she isn't afraid of our people. She's willing to Challenge the one being who most on a ship would never consider Challenging. It would be equal to fighting you or the first officer." Zh'oros tossed back her own tequila before turning the glass in her hand. "If an alien being is willing to Challenge the ship's esteemed policy master, then why can't our own people? Especially a being who has far more to lose."

"*Fark*," Mc'narrd said as he began to pace. Not that there was a lot of room in the office to do so. "I took a chance rescuing her. Then giving her freedom on this ship. She's been helpful in our assignment to open communications with her people. But this is a disaster. If she dies, we lose our only link to the humans. One who can help us turn the tide against them and their Va'nu'ian allies."

"Don't forget that after your night with her, there will certainly be tension," Zh'oros said as she poured more tequila into her glass. She glanced up at him. "You certainly didn't do yourself any favors by the scolding you gave her."

"Was anything I said wrong?" Mc'narrd demanded to know.

As Master Healer of the battlecruiser, Zh'oros was capable of overriding any comm she desired. And apparently, she'd done so during his conversation with Alyssa.

Zh'oros lifted a brow. "If you were to hear Policy Master ,K'rell speak, you would believe this woman to be plotting the downfall of all of us. That the humans and Va'nu'ians are on their way to find us this very second."

"That is another problem," Mc'narrd said with a groan. "Should he concede defeat by injury and not die, there will be even more xenophobic reactions. Those onboard will race to his side, supporting him and encouraging him until their voice is the loudest."

"And if he should die, the ship will be without a policy master. And though everyone in command is aware a ship can survive without that position, those who are sticklers for following the rules will think all is lost. That the ship will fail and no one will be able to continue their daily tasks without someone having that title." Zh'oros hummed in amusement. "We both know a policy master is not required, but this is not our first or even fifth expedition among the stars."

"That is because High Command has decreed no ship can operate without a policy master. Should a policy master die on assignment, the battlecruiser is required to return to K'lais and acquire a new one," Mc'narrd stated.

"The gym has been prepared, Commander," First Officer Ac'kyll's voice said in his comm. "Will you be witnessing?"

"I will be there. I'll inform Master Healer Zh'oros. We will be there shortly. Have Master Ra'dett escort Sergeant Zelaya," Mc'narrd replied, looking at the healer.

"Yes, sir," Ac'kyll said before the comm going silent.

"Let us hope for the sake of your human that she is a better Duelist than ,K'rell," Zh'oros said as she stood. She paused before saying, "Record private under Master Healer Keris Zh'oros."

"Something you don't want on the main record?" Mc'narrd asked.

"Yes. The policy master will not accept anything other than the human's death. Even if she were to concede defeat, he will not accept it. Should he survive this encounter, I will be starting the process to have him relieved of his duties due to excessive paranoid reactions towards an alien race."

Mc'narrd stared at the Master Healer. She had the ability to relieve anyone of duty for any medical reason, including psychological ones. Xenophobia was a psychological illness all healers on space-bound vessels watched for and were trained to spot. It was a concern his people took seriously.

,K'rell had been part of the military for years. Decades, even. He had a distinguished record. It would be extinguished faster than a flame in gale-force winds the moment Master Healer Zh'oros mentioned 'xenophobia' in the man's medical records.

"I have already spoken to those who heard his very loud, drunken declarations prior to the Challenge," Zh'oros continued. "I have spoken to him, as well. There is no mistaking the signs of blatant xenophobia leading to violent and aggressive behavior. None of that can be tolerated on a battlecruiser whose duties deal heavily with new, unknown races."

"How was this missed?" Mc'narrd asked.

When did the xenophobia begin? How had they missed the signs?

Zh'oros remained silent for a few moments, studying him intently. "His previous attitude towards those 'beneath' him hid his xenophobia. He used his arrogance as a deterrent away from it. It seems Alyssa and her openness to interact with us is what brought it to the fore.

Even then, he was able to conceal it. Up until he grew too drunk to hide it any longer." She frowned darkly. "Several empty bottles were located within his room. The bio suit was unable to cleanse his blood due to the amount he'd been consuming in such a short amount of time."

The commander merely nodded, unable to find words for the healer's declarations. In silence, he followed her from the office. She gestured to the same healers as before, and they fell into step behind them.

The somber silence grated on his nerves, but it was better than the anger he'd previously felt towards Alyssa and ,K'rell.

As they drew closer to the gym, he felt unease and nervousness settling into his body. This was one Challenge he was not eager to witness.

Chapter Twenty-Four

The gym held an entirely different appearance to Alyssa.

Not because anything had been changed, but because she was standing in the center of the floor with a growing audience. ,K'rell stood opposite her, full of anger and unhidden hatred.

Allowing her eyes to drift half-shut, she cleared her mind of everything but the task at hand.

This was just another assignment, she told herself. Her objective this time was to defeat the man opposite her. He was the foe. Her target. Her objective was to take him down using the weapon at hand, which happened to be the sheathed sword she was holding.

To survive at any cost.

Her opponent's black hair was pulled back into a tight ponytail. His gold eyes watched her as a sneer pulled his lips back. ,K'rell wore his usual bio suit and held a similar sword in his hand.

Between them stood First Officer Ac'kyll, her smooth features grim. A sword hung from her waist beside her standard service weapon. Once she was satisfied no more K'laisians were entering the gym, she raised her hands.

Silence blanketed the gym. Alyssa wished someone would drop a button or something, to see if it could be heard. The thought almost made her smile.

Almost.

"A Challenge has been lawfully issued between Sergeant Alyssa Zelaya of Earth's IMD and K'laisian Ardor ,K'rell, Policy Master of the battlecruiser *Laedschot*," Ac'kyll said, her voice echoing in the silent gym. "No Champions have been chosen."

That was different, Alyssa thought, glancing sharply at the first officer. She supposed it was for official records.

"The Duel need not be to the death," Ac'kyll stated, looking directly at Alyssa before turning her eyes to ,K'rell.

,K'rell glowered. "You are not following the normal speech."

"Nothing about this Challenge is normal," Ac'kyll retorted. "Do you accept the Challenge, Policy Master ,K'rell?"

"Yes, I accept it! Now let us begin," he said with a snarl.

The first officer glanced at Alyssa and sighed. "I'm not even going to ask if you wish to rescind the Challenge."

"Policy Master ,K'rell insulted me. He questioned my integrity and honor. I will not rescind the Challenge," Alyssa replied in a loud, clear voice.

"Very well," Ac'kyll said in a weary tone. She drew her sword and held it out between Alyssa and ,K'rell, even with their heads. She moved backwards. Swiping the sword downward, she called out, "The Duel may commence!"

Alyssa ignored everyone and everything except her opponent. Sliding her dominant leg back, she unsheathed her weapon and tossed the sheath far to her right side where she could see and mark its position. ,K'rell unsheathed his weapon and did the same, though his was thrown to the left. She memorized its position, also.

,K'rell didn't begin by trying to showboat. There was no twirling of his weapon, swinging to show his upper body strength, or anything that Alyssa had come to expect from overly-opinionated beings who felt they had an advantage.

,K'rell was holding his sword with only his left hand, so she prepared for the advantages he would have.

He came right for her neck with a backhanded swing of considerable speed. She blocked, managing to hold the unfamiliar sword in her own hands well enough to take the strike against the thicker part of the blade rather than the edge. The blades separated. He came at her neck from the other direction, still one-handed. She blocked again, this time pushing his blade away.

He stepped back. She did the same.

Keep space between yourself and your opponent, the voice of an old instructor whispered in Alyssa's mind. *Give no space unless it is by your own choice.*

Just as the last words rang gently in her mind, ,K'rell came at her again.

The forward thrust was a little sloppy, but his weight was behind it. Thus her upward swing to deflect the blade was unbalanced, meaning she had to move away from the tip. He stepped back and came with another thrust, this one more powerful and confident. The blade darted towards her face.

Alyssa stepped in and used her sword to push the opposing blade up and away from her.

With a quick sidestep and flick of her right wrist, she was a safe distance from him. They now faced the opposing directions they'd started in. She brought her weapon up one-handed, waiting for him to come again.

The wait was microscopically brief.

His hard overhead swing was too quick for her to dodge. She poised the flat part of the blade up, her left hand laid against the upper third of the sword to give more leverage without sacrificing her fingers to the sharp edge. She stopped the progress of his blade, and felt his weapon pushing towards her exposed left-hand fingers.

Using both arms. she pushed him away and down. The smallest of openings came as he had to recoup from the momentum. Alyssa stepped back and whipped her sword across from left to right. A three-inch gash split open where, on a human, the nerve cluster in the upper arm would be found.

,K'rell grunted and stepped back rapidly. His face was pulled together in anger and pain. Silver blood flowed into the bio suit's sleeve, which was already repairing itself and his wounded left arm. Still, he repositioned his entire body to take on a two-handed position with his weapon.

Alyssa made herself not smirk at drawing first blood. She knew she'd gotten lucky. Not lucky enough for the damage to take out the arm, but she'd take what was offered.

Small comfort, since ,K'rell doubled his efforts.

His two-handed swings came at her with more strength. He managed to give three hard attacks in rapid succession. She had to keep backing up to keep an effective amount of room between them.

The follow-up thrust came closer to connecting with her torso than any previous attack. She kept moving, blocking, losing track of how many attacks had come at her. He made her dance around the fighting area twice before he changed up his technique again.

Although she'd managed to keep the fight going using only her right hand, she was starting to feel the need to go into a similar two-handed technique to avoid her growing fatigue from getting the better of her. Before she could go through with that plan, ,K'rell came at her with an upward swing that she had to brace her body to deflect. The blades smacked off of each other, with the momentum making her overextend and turn to her right.

Her weapon was too far away to do anything about his sudden spin and downward swing.

She felt the skin of her thigh, maybe a handful of centimeters above her left knee, part and burn as the sword cut. Her hobbled turn and partial retreat was not graceful, but she kept upright.

He charged.

Alyssa could only move so much. She braced herself, meeting his attack with a strong defensive. The blades met, pushed and ground against each other. Between the crossed weapons, ‚K'rell's beamed at her.

"I'm looking forward to your death," he announced in a low tone.

He pushed harder, making her give another ten centimeters, and still their bodies were closer than they'd ever been. Alyssa leaned hard on her right leg, hoping the nanites would get enough work done for her to move soon.

She hopped just enough to get some movement to her right and push. The swords parted.

‚K'rell went into another spin. His weapon rose up to deliver a smashing blow down towards her torso.

Alyssa pivoted enough to block again. The edge of her opponent's sword was stopped less than two dozen centimeters from her scalp. This time, she managed to position her own sword so she could push more effectively. Leaning all her weight into the effort, she pushed both swords down to her left until their tips struck the floor of the gym.

He was wide open. His entire torso was right ahead of her. His weapon pointed ineffectively to the floor. Alyssa dove at ,K'rell, turning the sword in her hands.

The entire blade speared through ,K'rell's chest even before her body slammed into his torso. As Alyssa bounced off the policy master and stumbled to stay in a standing position, her hands released the hilt of the weapon she'd been using.

,K'rell stood there, right hand still clutching his sword. The hilt of her weapon was flush against the center of his chest. His expression was tight, still expressing anger, but growing slack rapidly.

"Did anyone hear what he said?" Alyssa gasped.

She'd given up her weapon, and ,K'rell still held his. Yet she still asked the question loud enough for all to hear.

"Our comms are all linked and recorded. So yes, Alyssa of Earth, we all heard him say he was looking forward to your death," said Master Healer Zh'oros. Her voice rang through the gym as clearly as if the healer were standing beside Alyssa.

Alyssa kept her eyes on ,K'rell. He appeared to be attempting to raise his sword. His whole body contracting inward, in fact. Alyssa felt her wounded leg become more agile. She slid into a better defensive position, not sure how ,K'rell was going to try and attack.

"It is over," she heard Mc'narrd say. His voice was neutral enough she couldn't tell what he was feeling or what the words might convey.

,K'rell kept drawing inward. Alyssa knew she had no idea of what kind of attack he might do. She'd never seen anything like what his body was doing. Even though his eyes seemed blank, the expression of his face slack, his body kept moving into a crouch.

The sword fell from his hand. She realized the fingers looked withered. So did the hand. The longer she watched, his entire form appeared as though it was growing smaller, or rapidly aging. The body collapsed to the floor.

She could not stop watching as what had been ,K'rell shriveled up and disappeared into the bio suit. Within seconds, a multifaceted lump of something was casually ejected out from the empty head hole of the suit.

The bio suit then began folding itself.

Confused, Alyssa looked around. The Master Healer walked past her, explaining while kneeling to pick up the lump.

"We do not eject our dead or vaporize them while traveling in space. The nanites in our suits remove all moisture so what remains of the body can be easily stored until returned home for proper burial."

"You are injured," Healer La'crou said, appearing beside her.

"Formalities need to be conducted," First Officer Ac'kyll said, stepping forward. Loud enough for the entire audience to hear, she continued. "The undisputed winner by death of Policy Master Ardor K' Rell is Sergeant Alyssa Zelaya of Earth."

There was loud murmuring once Ac'kyll finished speaking. Alyssa guessed that meant her words concluded the Duel. Zh'oros handed the package to someone, Alyssa couldn't see who, and knelt beside her. One knee touched the floor as the healer crouched.

"Can you walk?" Zh'oros asked, examining the injury.

Alyssa drew a breath and tried moving her leg. It was weak and hurt like hell.

"Stand, yes. Walk? Not without help," Alyssa said, adding more weight on the leg and grimacing with the pain.

Healer La'crou lifted Alyssa in his arms.

She glowered at him. "You could just let me lean on you and I could hobble along."

There was amusement in his eyes, though no smile curved his lips. "You are light. I will carry you to the medbay where we can attend to your injury and speed healing."

Alyssa followed his eyes to Mc'narrd who was watching with a stoic expression, though anger burned in his eyes. There may have been something else, but she wasn't foolish enough to think the commander would be jealous.

Zh'oros stepped in front of her, blocking her view. "Come."

Turning, the Master Healer strode through the throng of K'laisians. Her healers followed close on her heels with La'crou directly behind the master healer.

Alyssa had to content herself with being carried in the arms of a K'laisian who was not Mc'narrd. At least she would be healed. Though she would have preferred being carried by the commander.

Chapter Twenty-Five

The medbay was definitely not a foreign place to Alyssa anymore. Just like the last time, she wasn't being treated within what was basically a prison cell. Healer La'crou placed her on an actual bed before moving back and giving Master Healer Zh'oros room to move.

"This is a fairly deep cut," Zh'oros commented, examining the injury.

She motioned to La'crou who moved to a cabinet. She requested several different items that were not translated. La'crou moved with calm yet quick efficiency, grabbing the requested items and handing them to Zh'oros. From a drawer he removed a cylindrical tube with a tapered end. Lines wrapped around the tube, connecting buttons of various shapes and sizes.

Zh'oros' movements were fluid and steady as she mixed the items together into something very similar to the humans' version of a hypo. Except this one was sleeker and less clunky in design.

"This will help with the pain," she said.

Pressing the end of the hypo against Alyssa's thigh, she heard a faint whisper of air and felt pressure. But there was no pin-prick or any other sort of pain. What she did feel was the coolness of a liquid moving through her veins. It wasn't unpleasant, but it wasn't exactly pleasing, either.

Unlike most of the pain medications Alyssa received, this one remained only in her leg. She didn't feel it moving through the rest of her body, which she was thankful for.

La'crou said a word in question and Zh'oros paused, as she studied the laceration. She shook her head and took the odd device from La'crou. She held it over Alyssa's leg.

There was a faint tugging sensation followed by more heat. The warmth grew until it was on the verge of being painfully hot, yet it never got quite there. So Alyssa remained silent, accepting the sensations.

A short time later, Zh'oros moved away. She studied Alyssa before saying something else to La'crou. The healer gave Zh'oros a strange look, but retrieved another item from the cabinet. He handed it to Zh'oros.

"This will help you relax. It will allow the nanites to complete your healing," Zh'oros stated.

Zh'oros pressed the hypo against Alyssa's shoulder. Another faint whisper of air was followed by warmth this time. The healer hadn't been joking. Alyssa felt as though she'd finished several bottles of whiskey followed by a case of wine. Her head swam and she smiled sleepily up at the healers.

"Thank you," she murmured.

"How is she?" Mc'narrd's voice swam into Alyssa's ears.

She couldn't see the commander, but she could certainly hear him.

"Healing," Zh'oros replied.

A hand touched Alyssa's arm, and she turned her head to the side to find Mc'narrd staring at her.

"Will she heal completely?" Mc'narrd asked.

"Her body will be fully healed within three hours, provided she continues to respond well to the medications and nanites."

Mc'narrd moved closer to Alyssa, but she couldn't see any warmth in his features.

"Have her returned to her quarters. She is not to leave except under my orders," Mc'narrd stated. "Contact Master Ra'dett when she is well enough to walk."

"I didn't want to kill him," Alyssa said, forcing her tongue to form the words. She could barely keep her eyes open, but she reached for the commander anyway. "I'm sorry. I didn't want to kill him. He gave me no choice."

"There is always a choice. You could have simply walked away before Challenging him," Mc'narrd snapped. "I made a mistake in giving you freedom among my people. I will not make that mistake again."

With that, Mc'narrd turned and walked away, not giving her another look.

Alyssa's face grew hot, and her eyes stung. Tears fell as she forced her eyes shut. Her breath was ragged as she drew in one deep breath, let it out, then drew in another. It was all she could do to not give in to the pain of his refusal to accept her apology.

To refuse her.

Zh'oros brushed her hair back and wiped away her tears with a gentle touch.

"Men are not always the wisest beings," the master healer murmured. "Give him time and don't Challenge anyone else. He will come around."

"Maybe," Alyssa whispered. "But I am human. If he cannot accept me as I am, failings and all, then we have no hope for a relationship."

She didn't hear anything else as sleep overtook her. The last thing she remembered was a whisper of air, then blissful darkness.

Mc'narrd walked away from Alyssa, refusing to accept her apology. Refusing to allow her to touch him.

He now had to inform High Command that a human had Challenged the policy master and defeated him. Not only did she defeat ,K'rell, but she killed him as well. That meant issuing a letter of sympathy to his living family members.

How do you tell someone their relative was killed by a human in a Duel? Not only that, but the esteemed being who was killed had suddenly turned out to be extremely xenophobic? To the point of possibly jeopardizing their mission?

None of this would have been a problem, had he simply left the human in the medbay or brig. But no, he had to allow her to take up residence in the quarters meant for the commander's mate. Not only that, but he'd spent a night with her getting to know her intimately.

Ka'desh! He couldn't allow his feelings for the Earther to cause him to fail the mission.

If he kept her locked in her quarters, there would be no possibility for her to cause more trouble on his ship. To Challenge more of his crew to Duels.

"Commander, there is a communication incoming for you," Master Ar'ath's voice said through the comm, breaking into his thoughts. "It is Commander Cq'linns."

Mc'narrd frowned.

What was Vrehn doing in this sector? he wondered.

"I'll take it in my quarters," he replied as he quickened his steps.

"Yes, sir," Ar'ath replied.

By the time he reached his quarters, Mc'narrd's thoughts were solely on why his old friend and former battlemate was close enough to send a transmission.

"On screen," Mc'narrd said the moment the door to his quarters closed.

He crossed to his chair and paused, remembering Alyssa as she stood beside him. Eyes sleepy, but with a smile on her lips.

"Something certainly has you distracted," Vrehn's voice said through the viewscreen.

Startled, Mc'narrd looked up to find his fellow commander smiling at him.

Vrehn hadn't always been a commander. In fact, he hadn't even started out as a pilot. He'd been part of the military's guard, often conducting investigations. He had enjoyed drinking with the mechanics that worked on newly designed ships.

That is, until he jumped into a newly designed ship that hadn't been cleared for battle and attacked an invading force without authorization. Other pilots watched and followed Vrehn's lead by taking the other newly manufactured ships.

The pilots then followed his orders in the ensuing battle in space. His time flying with the mechanics planetside had gone unnoticed, until then. But instead of a court martial, he'd been given command and sent off planet.

A master strategist, the dark-haired K'laisian with rich tan skin and golden eyes commanded respect from those beneath him. Even while being a pleasant, charming being.

"A *kutchu mich*, my friend," Mc'narrd said, refusing to sit in his chair.

Vrehn Cq'linns' eyes swept over him, and he tilted his head to the side in thought. "Maybe I should transport over and you tell me all about it over a bottle of khok'kish." A favorite K'laisian alcohol of theirs, khok'kish put most of the humans' alcoholic beverages to shame in strength and taste.

"While you're over, why don't you tell me about why you're in this sector," Mc'narrd countered, a grin on his face. "I'm sure it's a good tale."

"Oh, it's rather boring, actually," Vrehn replied with a shrug of his shoulder. "High Command received word from an ally saying the humans were planning something nasty for you. Suggested we might want to send reinforcements if we didn't want to lose our ship."

"I'm surprised the Xoutians cared enough to send that," Mc'narrd said thoughtfully.

"Someone assassinated one of their ambassadors. Said ambassador had already begun the process of sending the message to us prior to his death," Vrehn replied. "They suspect the humans were behind it, but can't prove anything."

Mc'narrd stared at Vrehn for several long moments. "Come over. We'll have a private discussion about it."

Vrehn's gold eyes lit up in curiosity. "I'll see you soon. Commander Cq'linns out."

The viewscreen went dark, but Mc'narrd didn't stop looking at it. More pieces of the puzzle were falling into place, and he suspected he would need Vrehn's mind for strategy before this finished playing out.

Maybe Vrehn also had a suggestion on what to do about the human, also.

Chapter Twenty-Six

Sometime later with a half-empty bottle of khok'kish between them and full glasses in their hands, Vrehn Cq'linns sat across from It'zarry Mc'narrd in his quarters. Vrehn took another sip from his glass as Mc'narrd slouched in his chair.

"Let me ensure I have everything correct," Vrehn said, with amusement in his voice.

"None of this is amusing," Mc'narrd snapped.

"You have lost your sense of humor," Vrehn replied. "Or perhaps it's simply because you, of all people, are the one in this situation."

"Remind me again why I invited you to join me on my ship, Commander Cq'linns?" Mc'narrd asked. "I thought it was to help, not be yet another pain in my ass."

"You want help? Fine. Let me state what happened from my point of view. The humans sent one of their own out to die. Possibly to learn information about us, definitely to claim we killed her. Instead of letting this alien die on her ship, you brought her to your own where she was healed. She says she wants to help you in your mission with opening communications and trade with the humans." He paused in his commentary to ask, "How am I doing so far?"

"Accurate on all accounts. So far," Mc'narrd retorted, wondering where his friend was going with the conversation.

"Good. So, you allow this alien to use the quarters for the commander's woman. You, who refuses to allow anyone inside those quarters. Who will not even take a lover while on a mission, regardless of how long that mission may be."

Fark. Now Mc'narrd knew where Vrehn was going, and he didn't like it one bit.

"Go on," Mc'narrd said, downing half of the contents in his glass.

"I'll come back to that shortly," Vrehn promised.

It felt more like a threat to Mc'narrd, but he remained silent.

"The woman ends up proving she's not a threat. In fact, she respects our laws and rules and is willing to follow them. But your former policy master, who was a complete *númli,* doesn't approve of the alien and doesn't trust her for whatever stupid reason he had. Xenophobic? Oh, yes, that man was definitely xenophobic. He decides to make a useful suggestion of having her feign a distress call and setting the humans up to see what they will do." He smiled, and it wasn't a pleasant one. "I'll come back to that after I help you with your little human."

"I'm really starting to hate you," Mc'narrd drawled.

"So Challenge me," Vrehn retorted. "Your human ends up Challenging him after he makes a complete fool of himself. That is where the contention comes from, if I'm understanding everything."

"She could have just ignored him. Walked away," Mc'narrd said, glaring into his glass. Maybe if he kept saying it, he would eventually believe it.

Vrehn leaned forward in his chair, his forearm rested across his right leg, the glass held in his fingers. It was a casual enough appearance, but Mc'narrd knew better. Vrehn had insight and it wasn't anything he was going to want to hear.

"Let's remove the fact she is an alien. Alyssa Zelaya has accepted our laws, respects our culture. If she were of K'laisian blood, would she have been in the wrong to Challenge ,K'rell? Yes, he was the master of policies aboard the ship, but that doesn't make the being holding that position immune to Challenges. No more than being a commander prevents anyone from Challenging you if you commit a great error."

Mc'narrd stared at his friend, wanting to agree. "Very few people would dare Challenge a commander, let alone the policy master. As it is, there's going to be a price to pay for her doing this."

"Perhaps High Command will finally decide that Duels to the death will no longer be allowed on off planet missions," Vrehn said with a slight smirk. "It may also mean those who are policy masters finally realize they aren't better than anyone else onboard the ship. They may even stop thinking they are in the line of true command. You also didn't answer the question: If she were K'laisian, would you be this angry with her? Would you be willing to destroy a relationship with the one woman who has ever managed to get under your skin?"

"She isn't K'laisian, though," Mc'narrd insisted, refusing to admit what his heart knew.

Vrehn slammed the glass on the table beside him before standing. "You are being deliberately obtuse, It'zarry!" He glowered down at Mc'narrd as he continued.

"Then explain it to me," Mc'narrd challenged.

"If Alyssa were a K'laisian, the biggest problem you would be thinking about is needing to return to K'lais and acquiring a new policy master. You would have congratulated her, swept her up in your arms, and carried her to the medbay yourself! She'd be in this room right now and we'd be discussing your problem with the humans and their allies. Not why you refuse to see the obvious!"

"Are you finished?" Mc'narrd asked, leaning back in the chair. "The fact is, the woman is an alien."

"No, I am not finished," Vrehn said, turning and walking away. He strode to Mc'narrd's cabinet and pulled out a bottle of ve'qua. Pouring some into his glass, he continued. "Alyssa is an alien who obviously suffered some sort of mental harm if she decided you were the best choice of beings to be attracted to. Obviously, Master Healer Zh'oros should examine the alien closer. Perhaps after she's fully healed, she will find a better match."

Mc'narrd shot to his feet and was almost to Vrehn before he realized what he was doing.

"No one goes near her until I allow it," he snarled.

Not bothered by Mc'narrd's fury, Vrehn tossed back his glass of tequila. "What do you plan on doing? Keeping her locked in those quarters? Away from every other living being because you don't want her realizing there are other males out there? What about when you leave her on K'lais? I've seen the recordings of the lady, 'Zarry. She's a pretty thing. And if she is willing to live with our ways, she won't be alone for long."

"She's mine," Mc'narrd growled, snatching the bottle away from Vrehn.

No sooner had the words left his lips than he realized what they meant: He would fight anyone for her. That he cared deeply for her.

"Then start acting like a K'laisian warrior! Start treating her like someone deserving respect. And not like some *pet* to be cowed and caged," Vrehn retorted, snatching the bottle back. "You're acting like a child who is afraid to accept the situation in front of him and adapt to it. Not the warrior who takes the hits he receives and continues to fight."

"Do you honestly think High Command would allow her to remain on my ship?" Mc'narrd asked quietly. He grabbed another glass, grabbed the bottle back again, and poured the tequila into the glass. He tossed it back. "No. It's better if I keep her out of my sight."

"So you don't get further attached to her?" Vrehn asked, holding his glass out to Mc'narrd. Mc'narrd nodded as he refilled their glasses. Vrehn hummed, and he gave Mc'narrd a sly look. "If you take her as a mate, they can't deny you. Not without refusing every other mate who resides upon the battlecruisers. Including those who are not a part of our military."

"I cannot take her as a mate without her acceptance." Mc'narrd swirled the alcoholic beverage in the glass before finally meeting Vrehn's gold eyes. "Do you honestly think she would agree to a life with me? Always in space on one dangerous mission after another?"

"I believe if she feels deeply for you, she will be willing to see past the differences and accept you and that life," Vrehn replied, tossing back his tequila. "Of course, you'll have to do the same. And you both will have to accept the fact you're aliens to each other. With that will come with problems and headaches that you'll have to talk out."

"Something I haven't done so far," Mc'narrd said with a sigh. "Why do I get the feeling if she ends up as my mate, this will only be the first of many problems I will have to deal with?"

"Because that's what happens when we deal with women," Vrehn said pouring more tequila. "It'll only be worse since you're both aliens, and she's of a new race." He hummed louder. "Admittedly, I don't know if High Command had your method of 'opening communication' in mind when they sent you out here."

Mc'narrd huffed, then hummed a little. "Probably not, though I was told I could use whatever method I saw best. Ad'dari gave me complete freedom on this mission."

"Maybe you should keep that part out of the reports," Vrehn suggested. "Though, they'd probably suspect once you convince the woman to be your mate. Our women enjoy weapons and sweets. I wonder if the same is true for humans?"

"I'm not asking," Mc'narrd retorted.

Vrehn's eyes twinkled with laughter as he teased, "You must tell me how your brother and sister-by-marriage react to your methods on this mission."

"I may just Challenge you, instead," Mc'narrd retorted. Vrehn's humming had him joining in after a few moments. Both were aware his brother, Admiral Tr'oun Mc'narrd, was wed to Torlla Ad'dari. "I'm certain there will be many discussions about it."

"Good luck, my friend," Vrehn said.

"Thank you," Mc'narrd replied. "Now what about the humans?"

"I think your lady had a good idea about having her send a broadcast to the citizens of her world. So did former Master of Policies ,K'rell, in regards to luring them out here. We need to take the offensive back. Right now we're being defensive and reacting to what they do. They still think they've killed your lady love. Let's prove to them that she's still alive, and we aren't backing down." His smile grew cunning and Mc'narrd recognized the gleam in his gold eyes. "And let's locate the Va'nu'ian destroyer waiting in the proverbial wings. Remind them why it's unwise to take on their more advanced enemies."

"What do you have in mind, my friend?" Mc'narrd asked, thankful to be talking about military strategy now and not his love life.

"Bring up the schematics you have, including where Alyssa's ship was destroyed and your pod. We'll overlay those with the map of this sector, all the way out to Xoutsiis. They're willing to be a neutral territory, complete with offering up their own defenses to keep the humans from attacking us on sight. But we need a plan before we go, in case they try something on the way to or from the planet."

"What was the message the assassinated ambassador wanted to send?" Mc'narrd asked as he turned to the viewscreen and calling up the requested information.

"The humans have had contact with the Va'nu'ians for several decades. The Va'nu'ians intercepted information that we were wanting to open trade with Earth. It seems the admiralty was right to be worried: our 'cousins' have been sowing mistrust with the humans, hoping to start a war. The Xoutian ambassador learned they're trying to coax the humans into war with us. Probably to use it as a method to reclaim K'lais."

Mc'narrd studied Vrehn for several moments. "You realize Alyssa's last assignment was to assassinate a Xoutian ambassador."

Vrehn refilled his glass before tossing it back again. "I suspect it's why they wanted her dead, my friend. She killed the ambassador. As such, they needed to remove the one person who could tie them to the death of one of our allies. One who was trying to prevent a war between the humans, Va'nu'ians, and us. Possibly involving more, since we have many allies of our own, aside from the Xoutians."

"And if the Va'nu'ians are wanting war, she provided the perfect victim to set us up as cold-blooded murderers," Mc'narrd concluded. He grabbed a taller glass and filled it with the tequila before tossing it back. "I don't think I've ever wanted to find a Va'nu'ian destroyer so much."

The cold smile and burning gold eyes of his fellow commander told Mc'narrd he wasn't the only one wanting a fight. Mc'narrd filled their glasses again and they tapped them together before tossing the drinks back. As one, they set the glasses on the table and turned to the viewscreen.

First, he'd plan with Vrehn. Then he would seek out Alyssa and attempt to make amends. With luck, she would be willing to forgive him and move forward. Not just with helping with her fellow humans, but also with whatever was growing between them.

Provided he hadn't destroyed it with his anger and fear of losing her to death.

Chapter Twenty-Seven

Alyssa awoke to the door sliding open. She sat up, anxious.

Ra'dett stepped inside the room, looking decidedly grim. Several guards followed him into the room. Closing her eyes, she bowed her head, feeling as though her heart was shattering even more. Refusing to give into the tears that threatened, she swallowed several times, trying to control her emotions.

"Absolutely not," Zh'oros said in a firm tone. "Leave. Now."

Alyssa's eyes snapped open and she opened her mouth to say something, then closed it upon seeing the healer turning on the guards and Ra'dett.

"The commander-" Ra'dett began.

"Is being completely irrational," Zh'oros interrupted. "And I will be speaking with him shortly about his behavior."

Alyssa blinked, wondering if she'd heard the healer right. She could not have just heard Zh'oros say such in front of the guards. And Ra'dett.

"The guards are dismissed," Zh'oros repeated. She turned her back completely to Alyssa, giving the security detail her entire attention. "I am officially overriding Commander Mc'narrd's order. Now leave."

The guards turned in perfect unison and departed the room. Not a single one spoke against the healer. Alyssa stared in stunned silence at the healer and master of security.

"I couldn't do that," Ra'dett said, holding his hands up as he gave Zh'oros his attention. "I have to obey Commander Mc'narrd's orders. Unlike you, *I* cannot override him."

Zh'oros muttered a few words that Alyssa couldn't hear, which made Ra'dett's lips twitch slightly. She moved towards the bed, her eyes looking above where Alyssa sat.

"Shall we return you to your quarters, lady?" Ra'dett asked kindly, moving until he stood beside Zh'oros.

"No," Alyssa replied. She didn't even care if her pain came through in the voice. Who was going to object? "I will not return to those quarters. I'm not… I'm not his mate. I will not return there."

The healer and security master exchanged wary expressions before looking back at her.

"You have not been dismissed from there," Ra'dett said slowly.

"Give him time, Alyssa," Zh'oros implored gently. "He is… not thinking clearly."

"Does it matter?" Alyssa rejoined, her voice breaking. She took several deep breaths, trying to ease the tightness of her chest. "He made his decision. Allow me to make mine." Her eyes met Zh'oros, even as she wiped away tears. "Don't make me go back to those rooms. Please."

"It does matter," Ra'dett replied stubbornly. "Mc'narrd was concerned about you. He's attracted to you. We all know it. Give him time to calm down and be rational."

"Attracted," she repeated angrily. "Was it love? Or lust?" Anger was an easier emotion to grasp at and try to hold the heartache at bay. "He has not said anything about the former, though he most certainly has demonstrated the latter!"

"True, though that is an unfair statement. Both to you and him," Zh'oros replied calmly.

Zh'oros' statement cut through the anger faster and with greater ease than ,K'rell's blade had cut her body. She closed her eyes tightly and took a deep breath.

"Just… let me have other quarters, please," she whispered quietly. Looking up at the healer, Alyssa met Zh'oros' gold eyes. "Unfair or not, am I wrong? Please. Allow me space away from him to heal. To accept… what has happened."

Zh'oros sighed heavily. Her eyes shifted from above the bed to Alyssa. "Very well. There are quarters you can have, even if they are not the same as the ones Commander Mc'narrd assigned you."

Ra'dett eyes showed compassion, even though his features remained neutral. "I'll inform him of the change of rooms."

"Thank you," Alyssa whispered as she stood.

"I will take you," Zh'oros said giving Ra'dett a sharp look. Touching Alyssa's arm gently, she guided Alyssa from the room. "Ra'dett, ensure there are no guards outside her new quarters. If I even hear a hint of it…"

Ra'dett gave a brisk nod and departed the room, going a different direction from where Zh'oros led her. They traveled to the lift in silence, though Alyssa suspected Zh'oros wanted to say plenty. The sympathy and compassion in the healer's eyes warred with what Alyssa suspected was anger and irritation. Though she wasn't entirely certain what the master healer had to be angry or irritated about. Aside from perhaps Mc'narrd's response to the Duel.

When the doors opened on the same level as her former quarters, she narrowed her eyes at Zh'oros.

"The quarters for the command staff are on the same level as the commander's," Zh'oros explained gently. "Though you are not a threat to us, I would prefer you be among those you have come to trust. Who will not intrude on your privacy."

"That's very kind of you," Alyssa said, hating how her voice wavered.

Then again, she didn't think she'd been this heartbroken before in her entire life. Wasn't she getting to experience all sorts of new things? Eventually she'd end up on a new planet, also.

Alone yet again.

She hated how the thought brought a new round of pain. Her body felt far too hot. Unshed tears burned her eyes. The tightness in her chest had yet to lessen. Zh'oros, though, was true to her word. She led Alyssa along a different set of corridors before stopping in front of a new door. When Alyssa stepped in front of the door, it slid open to reveal the interior.

"There is an interface already in here," Zh'oros said, gesturing towards the desk along one wall. "And you have use of the console, also."

"Why?" she asked. She winced at how sharp the word came out. "Sorry."

"No need to apologize, Alyssa," the healer replied. She touched Alyssa's shoulder again and gave it a slight squeeze. "As it has been mentioned before, beings earn their positions. You've earned the right. Despite what the commander claims, you *are not* a threat to anyone. Other than perhaps him."

Alyssa turned to look at the master healer with a confused expression. "I won't get into trouble?"

"Not this time," Zh'oros reassured her. "I can and I am overriding his orders in regards to this. You need it for your mental wellbeing. Especially considering his current behavior towards you."

"Thank you," Alyssa said, trying to blink back her tears. But she knew a few had broken free and were trailing a hot path down her cheeks.

Something flashed through Zh'oros eyes. Shaking her head slightly, she took a step forward and pulled Alyssa into a gentle embrace. Alyssa didn't have the energy or desire to shove her away or pull back or anything. Instead, she leaned against Zh'oros, thankful for the healer.

"You are not alone," she said quietly. "And 'Zarry is a fool."

Zh'oros' words were the last thing Alyssa needed to hear. The statement opened the floodgates for the tears. Returning the embrace, Alyssa wept silently against the healer's shoulder. Zh'oros held Alyssa, the healer's hand rubbing her back in comfort.

"Sorry," Alyssa finally managed to say as the tears ebbed.

"There is nothing to apologize for, child," Zh'oros said kindly. At Alyssa's startled expression, the healer hummed deeply. "I am considerably older than you, Alyssa. This is not the first time I have encountered a broken heart. And I suspect that is an expression used even among your race."

"It's used among most races I know," Alyssa admitted. "Thank you."

"You'll be fine," Zh'oros assured her, the warmth in her gold eyes bringing more tears to Alyssa's own. "Try to rest. I will return later."

"Thank you," Alyssa repeated, uncertain of what else to say. "I appreciate everything."

The healer's gold eyes studied her for several long moments, as though appraising her. "I'll talk to Ra'dett about a comm. It's time you're allowed to communicate easier with us."

"That would certainly make contacting you a lot easier," Alyssa said, a wavering smile on her lips.

Giving her a nod, the healer turned and left Alyssa.

The room suddenly seemed considerably smaller and a lot lonelier to Alyssa. Turning, she studied her new, smaller quarters. Admittedly, the crew quarters were still larger than those on a human ship.

There were two rooms with a small separate bathroom. The bathroom had a small sonic shower and toilet, as well as a sink. There was even a small cabinet for toiletries and such.

The main room contained a desk and console, as well as a table and a pair of conforming chairs. There was also an interface similar to the one she'd had in her former quarters, though this one was perhaps half the size. The bedroom had a bed recessed into the wall, a dresser with shelves above it, and a small nightstand. Comfortable and spacious, it wasn't the luxurious room that belonged to the commander's mate.

Sitting in one of the conforming chairs Alyssa picked up the tablet and turned it on. There were words on the screen, but her eyes refused to focus on them. Nor did her mind want to read them. Closing her eyes, Alyssa propped her elbows on the table and dropped her head into her hands. Maybe she could eventually put the broken pieces of her heart back together again. But it wouldn't be anytime soon. And certainly not while she was aboard Commander Mc'narrd's ship.

Zh'oros may have promised to return, but Alyssa wasn't entirely certain she was ready to discuss her feelings with the healer. Regardless of how much she liked the K'laisian medic. She'd survived the Duel with ‚K'rell, but she wasn't entirely certain this was better than death.

There was a low buzz, signaling someone at her door. An interruption from her troubling thoughts. She opened her mouth, but only a choked cry came out. Clearing her throat, she wiped her damp eyes and tried again.

"Open."

The door slid open to reveal Commander It'zarry Mc'narrd standing on the opposite side.

"May I enter?" Mc'narrd asked hesitantly.

"What do you want? More orders? To gloat? To demand I go to the brig?" Alyssa asked, deciding anger was better than anything else.

Maybe if she could remain angry, she wouldn't break down into a weeping ball of pity. Or fling herself at him and beg for forgiveness.

Mc'narrd swallowed and drew a breath. "I am here to speak to you. I ask again, may I enter?" When she merely stared at him, he added, "I will not enter without permission. I will leave, if you so desire."

"Fine. Come in. Why not?" she retorted as she stood. Moving to the opposite wall, she leaned against it, folding her arms across her chest. "What do you want?"

"Why are you here? I did not order this," Mc'narrd asked, gesturing to the room.

Alyssa shrugged, looking away from him. The longer she looked at him, the more she wanted to break down and cry. It was easier to hold onto the anger if she kept her gaze averted. Not that she was completely successful. Her eyes kept glancing back at him.

"Those quarters were for your mate. It seemed only right that I have actual quarters. Not something that belongs to someone else. Even if you don't have one yet."

Something flashed through his eyes, but Alyssa did not know what it was. Instead, she lifted her chin defiantly and stared at him.

A small smile pulled at his lips.

"You definitely are not without a spine, Alyssa," he murmured. "I would like to apologize. I should not have reacted so strongly towards you Challenging ,K'rell. Had he said the same to one of our own, they would have Challenged him. Only the weak would dare argue any of what happened. You have accepted our rules. Our laws. I… should have been angrier at ,K'rell for allowing his xenophobia to threaten this mission."

"That's it? That's all you care about?" Alyssa demanded, dropping her arms in disbelief. She hadn't thought her heart could break more, but she'd been wrong. "The mission?"

"No. That is what Military High Command will be concerned about," Mc'narrd replied evenly. "His xenophobia is what caused him to be belligerent towards you. Despite the fact it was his plan. A plan that proved everything you said about your military. He refused to admit a single person could be different. Be better. That is what ultimately caused his death. That is what will be in my official report to High Command."

Alyssa blinked at Mc'narrd as she tried to wrap her mind around what he'd just said. "But… an alien Challenged him. Won't that cause you problems?"

"An alien who up until that point had done nothing to warrant his verbal attack. If you were K'laisian, none would think twice about it," Mc'narrd said gently. He bowed low to her. "I apologize for my words. For my anger."

The action stunned her. Until now, none had bowed low. He even lowered his eyes from hers. She had no clue what it meant, but she suspected it wasn't minor. Maybe she should've been reading up on K'laisian culture and traditions instead of their history.

As he rose, their eyes locked once again. "I apologize for allowing my worry to cloud my judgment. My fear of your death made me say things I should not have spoken to you. You have done nothing to deserve them."

Drawing in a deep breath, Alyssa let it out slowly. When she was confident her voice wouldn't break, she said, "Apology accepted."

"Thank you," he replied, his voice grave. Relief showed in his eyes and on his face. "Will you join me for a meeting? There is someone I would like you to meet. A fellow commander who arrived and is wishing to discuss our next move with your people."

Despite the fact she did not trust the commander's formal tone, Alyssa could not refuse his request. Mc'narrd was being far too polite and choosing his words too well. Whatever he had planned, she could only agree and hope for the best.

Whatever that might be.

The walk to the bridge was done in silence. An uneasy silence in Alyssa's opinion. It felt heavy and different compared to earlier times. Instead of dwelling on it, she kept her eyes straight ahead and considered the options before them in regards to the IMD and the four battleships currently trying to locate them. There was probably a Va'nu'ian vessel somewhere, but she had zero knowledge about them, and so didn't know what to expect from them.

When the door to the lift opened, it revealed the bridge of Mc'narrd's ship. A dark-haired K'laisian she did not recognize stood talking with First Officer Ac'kyll on the lower level. From the way Ac'kyll deferred to him, in addition to the subtle bio suit markings that were identical to the ones on Mc'narrd's suit, Alyssa guessed he was the other commander.

Mc'narrd did not stop at the pair. Instead, he led her in front of the viewscreen where all could see them without any obstructions.

Unclipping the sword at his side, he held it out to her using both hands to hold the weapon. It was only then she realized he had been wearing two, and this one was slightly smaller than its mate still at his side.

"I would be honored if you accepted this gift."

His comment gained the attention of every being on the bridge. Including those who had returned back to their stations after he'd entered. No one spoke. Or moved. In fact, the entire bridge was very, very silent.

Uncertainly, she accepted the weapon, taking it from his hands with her own. Stepping back, she slid the sword from its elaborate sheath. The weight was perfect for her, as was the length. She took a few experimental swipes with it, amazed at how perfect the blade felt in her hands.

Resheathing the weapon, she said, "It's a beautiful weapon and I accept it." She wasn't certain why she used those words, but they felt required. "But why are you gifting me a weapon that matches your own?"

"Among my people, it is a way to show one's affections. Their… love towards another."

"Do you love me?" she asked quietly, bowing her head and keeping her eyes on the sword in her hand.

She felt a hand lifting her chin up until she could not avoid meeting Mc'narrd's gaze. His eyes seemed to sear into hers as he said in a very soft voice, "Yes, Alyssa. I love you. And I will do whatever it takes to keep you by my side."

"I love you, too," she whispered before closing the short distance between them.

She pressed her lips against his. Someone took the sword from her hand, allowing her to wrap both arms around his neck, her fingers tangling themselves in his hair.

Mc'narrd returned the kiss and embrace, his hand moving from her chin to the middle of her back. He dominated the kiss until she was breathless, yet still wanting more.

"You two can continue this later in whoever's quarters you want," a voice said from behind them. "Though I would suggest returning to the ones adjoining his."

Breaking the kiss slowly, Mc'narrd glowered over Alyssa's shoulder, but he didn't say anything. The desire on his face said plenty, as did the hand holding her. She, however, could feel her face burning.

"You must be Alyssa Zelaya," the other K'laisian said. His olive complexion and hair reminded her of the Italians of Earth. His features weren't as chiseled, but he was still an attractive male. "A pleasure to meet the lady who finally managed to locate this man's heart." He gave her a very human wink. "Some of us were wondering if he even had one."

"Allow me to introduce Vrehn Cq'linns," Mc'narrd said. "Commander of the battlecruiser *Endis*. He is an old comrade and dear friend. Also, not always the most intelligent."

Vrehn Cq'linns smiled at Alyssa and bowed. "Ask me one day, when I am not in front of your commander, who talked some intelligence into him."

"I suspect it will be an entertaining story," Alyssa replied, not moving from Mc'narrd's side. She was still feeling giddy over Mc'narrd's proclamation.

"Especially since you're technically his mate now," Commander Cq'linns said, practically bouncing on his feet.

"What?" Alyssa exclaimed, looking up at Mc'narrd, who appeared very smug, then to First Officer Ac'kyll who was smiling and nodding.

"As his mate, Alyssa, High Command cannot force you to remain on K'lais once we return to our planet," First Officer Ac'kyll explained. "Our males are not always forthright in their words. They also seem to have forgotten you are not completely aware of our culture and ways of life. Or military celebrations of joining."

"I'm not sure how to respond to that," Alyssa muttered. "It seems that is another thing our peoples have in common. Do they often shove their foot in their mouth, too?"

Ac'kyll frowned and considered her words. "If you mean they speak without thinking, and therefore cause more problems than they should? Yes."

Alyssa giggled even as the two commanders glowered at the first officer, though the laughter in their eyes betrayed their true feelings of genuine amusement.

"Perhaps we should continue with why we are all here," Mc'narrd suggested, a smile on his face. "We need your assistance once again, Alyssa."

Between one heartbeat and the next, the viewscreen showed the sector they were in, as well as where her original ship had exploded and the pod the IMD had destroyed.

"What can I do?" Alyssa asked, looking between the K'laisians.

The two commanders smiled and Mc'narrd led her to his command chair. Commander Cq'linns and First Officer Ac'kyll followed.

Knowing she was not going to be forced to leave Mc'narrd and could find a place on his ship among his people was heartwarming. But more than that, she was thankful they'd finally moved past their differences. Maybe the next time something happened, they could talk about it instead of punishing each other due to egos.

Or, she thought in amusement, *they could simply Challenge each other. Since death wasn't a requirement, a Duel would certainly be a more entertaining method of settling disputes.*

There would be more time for thoughts, and more, later, she decided, as the two commanders, Ac'kyll, and Ra'dett began explaining the plan. At least now there *would* be a later.

"I only have one question." When the commanders gave encouraging nods, she grinned. "When do we put the plan into action?"

"After we hunt down their Va'nu'ian ally," Commander Cq'linns replied.

Alyssa snorted, swept her eyes over Mc'narrd as he sat comfortably in his command chair, then looked at Commander Cq'linns. When she turned her attention back to her mate, she burst out laughing.

"No, you most definitely are *not* lazy hunters," she finally managed to say.

Humming erupted on the bridge, even as Mc'narrd favored her with the human-style laugh she loved so much.

Epilogue

Later That Evening

Looking around at the Commander's Mate quarters, Alyssa began to feel like it was more of her own space. There was only a bit of her own to the room, that was true. Just the sword that Mc'Narrd had given her. That item stood against the wall, close to the bed. But that sword was *hers*. It was, in her mind, the first thing she could call her own in this new life.

She heard the adjoining door to her quarters open.

"Do you think you will be comfortable here?"

She smiled at the sound of Mc'Narrd's voice. Without turning, she replied.

"There's so much more to do. We have to confront another race, I have to see your home planet. Eventually, we have to go and deal with my own people."

"Indeed, each of those is a formidable task," said Mc'Narrd as he came up beside her. "However, I was referring to your place here, in this room. On this ship."

Alyssa felt her cheeks burn.

"Umm, I will have to find an actual job on this ship or I will go crazy. No," she said, "I will not consider 'consultant' or 'captain's woman' to be actual work. As for the room, it's fine."

"I am certain you will find a service to prosper in, Alyssa."

She chuckled and finally looked at Mc'Narrd. She had spent enough time around him to properly recognize his current expression. He was curious about her response.

"Isn't that your planet's motto, It'zarry?" she finally asked.

"My people adhere to a similar phrase," he agreed, "Which you will recall after enough exposure to it. Is that why you were amused?"

"To my silly human ears, you sounded like a recruiter trying to convince me to sign up for your planet."

"You pronounced my first name correctly, Alyssa. You are adapting quite well. I do not see a need to convince you."

She pondered that for a moment. Then she stepped towards him.

"Perhaps you can help me with one answer I definitely need," Alyssa cooed.

Her hands slipped over his chest, stopping as they clasped behind his neck. Without hesitation or concern, his hands trailed down her back to her waist.

"Remind me again how I remove the bio suit?" she breathed at him.

"Why would you need-" he began, and then smiled.

His right hand came around to take her left hand from around his neck. With his right hand fingers, he guided her hand into a closed loose fist with her thumb still out. He brought her thumb around to just below the artery beneath her ear. He pressed her thumb into the bio suit's material.

After a moment, there was a beep. Her bio suit seemed to sloth off her body and pool oddly at her feet. He then reached up and triggered his own suit. She watched the material ripple off his skin. Drank in the sight of his body as it was exposed, all the way to his feet.

"You'll... have to show me how it goes back on. It may have slipped my mind," she managed to say.

One hand lifted her chin until her eyes were locked with his.

"Later," he assured her.

Then their lips came together, and their night began.

END

Nebula (mixed drink)

Here's how to mix up Alyssa's favorite beverage, the Nebula:

Two parts sour appletini mix

One-part Bombay sapphire gin

Heavy splash of tangerine juice (or Sunny D, orange juice, etc)

Mix ingredients over ice, serve very cold.

We hope that you enjoyed this title and look forward to many more to come. Please, leave us a review! Reviews matter to all of our authors.

Take a look at some of our other award-winning series at https://threeravenspublishing.com/series-universes/

Visit us at https://www.threeravenspublishing.com and sign up for our newsletter for the latest and greatest news on upcoming titles and events.

Other series and titles you might enjoy.

THE RAVEN
AND
THE CROW
MICHAEL K. FALCIANI
FIND ME
ON AMAZON

You can also keep up to date with our latest release announcements on Scifi.radio and get some of the best fandom programing on the planet.

Scifi for your Wifi

And don't forget to check out our other Sponsors and Affiliates

Comprised of active or retired servicemen and civilian volunteers, Shepherd's Men enthusiastically raises awareness and funds for the SHARE Military Initiative (SHARE) at Shepherd Center in Atlanta, GA.

This nationally renowned program focuses on assessment and treatment for American military veterans who have sustained mild to moderate Traumatic Brain Injury (TBI) and Post-Traumatic Stress Disorder (PTSD) during post-9/11 service.

Find out more at: https://www.shepherdsmen.com/